THE SWORD

by

Ruth Elliott-Smith

Published 2018

Also published as an eBook on Amazon Kindle

ISBN No: 9781723805639

DEDICATION

FOR MY FRIENDS, ARAB AND ISRAELI.

MAY YOU FIND A LASTING PEACE

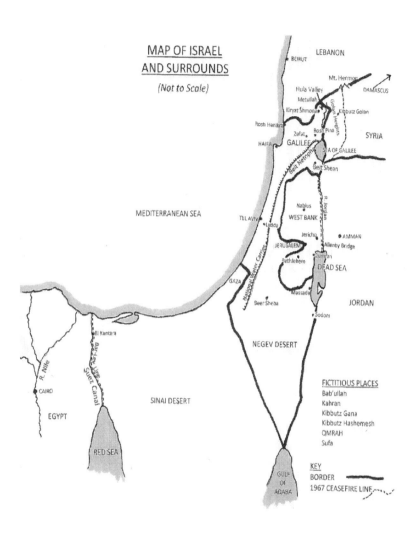

MAP OF ISRAEL AND SURROUNDS

(Not to Scale)

LEBANON

BEIRUT

Mt. Hermon

DAMASCUS

Hula Valley

Metullah

Kiryat Shmona

Kibbutz Golan

Golan Heights

Rosh Hanikra

Zafat

Rosh Pina

SYRIA

HAIFA

GALILEE

SEA OF GALILEE

Beit Netofa

Beit Shean

MEDITERRANEAN SEA

Nablus

R. Jordan

TEL AVIV

WEST BANK

Lydda

Jericho

AMMAN

JERUSALEM

Allenby Bridge

Qumran

Bethlehem

DEAD SEA

GAZA

National Water Carrier

Massada

Beer Sheba

JORDAN

Sodom

NEGEV DESERT

El Kantara

Bar-Lev Line

Suez Canal

R. Nile

CAIRO

SINAI DESERT

EGYPT

RED SEA

GULF OF AQABA

FICTITIOUS PLACES

Bab'ullah
Kahran
Kibbutz Gana
Kibbutz Hashemesh
QMRAH
Sufa

KEY

BORDER ⎯⎯⎯⎯

1967 CEASEFIRE LINE ⌁⌁⌁

THE SWORD

Prologue

The air ripped as the jets streaked in again, their engines drowning the screams below. Black bombs flew in graceful, curved and deadly descent, mirroring the Mysteres' ascent as they cleared the blast zone.

She bent forward, shielding her head with her hands, cradling the old man's head protectively in her lap as the shock waves hit, knocking the breath from her, showering them with debris.

Panic stricken refugees filled the street, women crying for children they could not find, men shaking their fists at the sky and shouting obscenities, dazed and bloodied victims stumbling, swept along by the crowd. The jets wheeled, diving, coming in low for another run. God, would they ever stop? The Browning peppered the air above, trained more in hope than expectation on the path of the killing machines relentlessly smashing the heart of the old town.

"Bastards!" she yelled, bracing herself, the word lost in the roar of engines, as the jets passed, their bombs already shed. The ground rocked. The blasts deafened her so she no longer heard the Browning, the cries of the stragglers. Nor did she hear the cheer that went up at the Mystere trailing a tail of black smoke, but she saw them point up.

"Thank God! Oh Jesus, thank God!" she whispered. Her hand closed on the Kalashnikov. She must start searching, she must find him, but she couldn't bear to leave the dying man. He was conscious.

"I see it," he whispered, so quietly that she bent her head close to his dry, cracked lips, her ears still ringing. She didn't catch his words. He smiled up at her, the pain gone, the eyes alive with happiness. A thin smoke trail curved across the blue sky, the pilot heading home. The remaining jet turned. Would it come in again? "I can see it!" the old man repeated. "You see the orange groves. Can you see?"

"Yes," she said softly, her eyes still on the jet. "Yes. I can see." She stroked his forehead. The breath rattled in his throat and he coughed blood.

"I said it was beautiful, now you know I spoke the truth." His eyes closed. "God has brought me home...my home," he mouthed the last word, "Palestine."

He lay still. She pulled his head to her and held it for a moment, rocking gently back and forth. Slowly she drew the *abba* over the shattered chest, the face peaceful in death.

She stood, alone in the street, the sky at last quiet. A dog dragged its broken leg, whining in pain. Wearily she turned to where a pall of yellow dust mingled with the black smoke which hung over the decimated buildings. Nothing in there could live. A few walls reared like jagged crags in a sand-storm. Otherwise it was rubble and somewhere beneath it he lay dead. She leaned against a wall, forearm across her eyes, and wept for the whole damned lot of them.

CHAPTER 1

1968

Jodi was one of seven crammed into the communal taxi, the *sheroot*. She could hardly breathe the cool breeze which blasted in through every open window, snatching at the blonde tangle of her hair. The vehicle hurtled onwards to Jerusalem as if it carried the very Crusades. Either side of the road pedestrians straggled, some trailing donkeys, the occasional camel, blissfully oblivious to danger as the *sheroot* veered drunkenly from one side to the other, narrowly missing them.

A huge and rather ripe woman in a shapeless black *chador* was wedged alongside her, forcing her against the side of the cab. Opposite, a thin young man with a thin shiny moustache and a shiny suit clasped a plastic document case to his chest and leered at her, his knees pressed against hers. Through the breeze she caught the call of the *muezzin*. It was time for evening prayer, when the greatness of God was punctually proclaimed in a determined battle between Muslim amplifiers and Christian bells, their minarets and steeples stabbing upwards to the blood red sky. People seemed unimpressed. Those who lived here allowed this timeless beauty to slip by unnoticed once every 24 hours. It was just another day ending.

"Oh Jerusalem, the choice of Allah of all his lands. In it are the chosen of his servants. From it the earth was stretched forth and from it shall be rolled up like a scroll."

Never had the words of the Prophet Mohammed seemed more poignant. Beyond the Old City rose the evening star, Saturn, known as Sharleem to the ancients. It sparkled like a clear blue diamond on a plush crimson cushion. Jerusalem was *Ir-u-sharleem*, the Town of Saturn or Satan and not, as so widely believed, *Ir-u-shalom*, Town of Peace.

It's just a heap of old stones, she thought dismissively. Yet it spoke to the soul; a place to be fought for and conquered and levelled and lost countless times; a monument to the pointlessness of material possession. It mocked possession. Last year the Arabs, this year the Jews, who next? And did it really matter so long as they were prepared to die in their hundreds and thousands for it?

"Allah akbar!" sang the *muezzin*. *"Yallah!* Move!" yelled the driver, leaning out of the window, gesturing impatiently at a cyclist towing a wooden cart of sesame seed loaves. The taxi weaved on dangerously through the packed narrow streets, finally jolting to an abrupt and merciful halt opposite the beautiful Damascus Gate. In the rush to get out she was half dragged onto the pavement. She staggered, straightening the crumpled pink dress while men, perched on small

stools outside the coffee house, broodingly appraised her. They ought to be used to mini-skirts by now, she thought with mild irritation. The city was full of tourists displaying alarming quantities of thigh beneath scandalously high hems. It rarely occurred to Jodi that she was attractive. Being a woman never got between her and the job, unless of course it facilitated things, in which case she exploited it shamelessly.

She was a journalist. Getting the story was what mattered. Jodi freelanced, barely surviving on the news features she sent back to England from her travels. Bare survival was all she asked. It was an exhilarating change from the stifling over-privilege she left England to escape. But in Israel even bare survival was difficult. The international media machine had a full stable of hacks here, still living off scraps from the Six Day War last year. Most were shacked up in the King David Hotel, rarely moving from the bar. Jodi saw them when she went into Beit Hillel, the press centre, to pick up her mail, file copy or sit obediently before the censor from *Aman*, military intelligence, as he scanned then rubber-stamped her stories. Otherwise she was a loner, shunning the pack, valuing her freedom. When money ran out she hitched lifts. She had seen more of Israel than most Israelis.

She hunted the unusual, demanding action, adventure. Not for her the stuffy newsrooms of middle-aged alcoholics reflecting on life from a safe distance. She needed to be where it was happening, telling it as she saw it, finding the angle; a peg to hang it on.

Truth was stranger than fiction Like the old woman who ran a rescue centre for dogs in the no man's land across which Israeli and Jordanian soldiers blasted each other last year. After three days the dog food ran out. The hounds howled with hunger, the bombs screamed overhead. The old lady waved a white flag, demanding a cease fire while she went shopping. Only when she returned safely to her sanctuary did the war resume. Hundreds died but the dogs ate.

"*Allah akbar*!" It was loud and very distorted now, coming from inside the Old City. She wondered idly how many of those now prostrating themselves at El Aksa Mosque would spend the rest of the night propped up at the Rainbow Bar.

Within the Damascus Gate a row of beggars reached out to her. Begging is no shame in Islam but Jodi's last *agrot* had gone to pay the *sheroot*. Lamps glowed in the narrow, dark *souk*. Shopkeepers put up the shutters. As she reached the tunnel where Damascus Street turned right into King David Street, the throng pushed against her. She kept to the wall, side stepping quickly.

A hand touched her arm and she turned to see a young boy standing in a doorway, smiling mischievously, stroking the head of a small yellow bird and holding the struggling creature up to her. She knew the game. He'd threaten to kill it if she didn't pay! Even the birds had full-time jobs here! But he wouldn't kill it or he'd have to catch another. She smiled, patting his cheek. "Sorry *walad.* You'll have to wring its neck. I haven't got a bean."

Then she was standing at the glass door of the Rainbow Bar, greeting Mustapha breathlessly. "*Salaam aleykom*!"

The barman beamed. "*Weh aleykom salaam.*" He was a rogue. Probably spent his childhood threatening to strangle birds. Now he swindled his customers but she couldn't help liking him. At the far end of the long, American-style bar sat Dahoud, the owner, reading the Arab newspaper, *Al Kuds*, and smoking a cigarette. He looked up briefly then went back to his newspaper. Dahoud was a miserable type. He didn't talk much. Most of his conversations were conducted with grunts and gestures.

Mustapha was the opposite. He still grinned broadly at her. "You gonna stand there or you gonna work?"

"Neither!" She seated herself on a barstool. "I'm gonna sit here and watch your beautiful Arab arse!"

Mustapha stopped polishing the glass, wagging a forefinger at her. "You talk like that in here, you gonna get in big trouble." She laughed. Was there ever any big trouble she couldn't laugh her way out of?

Jodi walked into the Rainbow by chance a week ago. As she sipped her Coke she noticed two obviously Western women on the other side of the bar leaning across and chatting to customers. She asked the barman about them. "Bar girls," Mustapha smiled. "Men come, lonely. We have two, three girls, young, foreign like you. Talk to men. Men buy them drink. We make money, pay girls."

Jodi sat up. What a story! Men here were starved of female companionship, jealously guarding their women from each other. Chatting to a woman in a bar was unthinkable unless it was a woman from the west. Even so, it sounded wanton for the Holy City. "Er, do they just talk?"

Mustapha looked shocked. "Just talk!" he affirmed curtly. Then a thought seemed to strike him. "You wanna job?" Jodi was about to laugh it off when she decided why not? She could do with the money. Getting paid for as much as she could drink and getting the story at the same time sounded like a journalist's dream.

"I don't speak Arabic," she confessed.

"You speak with your eyes!" he instructed. Jodi laughed. But, again, why not? She rarely passed up a challenge. It might even be fun. Just be nice to the punters, have a little chat with them from eight till two. It could be party time.

She was an immediate hit, extrovert and intelligent with an inborn curiosity about everything, everyone. In no time she had a devoted following who spent eight *lira* a throw buying her drinks. Sometimes she drank scotch. but usually it was the sickly purple sugar water Mustapha called "John Collins." Jodi had an easy confidence with people. She laughed a lot, spoke volumes with her eyes (the Arabs were big on eyes). She drove them wild. She filled the bar. Dahoud was almost happy.

Tonight was her last night, though they didn't know. It was sad but she was stifled and one week here was enough. She'd drafted her story. All she needed now was her wages, then she'd tell them.

It was early and there were no customers. Mustapha in his white shirt, dark waistcoat and long white apron continued to polish glasses. She joined him behind the bar, putting out trays of pistachio nuts while Umm Kalthoum sang passionately from the radio and Dahoud, chain-smoking, read his paper.

CHAPTER 2

Amin looked out at the land. It was his land, his birthright and he would walk in it freely one day. But for now he had to be careful, dodging Israeli patrols and road blocks, travelling only in the evenings in disguise.

Shin Beth, counter intelligence arm of the Israeli Secret Service, would pay a small fortune to know the true identity of the roughly-dressed unshaven shepherd travelling on the Nablus bus towards Jerusalem. They would pay dearly for not knowing and they weren't the only ones. Next to him, Fayez fidgeted, itchy in what was left of the filthy, flea ridden thobe, the folds of which hid a .9 Beretta. He fingered it nervously.

Amin placed his hand on his friend's: "You won't need it, my brother. He is fat and rich. Such men frighten easily."

Jerusalem was the last stop on Amin's tour of the Occupied Territory. Baseem would meet him there with guns and clothes. For six months Amin had operated out of the *casbah* of Nablus, collecting "donations" for the war against the Zionists. His face was not so well known as Yasser Arafat's who nevertheless had infiltrated the

West Bank only a year earlier setting up cells of resistance.

The *fedayeen,* the freedom fighters who would one day return Palestine to her rightful people, were no longer short of soldiers. They needed leadership, arms and the money to buy both. Young men gave their blood while fat Arab pigs grew rich and comfortable collaborating with the Jews. It was Amin's task to remind them of the struggle being waged on their behalf and persuade them to make a sizeable cash contribution. Generally he had little trouble. There had been one sad incident, the execution of a man's wife and young son. He paid in the end. They all did.

Any foreign currency would do. No one wanted worthless Israeli *lira*, least of all the Israelis. You couldn't buy foreign currency even from their banks. Once they had it they used it to buy arms, as did the *fedayeen*. Consequently a flourishing black market had grown up in the *souks* where foreign cash changed hands at inflated prices; cash that was never banked, never acknowledged. Amin had waited six months to discover whose hand held the purse strings of Jerusalem and now he knew. Tonight he would make a large withdrawal.

Amin was smiling at the thought when the bus braked and stopped suddenly, throwing him forward. There were shouts and heavy footsteps as an Israeli soldier swung up the steps waving an Uzi automatic. "Out! Everyone off," he shouted in imprecise Arabic. "Bring with you everything that is yours."

The bus was packed, carrying only Arabs. Many complained loudly as they filed slowly off; the children beginning to cry; the women scolding.

Amin nudged Fayez. "Be calm. Do as they say," he whispered. "It's a spot check. They aren't looking for us."

They climbed down to join the other passengers, standing before six armed Israeli soldiers. On the roof of the bus two more soldiers rummaged through the bundles and cases stowed there. They threw some down. One burst, scattering clothes and a few ornaments on the roadside. A woman ran to it.

"Get back," shouted a soldier, shoving her roughly so that she fell, howling.

"Your papers," ordered a sergeant, addressing the crowd, who began fumbling in pockets and bags for identification. He walked among them, checking each card as it was produced. He came to Amin who stood looking at the ground. "Papers!" He ordered again. Amin held out a piece of paper as filthy as the rags he wore. The sergeant looked at him in disgust, spat and moved on to Fayez who fumbled nervously. He was sweating profusely and his hand shook as it moved slowly to the gun. Amin acted quickly.

"This is my brother," he said to the sergeant, gripping Fayez's wrist. "He's sick. We're going to the hospital."

"Where's his identification?"

"He has it, somewhere."

The sergeant beckoned a soldier. "Search him."

"He's very sick. The doctor says maybe leprosy. We have it in our village."

The soldier, who was already eyeing Fayez's tunic with distaste, hesitated. The sergeant looked suspiciously from one to the other but stepped back just the same. "All right," he said finally. "Get over there, both of you." Muttering in Hebrew, hc moved on.

It was half an hour before the soldiers finished. A man and woman were questioned closely and there was a noisy scene as they were arrested and taken away. Finally the crowd was allowed back on the bus. The driver and those whose baggage had been thrown down, piled cases and bundles back on the roof. The bus drove off, its passengers shouting and waving their fists angrily at the soldiers as they passed.

The bar fell silent as Jodi and the Turk faced each other, before him a large tumbler of scotch filled to the brim, before her a glass of the sticky sweet coloured water "John Collins".

"So you think you can win?" he said smiling.

She didn't care if she could or not but that much coloured water would cost him at least 80 *lira*. At 10 percent that meant an extra 8 *lira*, nearly £1, in her pay packet, not counting the value of the scotch. Every little helped. She smiled back. "Yes."

"Begin," he ordered. Moving her hand to the glass, she paused, then snatched it to her lips, throwing her head back. The Turk was as fast. The crowd yelled encouragement. She looked sideways at him as she drank. His glass was emptying fast, whisky dribbling down his neck and chest. She slowed slightly. She ought to let him win. He'd soon feel bad enough without adding the shame of defeat.

He slammed the glass back on the counter a split-second ahead of Jodi. They both burst out laughing as the crowd cheered, slapping the Turk on the back, congratulating him. Mustapha marked up the Turk's bill by an extra 10 drinks. The state he'd leave in, he'd never know he hadn't bought them. He caught the signal from Haj Osman and went over.

"Arrack," said the Haj, "and ask the girl what she would like."

Mustapha approached Jodi. "The Haj wants you to drink with him."

Jodi looked over to where he sat, silently smoking and watching her. She smiled and waved, saying to the Turk: "Excuse me."

He grabbed her wrist. "Where you go?"

She jerked her head towards where Haj Osman sat but the Turk's eyes seemed to have trouble focusing. "Who?" he demanded.

"Haj Osman," she whispered.

"You stay here," he said, still holding her.

"I go where I want," she said, serious now but polite. With a sudden movement which took him by surprise, she wrenched her arm free. The crowd roared with delight. The Turk staggered slightly, shouting in Arabic after her. He was still shouting as she reached the Haj. Looking back she saw Dahoud pushing his way to where the Turk struggled, restrained now by some men.

"*Salaam*," she said.

"*Salaam*?" laughed Osman derisively. "You say 'Peace' and you do this?" he indicated the fight beginning down the bar.'

She shrugged: "I'm afraid he can't hold his drink."

"And you can?"

"Well I would say I'm managing a little better than he is, wouldn't you?"

"My dear, I am sorry to say you drink like a donkey."

Jodi was stung. True she drank a lot but she was popular. She couldn't tell him it was sugar water. Instead she said: "Then I'll have a bucket of water."

"Huh?"

"You asked me here for a drink." she reminded him. He smiled, relaxing a little.

"Mustapha. A John Collins!" she shouted above the din. She turned back to the Haj, fixing him with the amused, hypnotic gaze which seemed to get them all. Words were unnecessary as they read whatever they wanted to read into her eyes. It made conversation a whole lot easier.

Haj Osman was perhaps 55, overweight and immensely rich. He was a holy muslim who had already fulfilled the fifth commandment of the Prophet and made his pilgrimage to Mecca, a journey which earned him his title, Haj. He was supposed to refrain from drinking, smoking and womanising. Instead, on his return from the holy places, Haj Osman embarked on all three with even greater enthusiasm than before.

A regular at the Rainbow, he hadn't missed a night since Jodi arrived. Last night he gave her a pearl cluster ring. After he left she gave it away on impulse to a man who couldn't pay his bar bill and who in turn gave it to Mustapha.

"You come with me tonight?" said the Haj as he had said every night.

"Where to?"

"Where you want."

She smiled: "I'll think about it."

"I'll take you home. My car is here."

"No!" she laughed.

"Jodi," he stroked her hand, "I can make you happy."

"I am happy," she was still laughing.

"Give you what you want."

"Jodi! Jodi!" the Turk was yelling, waving his bar ticket. Mustapha beckoned her.

"Excuse me," she said to the Haj.

"If he asks how many drinks he bought you, say fifteen," Mustapha whispered.

"Fifteen?"

"Say it."

"He's spent enough."

"You say it or I in big trouble." He smiled that irresistibly helpless smile.

"Oh, Mustapha! Oh what the hell!" She walked over to where the Turk shouted loudly at Dahoud.

How many drinks I buy you," he demanded of

Jodi.

"I didn't count," she said.

"How many?" She was getting to dislike this man, drunk and swindled as he was. She caught sight of Mustapha.

"Maybe fourteen, fifteen," she lied, feeling wretched.

"No!" he lunged at her. Dahoud pulled him back as he grabbed a tumbler and hurled it at Jodi. She ducked. It brushed the top of her head and smashed against the wall.

As the Turk was dragged out she turned on Mustapha. "Don't ask me to do it again. Next time you're on your own." She was shaking as she returned to the Haj.

"Salaam!" he smiled. "Finish your drink. You will feel better." She downed it in one. "Mustapha," he called, indicating Jodi's glass.

"I'll have a scotch," she said. Mustapha brought the bottle.

"Leave it here," said the Haj. Jodi helped herself. She didn't feel well. It was so hot and the sound seemed to come from a long way away. Haj Osman's voice, through a long tunnel, said: "Are you all right?" His round face came close, the close-cropped hair, the pencil thin moustache, his teeth yellow from tobacco. The grotesque smile blurred and fell away.

The glass slipped from her hand as she sank to the floor.

***

Haj Osman dismissed the smirking chauffeur, thrusting a 50 *lira* note in his hand. He turned to the bed where Jodi lay, still unconscious, and sat beside her. Soon she would wake, soon she would be his. He wasn't used to waiting so long. Every woman had her price. He would find hers. There would be no trouble. He ran his hand down the side of her face and neck to her breasts. They were young and firm, her body smooth and silky beneath the rough cotton dress. He would buy her dresses such as she had never dreamed of. Women liked clothes and jewels. Yes, he would dress her as she deserved, and undress her too.

He slid his hand up the short skirt, feeling the flat stomach and taking hold of the cotton briefs. Jodi stirred. He moved away quickly smoothing her skirt. She opened her eyes, blinked and looked around sleepily. Above she saw her own reflection in a mirror as big as the bed. Either side, sugar pink and green damask curtains cascaded from ceiling to floor. The room was huge, with pale green and gold flocked walls. Gilded couches and big Queen Anne chairs scattered with silk cushions stood on a grey and pink marbled floor embellished with priceless oriental silk rugs. Her gaze finally rested on him. She tried to speak but gave up and passed out again.

Osman cursed. He must have misjudged. She drank so much alcohol she must have the constitution of a camel and he'd slipped a generous portion of the powder into her glass. It was careless and he sighed over his misfortune.

Standing, he shook off his jacket, loosened his tie and walked to a silver tray of decanters. He poured a large Arrack watching the clear liquid become opaque as he added water.

When Jodi "fainted" in the bar, he offered to drive her home. She was obviously distressed by the incident of the Turk, he said. Dahoud looked suspicious, but he couldn't leave the bar early and the 100 US dollars thrust into his hand seemed to settle the matter.

Haj Osman smiled as he walked back to where Jodi lay. She was so young, so lovely, so completely helpless for a change. Suddenly, he decided, he could wait no longer. He would take her now as she slept. She had teased and encouraged him, making sheep's eyes at him in the Rainbow Bar. She wanted him, didn't she? It would only have been a matter of time before she agreed.

Hurriedly he unhooked his belt, unzipping his trousers, trying to get them off over his shoes in his haste. He cursed again, as one leg stuck, half on, half off.

As he hopped ridiculously a loud laugh came from across the room. Haj Osman looked up sharply. In the open doorway stood three men. Aware of how foolish he must look, he was outraged at the intrusion and with as much dignity as he could command yelled: "Who are you? Get out!"

Amin and Fayez now wore casual shirts and trousers. They entered the room while Baseem, the biggest of the three, guarded the door. With a huge effort, the Haj freed his trousers and, pulling them up, walked to a bell on the wall.

"Don't touch it!" Amin commanded, adding gently, "if you want to live".

Osman stopped and turned, noticing now they were armed. From Amin's left hand, a Carl-Gustaf sub machine gun hung casually. With the other he was tossing and catching a grenade. Baseem also carried a Carl-Gustaf while Fayez pointed the Beretta.

Haj froze with terror. "Who are you?" he asked again, his voice low and trembling.

"We are your protectors, Haj Osman," said Amin walking to the bed where Jodi lay unconscious. He glanced down at her and then up at the mirror. "Heloa! You have good taste," adding with a smile: "But you cannot be an exciting lover. The lady is asleep." He laughed loudly. Fayez and Baseem joined in. Haj stood silently. Amin continued. "It would be a pity to wake her. We can make her sleep forever."

Still smiling at the trembling man, he tilted the short barrel of the sub machine gun towards Jodi.

"No! No!" Haj jumped nervously towards the bed. "You can't. She's not a Jew."

"Not a Jew? Of course not!" Amin said soothingly. "Such a loyal and prominent Palestinian would not fuck a Zionist." Haj shook his head quickly as Amin continued: "His fate would be certain death." Suddenly he swung the gun back to Haj. "Who is she?" he snapped.

"She, she's English, a journalist, but she works as a bar girl."

Amin looked thoughtful. He walked to the heavy curtains drawn across the window and parted them carefully surveying the lush gardens of the Haj's palatial mansion. After a moment he turned decisively. "We are here to give you the opportunity to make a donation to *El Fatah*," he said. "Young men are laying down their lives to win back freedom for our brothers and sisters who suffer under the Zionist yoke. If we are to succeed we need funds to buy arms, considerable funds. You understand?"

"Yes, yes," Haj said quickly.

Amin looked appreciatively around the room. "You live well. We're fortunate to have the support of one who has so much to offer."

"I'll give what I can. You must understand things aren't easy under the Israelis. I have lost a great deal. What you see is what remains of the prosperity we all enjoyed before we became victims of the racist regime."

Amin's eyes were cold. "Two hundred thousand American dollars," he said.

Haj swallowed hard. His eyes widened and he reached to loosen his tie, forgetting he had already loosened it. "Two hu...you're not serious. I haven't..."

"...you haven't the words to thank me? For allowing you to escape with so small a contribution?"

"Where can I get American dollars, and so much, at this time..?"

"Perhaps from your safe, the one behind the picture?"

Haj went purple. Sweat broke out on his face as he moved quickly towards Amin, then stopped. "I don't… *Kusumac*. You can kill me first!"

With his teeth, Amin pulled the pin from the grenade, holding the lever closed with his fingers. "With luck we shall kill you and open the safe at the same time." He turned to his comrades: "Get out!"

"No, no. All right, all right." Haj crossed quickly to a large, gold framed portrait of King Hussein, pushed it aside and began to turn the dial of the heavy metal door.

As it opened, Amin replaced the pin in the grenade. "Stand back," he ordered.

The safe was large, perhaps a metre high and almost as deep. Bundles of notes were neatly stacked there. Amin reached inside and examined some. "Deutschmarks, excellent! And, of course dollars. We'll take all these, and the Sterling. You can keep the rest."

Haj sat miserably on a plush chair while Baseem brought in two holdalls, which Amin filled with banknotes.

"Now my friend," said Amin as he zipped the bags shut, "we must leave you. You've been generous but we need one thing more, your car."

"My car?"

"The Mercedes below the window. No doubt it will be returned in due course, but you see we have a passenger." He looked towards Jodi. "It would arouse suspicion were we to carry her out into the street so I think it best we borrow your big car."

"Where are you taking her?" "

Where she won't be found until we get a nice fat ransom from the British."

"You can't..."

"Tie him up! Make sure he can't squeal. Then bring the woman."

Baseem ripped the flex from a lamp, pulled Osman's arms behind him and bound the wrists tightly. Pushing him to the floor and tying his feet with the same flex, he felt in the Haj's pocket, found a handkerchief and stuffed it into his mouth, gagging him with his own tie.

Picking up Jodi he followed Amin who carried the bags to the door and then put them down. As an afterthought he walked back to where the Haj lay and pressed the gun barrel hard into his cheek.

"*Ma salaam*, my friend," he said. "I warn you, if the Israelis hear of this we shall be back."

Haj lay still, the sound of retreating footsteps drowned by the pounding in his ears.

CHAPTER 3

Outside the air was hot and still. A few children played along the row of rough stone houses opposite. On a step in the shade, two *fedayeen* drank coffee and played backgammon, AK47's propped up beside them. Beyond, a group of recruits were at target practice.

The lower ranks were hardly more than boys, mostly uneducated above primary school level. When they joined *Fatah* they had no discipline, no weapons training, no real idea of what they were to do. What they shared was a burning hatred of the expansionist Zionists who drove their parents and families from their homes, usurped their land and forced them into the squalor of refugee camps. Like Amin they were stateless and destined to remain that way, manipulated by the Arab states for their own political ends, left to rot in refugee camps as a reminder to the world, a festering wound on the Middle East which would never be allowed to heal.

There was only one path home, the path of violence, and the Palestinians had to beat it themselves, dragging the whole Arab world reluctantly behind them if necessary.

The 1948 War of Independence left Amin a homeless orphan. For months he begged and stole, unable even to get into to the refugee camps, which took only families. There was no work, the whole Arab world was in turmoil.

He heard of a man setting up an orphanage near Amman. Along with hundreds of other half-starved, louse-infested urchins he somehow reached the place and fought to the front of the queue. The man was taking only 20 boys and Amin was too late. He was turned away but unlike the rest, Amin did not go. Instead he crept back at night and into the man's room. There he begged to be taken in, promising to do anything, so the man fed and bathed him, burned his filthy clothes and, before giving him new ones, put Amin's promise to the test.

The boy did not make a sound, aware that his pain and humiliation were the price of survival.

Throughout his years at the orphanage, Amin was the focus of the man's deprivations. In return he was fed and educated, showing a determination to get through, using subterfuge and flattery. At puberty Amin understood that sex was both sadistic and masochistic, soft words and gentle caresses followed by violence, the inflicting and bearing of pain. With the man he bore it and the favours he gave won him a position of unchallenged authority over the others. He selected lovers from among the younger boys and found it more exciting if they were unwilling.

By sixteen he was brash and self-confident, a ruthless, cunning leader who learned nothing of importance in class but still knew all that needed knowing. The man got him a United Nations grant and a place at the newly renamed Cairo University.

"Come back to me in the holidays, Amin," ordered the man, squeezing his genitals. But Amin, poisoned with resentment, vowed silently never to return.

The man drove with him to the station but Amin did not board the train. He waited unseen until nightfall and for the second time in his life crept into the man's room. The man sat, the flat pita bread in his hand onto which he shovelled humus from one of the many dishes of a *mezze* spread on the table before him.

He stood up, surprised as Amin entered but had time to say only "Amin..!" before the boy crossed quickly and crashed his fist into his face. He fell back into his chair but Amin grabbed his hair and crammed the slab of bread and humus into his gaping mouth. As the man choked, he dragged him from the chair, pushing his face down into the sticky yellow bowl, still holding him firm by the hair. The man struggled, sending plates crashing to the floor, but Amin was fully grown, taller, younger and stronger than the fat, pathetic, blubbering creature whose life he was choking away.

The struggle was much weaker when Amin saw the knife, its long, serrated blade protruding from a bowl of fruit. He took it by the wooden handle and plunged it into the man's rectum. The body heaved convulsively as if making one last massive effort to break free. Amin twisted the weapon sadistically, bereft of feeling except for disgust at the foul-smelling substance that oozed through the dying man's trousers. Then he was still. Amin became aware of his own rasping breath. It was so loud someone would surely hear. He walked quickly to the door, opening it just enough to see out.

The courtyard was empty and dark except for a light over the door to the boys' dormitory some distance away. Amin looked back at the body slumped across the table. Then he slipped into the night, to the train, bound for Cairo and freedom forever from the one person who dared abuse him.

His freedom, won with killing, was a natural step towards winning freedom for his country. In Egypt were many students like Amin.

Cairo was a city in turmoil. The Egyptian Army revolt the previous year had ousted the monarchy and cleared the way for Nasser, who was rapidly rising to power. By 1954 Nasser was prime minister and wrangling with the British over ownership of the Suez Canal. The students who carried out attacks against British troops in those years were encouraged, among them was Yasser Arafat.

Amin liked what Arafat had to say, joined his Palestine Student Federation, becoming one of the Generation of Revenge pledged to purify Palestine and drive the Jews into the sea. Only the British guarding Suez stood in his way.

Federation meetings were noisy, sometimes violent, which was why Amin first noticed the bedouin boy. He was much bigger than the others and sprawled in his seat, listening casually, while all around him young men jumped up and down, shouting excitedly.

David was a year younger than Amin but he knew the desert and could shoot straight. He was not true bedouin, half British half Arab, but the Jews killed his father and the British shamed his mother by shunning her.

Amin recruited him into his unit, carrying out hit and run raids at Suez. He was a solitary youth who would rather keep watch than sit with the others, rather scout ahead than follow. Amin could never fully manipulate him as he did the rest, but he took orders unquestioningly, was swift and silent and deadly accurate with a Mauser. He found paths through the desert, so the unit could attack from unexpected quarters, covering their tracks and retreating as quickly as they'd struck. Amin wished for half a dozen Davids. He could drive the British from Suez himself.

David learned how to handle explosives, used them well and quickly became proficient at sabotage, knowing almost instinctively where to do greatest damage. As a sniper he needed only one clear shot. The enemy never had a second chance to pinpoint him. "You strike like a sword, my friend," Amin said. "You are our sword, our *hussam*. It is a good name for you, an Arab name, Hussam, better than David, the Jewish king."

The name stuck. Amin gave him command and his own unit. Hussam, the Sword became a legend, famous throughout Egypt and Palestine and in his own small country, Qmrah.

Then began the real business. Backed by Nasser, Amin ran raids into Israel. This was what he wanted, the beginning of the revenge he had patiently awaited. Hussam had more success than he, destroying a radio transmitter, laying mines, ambushing army patrols. Sometimes he waited behind on the border for the inevitable reprisal, picking off the officers with sniper fire.

Then came Suez. Pitched by Nasser into the heart of battle, the *fedayeen* were all but wiped out. Hussam's talent for sabotage, scuttling ships in the canal, blowing up British installations, ensured his unit was one of the few which survived and continued harassing the Israelis after their ignominious retreat from Sinai.

But Hussam abandoned Palestine. He left suddenly and, though Amin sent for him many times, refused to return.

Amin sighed. They were good, those days in Egypt. Here at Sufa things were different. Like the other refugee camps it was a breeding ground of discontent, the ideal place for a *fedayeen* military cell. Recruitment was high. Amin's soldiers were popular. They protected their fellow Palestinians from harassment from government troops and in return received food, shelter and support.

In the distance, rose the pink and purple slopes of Mount Hermon which sheltered the Druze villages. Amin spat in disgust. The Druze were a curse. They collaborated with Israel and protected the cease fire lines. They were good too. It was hard to get *fedayeen* missions through Druze country.

He stretched, looking at his watch. It was three o'clock. He had slept most of the day but not well. He sat back on the low bunk, clearing the sleep from his mind and trying to identify the source of unease. It was the woman! Ah yes, the woman.

It was easy enough taking her. Whatever that miserable dog gave her kept her lifeless all night. Getting over the border was the difficult part. Crossing it anywhere was risky, so many minefields, so many patrols. It had to be done on foot, and quickly. The money and the woman slowed them down but what they would buy would be worth it in the end. Or would it? Would the British pay up?

He shrugged. If they didn't her family would. And in any case she would be easy to dispose of. Still he was uneasy. He paced the bare room impatiently. Last night it seemed a good idea. Now he wasn't so sure. Women were trouble where there were men.

Snatches of his dream returned. The woman was screaming and he hit her but she screamed louder. Try as he might to shut her up, he could not. Even with his hands round her throat, crushing the life from her, God knows how, she still screamed.

Where was she now? He'd left her with Kushi while he slept.

"So, this is what they use for money in Jerusalem?" Kushi joked when he met them with the Jeep a mile from the border.

"This is what they use!" Amin replied throwing the bags in the back. "The woman is a little extra British currency."

Back at camp he gave instructions before going to his room. "Find out more about her. We'll talk later."

Amin walked the few yards along the narrow dirt street to the command post. The room was sparsely furnished with a few wooden chairs grouped around a central table. Cardboard boxes along one wall held papers, mainly old newspapers mixed in with communiques from Beirut. Empty tins, bottles and dirty plates were scattered around.

Kushi lay on a threadbare sofa studying a piece of paper. He was a short, squat man with narrow, cruel eyes, a moustache and half-grown beard. A chewed cigar hung from the corner of his mouth. He looked up and smiled, showing bad uneven teeth. "Ah! The hero wakes," he said sarcastically.

Amin smiled. "Hero eh? We are all heroes!" He flung out his arms to the others in the room. They were five in all, including Baseem and Fayez. The other was a young recruit whom Amin embraced vigorously, kissing him exuberantly on the cheek.

Kushi continued unenthusiastically: "But you, my friend, are an official hero. We've heard from High Command in Beirut." He waved the paper. "They want details of your mission to give to all the newspapers of the world."

Amin looked irritated. "*Y'allah*, to boast! That's all they ever do. Who will believe them?" He paused, looking at each in turn. Suddenly he smiled again, punching Baseem playfully on the arm. "Eh, but we did well, my brother, we did well."

"What shall I tell Beirut?"

"Tell them to make a hero of someone else. We have work to do. Where's the woman?"

Kushi jerked his head towards a door; the room he reserved for interrogations for which he had an extraordinary talent, learned in the training camps of Syria, and for which he earned the name Kushi, "the Black One".

Amin glanced at the door. "Was that necessary? For a woman?"

"Maybe not, but it's good to practice sometimes."

Amin slammed his fist on the table. "We need her alive!"

"She is alive," Kushi said soothingly. "She won't cross her legs for a while, that's all." He winked and chuckled while Amin eyed him coldly.

"Is this all they teach in Syria?"

"In Syria?" Kushi roared with laughter. "I taught them some things in Syria." He stood up, opening the door and holding it for Amin.

The room was small, an old store with one high window. A metal bar with hooks from which meat once hung ran below the ceiling along one wall. There was a small wooden table and chair, nothing more. It stank of sweat and cigar smoke, and fear. In a corner on the floor was the woman, her knees drawn up in front of her. She whimpered and looked up with dull, frightened eyes, trying to push back into the corner. Amin would not have known her as the one Baseem lifted from the sugar pink bed in Jerusalem. He raised her chin. Her face was swollen, cheeks streaked with dirt, eyes rimmed with red, lips split and congealed with blood. Her head dropped back on her arms. She was barely conscious.

Amin's dream returned, the dream in which he couldn't stop her screams. So it wasn't altogether a dream. Furiously, he turned on Kushi. "What good is she like this. We need a photo for the ransom."

"So take one. Let them know we mean business."

Amin considered it. Maybe he was right. "What did she tell you?"

Kushi smiled again. "She's a smart one. Tried to be clever. I like the clever ones." He paused but Amin said nothing so he continued sulkily: "She's English.

She's a journalist. She's *Nazrani*, a Christian, with a Christian name, Josephine." He spat.

"Is this all?"

"No."

"What then?" Amin grew impatient.

The smile slowly returned to Kushi's face. "It's as you believed."

"Dimbleby?"

Kushi nodded: "One of the biggest arms makers in the west. He's her daddy!"

CHAPTER 4

On instinct the gazelle raised her head. Her eyes darted towards a rocky outcrop, a bush and then away to the vast lowland. Was there danger? If so where? Ears pricked and nostrils flared she sniffed the hot air, making quick little movements with her delicate head.

She sensed something, heard nothing, not even the shot which killed her instantly. By reflex the graceful body leapt in the air, dropping like a stone as the crack of the rifle echoed and faded.

The danger came from the rocks. It was a man, standing now and easing the tooled leather strap of the rifle onto one shoulder. He jumped down over the loose stones towards the spring where the gazelle had been drinking. In spite of his size, he was as silent and sure-footed as the creature once was which now lay dead at his sandaled feet.

Hussam was tall and powerfully built, western traits inherited from his father. But he was Arab in all other outward appearances, olive-skinned and dark-eyed. He wore a black tunic top and loose-fitting trousers. A black *kaffiyeh* covered his dark hair, shading his neck and face from the glaring sun. He allowed himself one embellishment only, an ancient scarab ring on the little finger of his left hand.

The bullet had entered the head. It was a clean shot, a quick death. Easily he hoisted the animal over his broad shoulders and climbed back to where the camel waited.

He stopped at the spring when he journeyed back from Kahran, dismounting a way off and stealing up behind the rock. Often there would be game grazing or drinking at the water's edge and he took fresh meat home to Bab'ullah. It was still a half-day's journey. He wouldn't make it by nightfall. The late afternoon air was dry and dusty. Here by the spring was a good place to camp.

He gathered wood and foliage for a fire, unrolled a blanket and, in the fading light, sat down to a meal of goat's cheese, olives and bread. From Kahran, the busy capital of Qmrah, to the oasis of Bab'ullah was almost a day's drive following the low ground. The same route took three days by camel but Hussam did it quicker than any vehicle by cutting across the steep and dangerous rocky ridge which separated fertile coast from desert interior.

The Prophet said the camel was an example of the wisdom of God. For three and a half thousand years camels had carried people and their wares across vast oceans of sun-scorched sand, thriving on desert scrub which no other creature could eat. The camel opened up the world to the Arabs and a good camel could still beat a Jeep unless the distance was short, the ground firm and flat.

Hussam could have chosen a Jeep. His work was with any vehicle which would serve a military purpose. He disliked it. Improving the irrigation system he built at Bab'ullah was more constructive. But vehicles made money. They were part of Hijazi's contribution to the Palestine war effort.

Hijazi, his stepfather was shrewd. He believed in the cause but he also believed in charging the *fedayeen* a high price for vehicles and arms. Hijazi was wealthy now but still lived the simple life of a bedouin.

Twenty years ago the family fled Jerusalem and the big house in Kattomon before the advancing Israelis. The suburb was Arab territory before the so-called War of Independence. So was the Jaffa Road in the city centre where, in just five years, Hijazi built up a profitable business as a merchant dealing in carpets.

The oldest son of a bedouin family, he had quarrelled with his father and come to Jerusalem to make his fortune. He was already rich when he married Hussam's mother.

In 1948 came the Israeli War of Independence and they lost everything. He remembered holding onto the hand of his mother, hugely pregnant, as she trudged along the roadside, carrying Ahmed the baby, Hijazi's firstborn. Hijazi staggered under the weight of a large bundle containing the most essential of their possessions; a refugee family among thousands pouring along the road to Transjordan out of a city from which rose columns of black smoke and the sound of gunfire.

The refugee camp toughened Hussam. There was no room in the tiny tent for him and he slept outside, even in the rain. At 11, big for his age, he had rarely found it necessary to fight. Now he fought not just boys. but full-grown men. He fought for life itself: the food, clothing, medicine and blankets the strong tried to take from the weak. He won respect and for the first time understood the value of strength and independence.

He was street wise, old beyond his years when Hijazi took the family and returned to the desert. Hussam faced yet another big change, from the cramped, filthy, hostile camp to the massiveness of the untamed wilderness. He withdrew more into himself, overawed by the vastness of it all, the emptiness, the harsh and unrelenting starkness of rocks, sand and sun. Here were no walls to hide him, no rubbish dumps to scavenge, no food except what one raised or hunted.

Hussam was old enough to go with the caravans on their long journeys. From the camel drivers he learned the ways of the desert, where there was water, where one must ask permission or wait to drink and where one could take regardless. He learned the law of the desert, the swift and cruel retribution which both bedouin and nature mete out to the weak.

When Hijazi became *sheikh*, the family moved to the oasis of Bab'ullah and made it their home, Hussam was 15 and considered himself a man. He was already over six foot and a match for any bedouin. He could shoot and ride well. On both camel and horseback, he challenged the best.

With money left by his British father for his education, Hussam was sent to Egypt, to school. If he were clever there was money enough for university too. When he returned, a graduate engineer, Hijazi was already tapping an insatiable market for guns. He rolled sheaves of them in carpets for the caravans from Qmrah to the borders of Israel.

But apart from his hunting rifle, Hussam would have nothing to do with weapons. Hijazi was at first mystified and later disgusted by his refusal to help. "You killed Jews. How can you kill without guns?" he demanded. "You think they come from Allah? They come from me!" he thundered.

There was no defence. He had killed and God knew where his gun came from. But Hussam stood firm as his stepfather railed. He busied himself with the task of irrigating the land around the small oasis tended by his mother, goaded constantly by Hijazi. "You work for women. I work for Palestine," he jibed.

His mother begged them to stop and find a way of working together. Grudgingly Hijazi outlined his plan. He'd located a cheap source of old and damaged ex-military vehicles. Hussam had the knowledge to rebuild them. Would he do this? It was poor work for an engineer but, with a glance at his mother's anxious face, he agreed. An uneasy peace had since existed between him and Hijazi. They kept out of each other's way.

Hussam was in Kahran one week in every four to check over the latest two or three arrivals. Some were beyond repair and he broke them for spares. He telexed direct for parts not available in Qmrah or which he could not make or recover and had them flown in. It cost more but the turnover was faster and Hijazi's customers were impatient.

Jamal acted as the front, importing and repairing trucks. He was a good mechanic, well paid to share his workshop and ensure that what Hussam ordered arrived, ready for Hussam's next visit. Jamal learned much from Hussam, often able to carry out repairs on his own. For Hussam there was at least peace and distraction in the job. As each vehicle was finished he told Hijazi. Next time he went, it was gone.

He built up the fire, pulling the blanket around his shoulders. It was bitter at night. He lay back looking up at the clear starlit sky and listening. A sound unfamiliar in the desert grew slowly from the distance. He sat up, turning to the lowland. A single bright light pierced the darkness, rising and falling with the undulations of the land. The light became two. It was a vehicle, a Land Rover by the engine pitch labouring over the rough ground. Hussam watched the white lights become red as the vehicle passed below, continuing through the darkness deeper into the desert.

Hijazi would have a visitor.

43

"*Abu, abu*!" young David, who had been scanning the desert since he woke, ran fast, rapidly closing the distance between himself and the approaching camel. "*Abu, abu*!" he panted as Hussam reached down, took his son's hand and swept him up on the front of the saddle.

Hussam laughed and kissed David's head. His son was now five but already bigger and stronger than boys two years older. "I knew you would come today, *abu*." David was still breathless, talking rapidly. "*Umma* said she didn't know, but I knew, so I watched and watched. I saw you a long way off but *umma* wouldn't let me come. I had to wait by her till you reached the bamboo."

Hussam looked towards the tent but there was no sign of Leila. If she waited with their son, she had already returned inside. There was no one but the boy to greet him. He couched the camel and, swinging David to the ground, turned towards the Land Rover. A vehicle was a rare sight at the oasis. It was ex-British army, camouflaged and open under a tattered canvas canopy. It stood alone in the central clearing around which the fifteen low black tents clustered.

Hijazi hurried from his tent, looking old and frail compared with the younger man who strode behind him, dressed in battle fatigues. Hussam felt a coldness which the scorching sun could not pierce.

"You arrive in good time, my son," said Hijazi excitedly. "We have a visitor."

They faced each other for a moment in silence. The visitor spoke first, throwing his head back in a laugh and holding out his hand. "Hello, old friend. It's been a long time."

Hussam slowly took the hand. "Peace, Amin," he said in a voice which lacked warmth. Amin was big now in the *fedayeen*. In Kahran, Hussam read of his latest exploit into Jerusalem, the new heart of Israel. *Fatah* were proud of him; the papers were full of it.

Amin caught sight of the gazelle still tied across the camel's shoulders. He smiled broadly. "Through the head! You still strike true, my Sword. Ha! You remember?" Hussam remembered. The name Amin gave him reached Qmrah ahead of him. The people had few heroes. Anyone fighting the British, whose rule in the Middle East had been as unwelcome in Qmrah as elsewhere, won instant acclaim. That Hussam was also active against the Zionists endeared him to them the more.

Hijazi shook him from his thoughts. "Hussam! For shame! Amin is our guest," he said angrily.

"Peace, my friend," Amin soothed, "Your son and I go back a long way. Words are not necessary with us."

"He should at least bid you welcome."

Amin clasped the older man round the shoulders. "You are a good friend of Palestine," he said.

"And you, my enemy's enemy, are my friend," responded Hijazi.

Amin turned again to Hussam. "I need your help. You won't refuse me?"

"He cannot," interjected Hijazi. "I am *sheikh* here."

Amin's eyes stayed on Hussam. "I've brought you a guest, a woman. I need somewhere to keep her which is, let us say, secure. Here in the desert is good. A day's journey anywhere and that only if you know the way."

Hussam looked at the Land Rover. He could see no woman. Hijazi pointed to a tent. "She's in there. She won't give us any trouble," he chuckled. "Amin has seen to that."

Hussam stroked his son's head. All the time the lad had stood listening. Now his father crouched beside him. "Go to *umm*. I'll follow." The boy flung his arms round Hussam's neck and then ran off.

"Your son," said Amin, watching David with interest, "is fond of you."

Hijazi was irritated. "Such affection in a boy is unseemly!"

Hussam walked between them towards the tent Hijazi had pointed out. He lifted the thin canvas flap and

46

went inside, followed by Hijazi and Amin. A woman lay on the rugs covering the sand, a rough blanket thrown over her. She was motionless, her face swollen, eyes closed. He crouched beside her looking at Amin but Amin's eyes told him nothing so he felt beneath the woman's chin, finding, after a few seconds, the faint pulse which betrayed life. His fingers traced a series of vicious red burns from the neck down to the shoulder and he looked again at Amin.

"Kushi," Amin nodded.

Hussam felt the coldness descend again. "Why?"

Amin shrugged: "Kushi is Kushi."

"Are these the marks of Palestinian courage?" Hussam asked derisively.

"Be silent!" Hijazi cut in sharply. "Amin is our guest. Show him respect."

Hussam still watched Amin. "Who is she?"

Amin was unashamed. "She's a hostage," he began, taking his time. Casually he pulled a cigarette from his shirt pocket and lit it, inhaling deeply. "We have soldiers now. There are many *fedayeen*, though they are not as we were in Egypt. You talk of courage. They have courage. But it's not enough. They need guns, many and quickly. We were in Jerusalem, our last night, our last town. We had a tip-off from a friend that this woman was worth more than everything we collected in Palestine. Hussam, she was a gift to us, a gift from God. Her father is the chairman of Armature."

"Good guns," put in Hijazi, "good and true, and," he looked sideways at Amin, "expensive."

Amin continued: "We want one million pounds Sterling in arms and ammunition for her return." He turned to Hijazi. "They'll come through Kahran. You, my friend, will bring them to us. You'll be well rewarded." Hijazi beamed.

Hussam was unimpressed. He pushed past them and went outside. In the shade of her tent, his mother sat talking to Nooria, the little sister he loved. They fell silent as they saw him. The whole camp was silent, waiting. "Come quickly," he called. They hurried across, following him inside.

"*Y'allah*," his mother exclaimed. "Is she alive?"

"Bring water and what medicines you have. Do your best."

Hijazi was furious. "Since when do you give orders in my camp?" he stormed.

Hussam ignored him, turning instead on Amin. "You still do such things Amin? In the name of Palestine you do them?"

Amin faced him. "For my country I will do what's necessary."

"I won't help you in this."

"Have you forgotten your father? Murdered by the Jews?" Hussam was silent.

Hijazi joined in: "What of your family, I, who raised you as my own? We lost all. Do you remember the camp, what it did to your mother?"

"Hundreds of thousands of our people still live like that," Amin continued. "O.K., forget the woman, she's nothing. But don't betray your brothers. Soon they'll have guns but who will lead them? Hussam, they would follow you to death itself. Fight with us as you once fought. Remember Arafat? You wanted to be like him."

"Arafat is Palestinian, so are you."

"Arafat is Arab, so are you!" thundered Amin.

"I am only half Arab."

"Then you are only half a man!" railed Hijazi.

"Perhaps."

Amin sighed, throwing out his arms expansively. "Hussam, we were as brothers. Your brother needs you. This is no war of halves. We cannot be half Arab, have half a home, half a country. We must have all, or nothing!"

Hussam looked down at the woman. Nooria was tearing linen into strips, while his mother bathed congealed blood from the swollen face. "In Egypt I was young. I knew no better until Kibbutz Hashemesh. What you..." he paused, "What we did will sicken me until I die. I have no more stomach for your war."

Hijazi raised both arms: "Would I were younger."

Amin walked to the tent flap looking out silently. Then he turned and indicated the woman. "You want me to take her back?"

"She wouldn't make it. You know it."

Amin snorted. "It matters little. If her father refuses our terms she'll die anyway and if he doesn't he won't know until it's too late."

"Then choose, Amin. If you leave her, she's under my protection, no one else's, understand?" he looked at Hijazi meaningfully. "Otherwise, take her. I want no more death on my hands."

"Then she's yours," Amin smiled, "until I want her back."

"Why? To play with her some more?"

Hijazi interceded. "Enough! He'll do it. If she lives she'll stay as long as you want. If she dies, well, the desert keeps its secrets. You are welcome Amin. Excuse your brother," he glanced with contempt at Hussam who crouched by the woman, "he is not as he was."

The scene interested Amin. Hijazi was wrong, he thought. Hussam was a born warrior. He'd never be anything else. But every warrior had weakness which a good leader could find and use. With most *fedayeen* it was their inherent vanity, self-delusion or burning hatred. Hussam was strong but he was, as he said, only half Arab and betrayed affection for his son, compassion for the woman.

Amin smiled. His journey might prove more fruitful than he hoped. Putting his hand on Hijazi's shoulder he allowed his host to lead him from the tent.

CHAPTER 5

The noisc of London's traffic was muted. Little of modern life penetrated the well-worn, comfortable red plush and oak panelling of the Carthonian Club. It smelled of last night's cigar smoke and this morning's Mr. Sheen and the early sunshine slanted in through tall dusty windows throwing squares of brightness onto the fringed rugs and deeply polished floor boards.

His back to the newly lit fire, Sir Roland Dimbleby rocked agitatedly from heels to toes, glancing for perhaps the twentieth time at his gold Rolex watch. He was a large, good looking man in his fifties, greying at the temples. His face normally assumed an expression of bonhomie but today he frowned, deeply thoughtful.

Footsteps echoed on the boards as a man entered at the far end of the long room. Sir Roland waited for the new arrival to reach him, his eyes fixed on some distant point ahead. The man stopped directly in front of him, smiling rather too readily. He was red faced and breathless, carrying too much weight. He extended a hand which shook, though almost imperceptibly.

"Roly, old chum."

The big man took it briefly. "Jack," he said. "Good of you to come."

"Damned sorry about this whole business. Sorry your daughter's mixed up in it."

"Josephine's a headstrong girl. Insists she can look after herself. Always could till now. You saw the ransom note?"

"'Fraid so."

"So you know what they, want?" His voice was matter-of-fact.

Jack nodded. "Sit down Roly. Let's have a drink." He hailed a waiter. "Gin and tonic. Make it a double. And you, old boy?"

"For God's sake Jack, I'm not here to socialise. I want to know what you're doing about it!"

"Everything we can," Jack was magnanimous. "You've seen the Foreign Office boys. First class Arabists y'know."

First class bullshitters, thought Sir Roland but restrained himself, leaned forward conspiratorially and said: "Jack, we've been friends since the old school. I want to know the score. What are the chances?"

Jack's drink arrived. "Put it on my tab, that's a good chap." He took a large gulp then sat back meditatively. "Tricky bastards the Arabs, excitable, emotionally unstable. Remember them in Egypt. About to slit our throats they were till Monty won at El Alamein. Suddenly they were all pally again."

"Jack, we've been selling to the Arabs for years. Things have changed a lot since then."

Jack held up his hand. "Not your average customer these. Not likely to be the mainstream PLO either. Too much bad publicity in kidnapping. According to our chaps, there are ructions in the Palestinian camp. Big power struggles, splinter groups, private militias and so on. Dozens of them. No one with overall control." He sipped his drink. "Not to put too fine a point on it, it's a bloody mess. God knows where it'll end."

"Which of them has Josephine?"

He shook his head. "Could be any of several. Small time leaders with inflated ambitions. Big frogs, little ponds and all that. We don't know where she was taken after Jerusalem. The Israelis say the ceasefire line's impregnable but that's rubbish. As to where she is now, well..." He finished his drink and hailed the waiter for a refill. Jack glanced uneasily at his friend. Not even MI6 could keep track of all the breakaway factions. He doubted the Arabs themselves could. Some were led by bloody lunatics, some by religious fanatics. In the unlikely event they did find the right gang, there'd be no talking to them. They'd kill her instantly.

Sir Roland interrupted his thoughts. "What the hell do the Israelis have to say for themselves?"

Jack waited while the waiter placed another gin on the table, half filling the glass from a small tonic bottle. "Thanks, old chap," he said, lifting the glass. "According to them she wasn't having too much luck as a newshound. Short of money. Took a job in a bar chatting up the customers. Damages a girl's reputation that sort of thing you know."

Sir Roland was silent. It was typical of Josephine that she should try to sort out her own problems instead of cabling home. She had an independent streak which he could hardly condemn. It was obviously inherited from him.

"Well," continued Jack, "they reckon these bar girls vanish with their Arab boyfriends all the time. Turn up again a few weeks later when the eastern promise wears off."

"That's ridiculous. Josephine's not like that. And what about the ransom note?"

"Ah, yes. Calm down old man. I'm only telling you the score." Jack looked around as if to ensure no one was listening. "We thought it best not to mention the ransom. As we see it, it'd shut off your last recourse. Let's face it old man, you may have to give 'em what they want. If the Israelis knew, there's no way they'd let it happen. A million pounds worth of guns in terrorist hands? You'd be damned lucky to get 'em out of Southampton."

Sir Roland stood impatiently. He walked to the window. "The Israelis don't have a bloody say in it. We're big suppliers of theirs. They wouldn't jeopardize that."

"Come on, Roly. There'd be nothing to link it to Israel. A lot can happen to a ship at sea."

Sir Roland was pensive. Over his shoulder he said: "Will it really come to that?"

Jack was looking down into his drink. "Our chaps'll probably tell you to stall, ask for proof she's alive and so on." He looked up. "But if it doesn't work and you have to go ahead, we won't intervene. Just be discreet. Officially, the Foreign Office will deny all knowledge. If it leaked out we're sending arms to terrorists there'd be an international outcry. On the other hand there are no diplomatic channels for this sort of thing. Sorry old chap."

There was a long silence as Sir Roland looked out unseeingly. At last he said: "If these arms get through there'll be an escalation in attacks on Israel."

"Off the record Roly, the minister isn't too concerned about Israel. They've just thrashed the Arabs. He doesn't feel a million pounds worth of guns to the *Fatah* rabble will make much difference. They'll more likely shoot each other than the Jews."

Sir Roland nodded thoughtfully, then looked back to the room. Decisively he returned to Jack and shook his hand. "Thanks for putting me in the picture. I appreciate it." He walked towards the door, footsteps echoing across the polished wood.

"What'll you do?" Jack shouted after him.

At the door Sir Roland shrugged but did not turn. "There's always someone prepared to supply these bastards. If they don't get arms from us, they'll get them somewhere else," he said and left.

***

It was hot and the heat was all she knew. Everything else seemed a throbbing numbness. In her ears was the sound of a big diesel truck going up a steep hill in low gear. The truck wasn't moving away. Her mouth was dry and she had no interest in opening her eyes. Pain shot through her as something under her neck pushed her up and then her lips were moist. With the pain the panic returned.

She choked on the water, feeling for the sadist's hand, trying to stop it. Her mouth tried to say "No!" but all that came was a hoarse moan. Her lips were moist again and this time she swallowed, her hands finding his hand and holding onto it feebly. She opened her eyes. They wouldn't focus. But it was him. She couldn't escape. She couldn't stop him, couldn't stop him hurting her. Her body ached now. Her head was shot through with pain and all the time the truck went uphill. She closed her eyes and opened them again. Still there, he was still there, smiling cruelly.

Now she could feel her hands. They were free! If she moved quickly, took him by surprise…With a massive effort she threw his hand from her face, lunging forward and turning her body until she knelt, dazed, facing him. He too was kneeling, swaying, reaching for her arms and pinning them to her sides.

"No! No!" she fought free, falling backwards, then rolling onto her stomach, trying to crawl from him. She was tired, so tired. Every move was agony.

Hussam watched her. She would pass into unconsciousness again soon. He could carry her back then. He looked at his mother.

"Hussam, go. You can't do anything," she said gently. "It is better that Nooria and I nurse her. She's afraid of you."

He nodded and walked out of the tent. It was the fifth day of Hamseen, the lazy but searing desert wind which resolutely blows dust and sand through a merciless, scorching heat, sapping the strongest man's strength, fraying the mildest temper, turning the meek into murderers. Above, the sun was hazy in a yellow sky and below the world was colourless, formless. Nothing moved in Hamseen. The desert stood still. If the wind didn't change soon it would be worse for the woman.

For a week she had lain there, lapsing into troubled sleep between bouts of hysterical ranting. Amin did this and now he had brought her here. Hussam felt the turmoil within him rise. The war threatened to suck him in again. It was not his, this war of women and children, of helpless and innocent victims, of any living thing which could be abused to wring horror, pity and revulsion from the world and focus its attention on Palestine. He wanted no part of it. One night, long ago decided that. The weariness which descended on him then had never fully lifted. He felt it now with all its guilt and remorse.

He entered his tent. Leila looked up. She sat listlessly, her hands on her swollen stomach. He sat beside her, putting an arm around her shoulders. "It's the Hamseen. Soon it will change. It must be difficult for you," he said.

She sighed. "I must go to Ein Mara again before the baby comes."

"When?"

"Another week."

"It's too far for you like this."

She smiled wearily. "The walk will do me good."

"I'll come with you."

"You're a man, you've done your part," she teased. "I need women now. Your mother will come, Nooria too."

She came from a traditional Arab family where a man's right to do as he wished was unquestionable except in the matter of childbirth. In that, women reigned supreme. Even when the baby was born, the father had no right to hold it until it had been passed around the women, sometimes a whole village of them, who attended the birth.

When Hussam first met her, Leila was veiled. Being a distant relative, his mother made the approach and the families agreed to a match. It caused a considerable stir in the neighbourhood and Leila's father was overjoyed such a celebrity should ask for her.

She glimpsed him from her window as he arrived with Hijazi to talk with her father. Her sisters' giggling caused him to look up and she closed the shutters quickly. Later, when the women were summoned to serve them, she had more time to observe him. She was disappointed. He wore such dull clothes for an important visit. She had expected one with his reputation to be altogether more magnificent. He dressed then as now and looked out of place, awkward in the opulent surroundings of her father's house. He watched her too and she blushed, glad of the veil.

The wedding date was set. It was to be in six months to give the families time to invite sufficient guests. But Hussam came back sooner than expected. As she left the house for the *souk* one day, accompanied by her mother and sisters, Hussam appeared from behind a wall and tore the veil away. She was so startled she stood dumfounded. Her mother leapt at him, yelling and beating him about the head with the large palm-frond basket she carried. Fending off the blows, he smiled sheepishly, dropped the veil and fled.

The family was outraged. Hijazi calmed things with an expensive gift and an explanation that it was only the young man's curiosity to see his bride's face before the marriage which caused the incident. He meant no harm and had been severely reprimanded.

Hussam obviously liked what he saw because from then on things went smoothly and the wedding took place as planned, but not before Leila got her own back.

She was allowed to take him to a room where, observed by all the women, but without any support from the men, the groom traditionally watched the bride demonstrate her housekeeping skills. Aware of Hussam's indiscretion, the women were keen to make him as uncomfortable as possible. All, including Leila, removed their veils and eyed him seductively, beckoning and blowing kisses, until he blushed crimson. He was barely able to pay attention to her mime of housework and all the tasks she would henceforth assume. Around him, the women laughed and fell into each other's arms giggling as he looked about in confusion.

When they led him back to the men, Hussam was suitably humbled but only until the feast ended. Alone with him, with any man, for the first time, it was her turn to feel embarrassed, and afraid. He was a stranger. She had seen him only three times and they had never spoken. Now she had nothing to say.

This was the first time a young man should see the face of his beloved and many a bride waited in terror for her groom's reaction, but Hussam had already cheated, so had she, and the lifting of the veil held no surprises. He kissed her and his lips felt warm and full on hers. Patiently he undid the many tiny buttons on the front of her white and red wedding tunic, slipping it from her shoulders so she stood naked. Her eyes closed as he looked at her body and then, lifting her, laid her on the low couch that was their marriage bed. Kneeling on the floor beside her, he kissed her mouth, her throat, her breasts and then her mouth again.

The terror in her was subsiding. In its place came a longing, a compulsive stirring in the pit of her stomach. He parted her legs and kissed her there too. Leila thought she would die, but whether of embarrassment or excitement she didn't know, didn't care. She cried in pain when he first entered her, but he covered her face with light kisses, filled her mind with his whispered endearments, drew her to him and around him, placing her body beyond her control until she cried out again no longer knowing herself to be anything other than a part of him.

Then she was guilty because she had known a pleasure reserved for harlots. As a wife, her body was her husband's to enjoy, hers only to bear his sons. But she never learned to suppress the ecstasy he aroused and prayed he would not despise her.

Hussam brought her to Bab'ullah which, though small and remote was noisier than the city. As if to mock the silence of the great desert the bedouin kept up heated and animated conversations all day long.

At first she was homesick and Hussam was kind. Sometimes, when he went by Jeep rather than camel to Kahran, he took her to visit her family. Now she was heavily pregnant with her second child and the journey was too long and difficult. In the last eight months she had left Bab'ullah only once to walk the day's journey to Ein Mara where, three times a year, a doctor from the antenatal service visited. It was time to go again.

Leila would not have bothered, but Hussam's mother insisted and, as her mother-in-law, must be obeyed. A group of the women would go with her, with two men for protection, camels to carry provisions and an ass to carry her when she tired of walking. It was quite a caravan and Leila enjoyed being the source of such attention.

CHAPTER 6

The *kibbutz* truck halted briefly. Behind it vehicles began hooting impatiently while a man dressed in pale khaki trousers and short-sleeved shirt jumped down onto the pavement. He turned to shout his thanks to the driver, waving the hand which held his rolled-up beret before slamming the door and crossing to mount the-steps of an unremarkable yellow concrete building.

Uri Gershon was a paratrooper, a colonel in the reserve, but his ambling gait, wiry frame and good-natured expression betrayed him as a *kibbutznik*. In north Galilee he lived a life dedicated largely to the glorification of apples, a cash crop of that lush green province whose malarial swamps he helped drain into the River Jordan fifteen years earlier. The Hula Valley now stood beneath acres of apple orchards, alfalfa, cotton and water melons, the abundance of water there utilized to provide carp from big shallow oblong fish ponds.

Here in Jerusalem, he was a soldier. Every Israeli, man and woman was called for national service and thereafter the men were recalled for eight weeks every year.

Israel was at her exuberant best now. Only last year the Six Day War brought her the prize for which every Jewish heart longed: the Old City of Jerusalem. Throughout the country they still danced Horas and sang war songs, one in particular. There wasn't a dry eye in the house whenever singer Noomi Shemer sang her hauntingly beautiful *Ir-u-shalyeem Shel Tzahav*, Jerusalem of Gold.

Uri had been one of the first through St. Stephen's Gate in the old city wall by which the Jews broke in once before to win back Jerusalem more than 2,000 years ago under Judas Maccabaeus. Then they had lost it. They wouldn't lose it again. Uri vowed it as he wept with the others at the Wall.

He returned again and again to the Old City. Who had captured whom, he thought, entranced by the aura, the people, the soul of it. Soon the shops and bars were open again and he bargained with the merchants, drank Turkish coffee or mint tea with them, made friends, good friends. Why couldn't it be like this? Arab and Jew sitting together?

In the war he was a major. Now, a colonel with military honours, but Israel was full of brave men. Every soldier had his moment of glory and a story to tell, a proud boast. They were boys whistling in the dark. Israel longed for peace in the certain knowledge there were more wars to come. Already the cease fire lines were under attack. In too many border *kibbutzim*, the sun rarely shone on the children. They ate, slept and went to school in underground bunkers. How long could a small country go on under such siege?

It was common purpose which held his people together. Remove the Arab threat and Israel would destroy itself from within. Put two Jews in one room and get three opinions, they joked. Well, soon he would see.

Uri took the steps two at a time. On the first landing, without knocking, he entered a small high room. The shutters were closed against the midday sun but there was light enough for him to recognize the two men present.

"Shalom, Uri!" A small man rose from behind the big desk to shake his hand. He was old now, slightly built with a pronounced stoop, but Avrom Ezer was a statesman of massive political stature. "You know Ytzak." Uri shook hands warmly with both men, slapping Ytzak on the back.

Ytzak Weissman was advisor to the *Memuneh*, that curious father-figure, answerable only to the prime minister, who headed *Mossad*, Israel's Secret Service. He was a gaunt, pale man and looked unhealthy next to Uri. He spent too much time in an office. On his wrist was the tattooed number they gave him as a child in Auschwitz.

Ezer sat, clasping his frail hands in front of him on the desk. He was renowned for coming straight to the point. "We have a kidnapping. A woman was taken from Jerusalem, right under our noses. Who took her, where she is, we don't know. We want you to find her and bring her back unharmed." He pushed a file towards Uri who opened it.

"A good-looking woman," he nodded appreciatively, holding up the immigration form to which a passport photo was stapled.

"We intercepted this message," said Ytzak. "It came from Damascus, but that means nothing." Uri read the photocopied sheet of Arabic slowly. He had learned it on *kibbutz* where a *sephardi* immigrant from Iraq taught lessons to any *kibbutznik* wanting to learn. When he finished reading he let out a whistle.

Ytzak retrieved the note. "The British want to know where she is. They said her family were worried because she hadn't written for some time."

"They didn't let us in on the ransom," said Ezer. "It means only one thing."

"That they'll do it," said Uri.

"I believe that in the end the decision will be her father's," Ezer continued. "What would you do if you were him?" He shrugged turning his hands palm upward on the desk. "He's a loving father and a rich man."

"He also supplies us," Ytzak put in. "Politically and militarily our hands are tied. In fact, we're almost duty bound to make sure the arms get there. If anything happens to them Israel will be the only suspect. Already France won't sell to us and we daren't risk a British embargo."

Ezer sighed and shrugged again: "What can we do? We must have Armature assault rifles, at least until we get our own Galil into production." He narrowed, his eyes, wagging a finger at Uri: "Yet we cannot let these guns get through. The price for us is too high."

"Did we know who she was?"

"Sure we knew," said Ytzak. "She registered with the press bureau at Beit Hillel two months ago. *Aman* kept an eye on her but only for the military, no more than any other journalist. She took a job two weeks ago at the Rainbow Bar, you know it?"

"A bar girl?"

Ytzak continued: "It happens with a few foreign girls, particularly *sikshes*. We don't give out work permits to non-Jews, so they can't get legitimate work. Or she might just have been writing about it. She's that sort. Still, we had no reason to believe she was in danger. She didn't shout about who she was. *Aman* say whoever has her just struck lucky."

Uri snorted. "A big coincidence huh?"

Ytzak and Ezer exchanged a quick glance.

"We think so too." Ezer leaned forward: "Uri, you have friends in the Old City. Talk to them. The Arabs respect women. They won't like this."

"We want you in from the start. Now you know as much as we do," said Ytzak. "You have the resources of *Shin Beth* at your disposal. The bureau has both Arab and anti-terrorist sections on it. They're reporting back later today."

"How long do we have?"

Ezer spread his hands again. "Without wishing to hurry you may I suggest you start now?"

***

Jodi woke. Above her a ceiling of thin black canvas rose and fell to the breath of a gentle breeze. A woman, older than she, in a long black embroidered gown, like the hundreds that hung in the *souk* of Jerusalem, looked down at her. She had a kind face and smiled as she carefully removed a damp cloth from Jodi's forehead, wrung it out in a bowl of water and replaced it, beautifully cool.

Her mind was clouded. Where was she? Was this Jerusalem? She ached all over, her body was sore. Her mind struggled on the edge of a terrible dream, hazy and disjointed like a dream.

"Don't try to move," said the woman in excellent English. "You've been ill. You will be very weak."

"Where am I?" Her voice was hoarse, her jaw aching.

"That doesn't matter. What matters is that you are safe and will get well."

"Who...?"

"My name is Fatima," the woman interrupted quickly. "Now be quiet and rest. You will have plenty of time to ask questions when you are stronger."

Her flesh burned and Jodi caught sight of her bare arms, running her hands over the red marks. Lifting the sheet she looked down at her naked body. She recoiled suddenly from the woman who did not move but said simply: "You are safe now. The man who did this is far from here."

Confusion, deep hurt and helplessness mingled inextricably. Tears welled in her eyes. "Hush now, hush," soothed Fatima, cradling Jodi in her arms. "Hush and sleep if you can."

Jodi allowed herself to be held. "Sleep," she murmured, closing her eyes. The woman was soft and smelled good. As she inhaled deeply the smell of cigar smoke returned. She fought free with sudden and startling violence. Fatima watched silently as she struggled to stand, clutching the sheet to her. "Where are my clothes?"

The older woman sighed and stood up. "I have some clothes for you," she said, walking to an ornately carved wooden chest. Opening it, she lifted out an embroidered dress, almost identical to the one she wore. She held it by the shoulders as if to inspect it then, gathering it up from the hem, helped Jodi slip it over her head. Standing back she looked at her, then, reaching into the wooden chest, produced a hand mirror. Jodi's hand trembled as she held it up. Her fair hair fell around her shoulders, thick and dishevelled, framing a face which was deathly pale between the yellowing remnants of several bruises. The garment was loose, the hem at least nine inches from the floor.

"You are tall for a woman, and thin. I'm afraid this will have to do." The cotton was light and soft but Jodi winced. Her skin was still tender and every joint ached. Fatima caught her pained expression and gently took the mirror. "Sit and we'll talk," she said, sitting cross-legged on a soft rug. She poured a drink from an earthenware pitcher and, smiling, offered it up to Jodi.

Perhaps because she was weary, perhaps because she sensed the woman was kind, Jodi sat and drank. It had a minty, medicinal taste, not unlike lukewarm mint tea. Fatima smiled encouragingly as she retrieved the empty cup. "You're impatient, but then you're young," Fatima said. "I can tell you little. You must wait until you are stronger and then you must ask Hussam, my son. He's a good man. No harm will come to you while he protects you."

Jodi listened in silence, trying hard to concentrate, to keep her mind from clouding over as the woman's gentle voice soothed and lulled, coaxing her irresistibly into a deep sleep. How long she slept she had no way of knowing but she woke suddenly, a shrill scream echoing in her ears. There was a beating sound and a shadow crossed swiftly over the tent. She was fully awake now, sitting up, trying hard to listen above the loudness of her breathing. She looked around but Fatima had gone.

Quickly she stood and quickly moved to where the tent flap parted slightly. Looking out she saw the oasis for the first time. Low black tents clustered together around a central clearing, beyond which a belt of lush greenery gave way to a merciless desert. In the distance were mountains, reflecting rose-coloured light from a sun which might be rising but which instinct told her was setting.

The cry came again. She looked up to see a bird hovering, motionless, black against the pale sky, its wings stretched, the only sign of movement coming from the quick tilting of its fanned tail, first one way then the other. In a second it fell like a stone. Jodi watched it vanish beyond the palms behind her tent. She waited for it to reappear and when it did not, began walking in the direction it disappeared.

The sand was warm and comforting on her bare feet. The pain seemed less. She felt stronger. Either side of the winding path were tall green bamboo plants, beyond which she couldn't see until suddenly it ended just short of a wide pool, surrounded by date palms and flowering shrubs. A slow clopping sound came from one side, near rough stone walls which channelled water into a stream: some sort of primitive irrigation system, she supposed.

It was then she saw the falcon again. It perched on the gloved hand of a man who, though he stroked and talked to it, looked directly at her. Jodi jumped slightly at the shock of seeing him. He was Arab, bigger than most, and dressed in black. As he looked at her she was aware of the absurdly short and baggy dress she wore. She glanced down at it. When she looked up he was smiling.

"*Ahlan weh sahlan, annisatti*," he greeted her. "You make a good bedouin."

She stared at him and he turned his attention to the falcon stroking the white feathers of its throat gently. The bird watched her with sharp dark eyes, its curved yellow beak, tipped with grey, held the remnants of some red flesh.

Jodi felt irritable and short tempered. "Are you Hussam?" she demanded.

"They call me that," he replied still watching the bird.

"Then tell me where I am and what I'm doing here."

He looked at her. "It's better that you don't ask. All you need know is that you are a guest of the bedouin. You'll be treated with courtesy and respect while you stay."

"Supposing I don't want to stay."

His voice was impassive. "For now you must, until your father pays the ransom."

"Ransom?"

"A million pounds Sterling in arms and ammunition."

Jodi was stunned. "You're mad!" she said.

His voice was suddenly cold. "You are the mad one. Mad to take such risks when you are who you are."

She was silent, trying to be calm, to think clearly, but her brain was still fogged. He turned his attention to the falcon again. With a swift upward movement of his arm, he launched it into the air. Beating its wide grey wings, the falcon took full advantage of the thrust and soared.

"I haven't come to watch you play with your bird," she stormed. "I demand you release me. You've no right to hold me here against my will."

"Sometimes it is not as we will but as Allah wills."

Her eyes narrowed and she raised her chin defiantly. "I can't believe it makes a blind bit of difference to Allah whether I stay or not!"

"Then go," he said absently, looking upwards at the circling falcon.

Go where? She looked out beyond the green-fringed oasis to the empty landscape. It was futile to think she could cross it without even knowing where she was, let alone where she was going. Fighting frustration and self-pity, a rage swelled within her and she flew at him.

"You smug bastard!" She wanted to fight, do anything to try to stop the murderous plot to which it seemed she was central. A million pounds worth of guns! He was right, she was mad. How could she ever have thought her identity would stay a secret in a city like Jerusalem. And now how many innocents would die for her lunacy?

Before she could strike he grabbed her wrists. She had no chance against him but she needed to struggle, to yell, to assure herself she'd done all she could to escape. But he barely moved and the strength of her anger flowed out through his grasp. His eyes reflected the sudden confusion she felt. For an instant they made sense of it all. The struggle ceased. It was pointless.

A shrill cry rang out above. The falcon plummeted earthwards, striking its prey and deftly trapping the floundering bird with strong talons before spreading its wings to glide downwards. He let her go, raising his gloved hand to the falcon. She heard the beat of its wings, felt the rush of air as she turned to stumble back along the path.

CHAPTER 7

Palm leaves brushed disrespectfully against the arches of the marbled veranda, their asymmetry spoiling the perfect proportions of the Sultan's palace. To the small fat man whose leather slippers made a faint shuffling sound as he hurried past at a speed which made him perspire, the journey seemed longer than usual. He halted outside a wide, open lattice door, guarded on either side by soldiers of the royal household in western military uniform. They stood to attention as, half apologetically, he announced himself and glanced down to check that the official insignia of his high office hung straight on his chest. Adjusting his gold-edged black *abba* over the ankle length *thobe* he stood as tall as he could and made the most imposing entrance possible under the circumstances.

He exchanged customary greetings with a particularly handsome youth, once a favourite but who had now outgrown the Sultan's sexual preferences. Showing a keen intelligence and cunning he had managed nevertheless to remain his master's confidant and won position as his Majesty's personal secretary. The boy's manners were impeccable. He greeted the Minister warmly, inquiring as to his family and his health. He repeated the greetings. His whole demeanour was sincere, his face open and honest. He was a most dangerous young man.

Leading the Minister through the double doors from the ante-room to the Sultan's morning room, he bowed low and announced the visitor. Then he withdrew, closing the doors.

A small, serious voice which seemed to be reading something important fell silent. The Minister heard only the low hum of the air conditioning. The room was large, though small by palace standards and was furnished mainly in his Highness' favourite colour, yellow. Large, low gold-framed chairs and couches with squat, ornately embellished cabriole legs surrounded a marquetry coffee table on which stood a bowl of sweets and chocolates. Silken rugs from Tabriz and Tehran were scattered on the floor of dark polished cedar. A vast crystal chandelier hung from the high domed ceiling.

The Sultan reclined on a chaise, wheezing slightly, his hand stroking the blond head of a boy whom the Minister judged to be about seven and who sat cross-legged on the floor, a big book open on his lap.

Sheikh Abd'allah, servant of God and Sultan of Qmrah, was a large, obese man whose family and friends had amassed sizeable fortunes from the positions of power to which he appointed them. He was decadent in the extreme, sparing himself no indulgence. In younger days he travelled the Mediterranean on his yacht, visiting the famous casinos, where he would pick a roulette table by whim and order it to be cleared for his own private use, placing 500,000 dinars on the spin of a wheel. Now he no longer had the energy for such strenuous pastimes and contented himself with a luxurious, homely existence lived mainly here in his palace or at his summer house in the high, cool mountains which rose from the coastal plain to the south.

He nodded recognition as the Minister gave the formal greetings, then waved him to a chair. Silently, the boy regarded the newcomer, his eyes wide but dull. Perhaps he was drugged, perhaps just tired.

"He is beautiful," said the Sultan, still stroking the head of fine fair hair.

"Very beautiful, your Highness," agreed the Minister.

"Expensive, but then the blond ones always are. Clever too. Already he reads Arabic."

"He is fortunate to have your patronage."

Abd'allah, servant of God, wheezed a sigh as if preparing to meet some disagreeable task. "I have given considerable thought to the matter of the Israelis."

Shifting uncomfortably in his seat the Minister was silent, nervously fingering the string of beads in his pocket.

"Their impudence is appalling."

"No direct threat has been received," the Minister hastened to assure him.

"But aggression against neighbouring Arab states has become so commonplace that strikes further afield cannot be discounted."

"Your Highness so accurately assesses the situation."

"I am therefore, unfortunately compelled to take note of their warning." The Sultan's eyes rested coldly on his Minister. "What do you intend to do?"

"I...I can mobilize the forces."

The Sultan waved away the suggestion as absurd. "It wouldn't stop them. Four of Arabia's strongest nations were routed in six days by the Jews."

"Then, with your Highness' permission, we must stop Hijazi." Hijazi's gun-running provided a modest supplement to the personal incomes of both Minister and Sultan. What entered Kahran in the boxes labelled "machine parts" was of little interest to either, until the Israelis found out.

"That could lead to complications," the Sultan wheezed. "You're forgetting that cursed son of his."

His Highness had never met or publicly recognized Hussam. The Minister recalled the fury with which he received news fourteen years ago that a hero was born. It was the Sultan's dearest wish that Hussam would die a hero before returning to Qmrah. His Highness unfortunately did not enjoy the popular support of his ungrateful people and immediately saw Hussam as a direct threat. Regrettably, the passing years had not diminished Hussam's popularity which seemed rather to have grown in the air of mystery which surrounded his wish for anonymity. The stories of his deeds were exaggerated: he defeated an army single-handed; it was his daring exploits which finally drove the British from meddling in the Middle East; with a rifle he brought down Israeli bombers; he scuttled tankers which completely blocked the Suez Canal. They made good telling. They were folklore now, handed down to a new generation.

Hussam had never shown inclinations of political ambition but his Highness was clearly wary of waking a sleeping snake. Removing the family's livelihood might be dangerous. The Minister would need time to think.

Already the Sultan had lost interest in the problem. He tired quickly. Taking the boy's chin in his hand and lifting his face, he popped a chocolate into his mouth and stroked his cheek.

The Minister rose. "I shall give the matter my immediate attention your Highness."

He bowed low, wishing the Sultan peace and happiness, both of which he undoubtedly intended to have.

Fatima reached for the small oblong tin. When she was troubled it calmed her to look through the photographs. Her memories and the certainty of yesterday made tomorrow more certain.

She was troubled now. She knew her son. In ten years, since his sudden, unexplained return from Egypt, he hadn't settled. She thought marriage would change that. He had a good wife. She had chosen Leila herself. But his heart was not in the bedouin life. Inside he burned for something more. With a sense of foreboding she knew this western woman completed some part of her son's destiny. Everything would change because of her.

Only the past could not change. Fatima leafed through the small bundle of faded sepia. She was so absorbed she didn't hear Jodi approach.

"Hello." Fatima looked up. Jodi smiled nervously. "I hope I'm not disturbing you. It's just that not many people speak English round here."

Fatima understood. "I am your mother's sister," she said, patting the ground beside her.

Jodi sat, looking with interest at the bundle Fatima cradled in her lap. "May I see?"

Fatima knew she shouldn't. Hijazi had warned her it would be dangerous to let the woman know too much but her heart went out to Jodi for what she had suffered already and for what might happen yet.

She bore it bravely. It was three days now since she'd regained consciousness and there had been no trouble. Once in the night she screamed: a bad dream. Usually Jodi kept to herself sitting in the shade of her tent flap. She wasn't strong yet but she walked to the pool sometimes; other times to the edge of the vegetation where she looked out hopelessly across the desert.

She placed the first photo in Jodi's hand. "This is my father. He was a merchant in Kahran but he's dead now." Jodi saw a proud, bearded man in a long grey coat, posing self-consciously with a scroll of papers in one hand, the other resting on a table. "I was his only daughter, his only child. He is the reason I speak English, French too. You wouldn't understand but for an Arab to have no sons is a tragedy and to have only one daughter is less than useless." She laughed lightly. "I think he educated me so well to show our friends he was not ashamed.

"This is his shop, and that's my uncle outside. When I was eighteen I went there to help them. My mother wanted me at home but much of their business was with the British and French who were in Qmrah then and I spoke the languages. I had also learned arithmetic. I was lucky to have such a father."

Fatima lapsed into silence as she recalled the day she sat alone with her accounts books at the back of the large shop, her father and uncle having gone to the mosque for afternoon prayers. A tall, blond man in a British lieutenant's uniform walked in. She watched him quietly for a few minutes as he looked around, not noticing her in the shadows. Few Arab women appeared unveiled in male company in those days. Fatima considered herself very modern, and though she dressed traditionally for family occasions, for business she wore fashionable Western clothes. She was used to being with men, though not alone, and on this occasion felt particularly shy, finding it difficult to meet the stranger's gaze as she approached. "Can I help you?" she asked.

Smiling self-consciously, he said: "Er, yes. I want a carpet."

Her hand gestured around the shop where hundreds of rolled carpets and rugs of all sizes leaned in bundles against the white walls. Rich, earthy aromas of lanolin and wool saturated the cool air. "Then you are in the right place," she said gently. They both laughed.

"I suppose I am," he said. His name was David Allenby and when she wrote it in Arabic on the bill of sale she sat back in surprise. "Allenby?" she repeated, checking the pronunciation.

"Yes. Is anything wrong?"

"No. But it is written as we write 'prophet'."

By the time her father returned, Fatima had sold the English lieutenant five carpets and they were talking together as if they'd known each other for years. Her father, who sometimes invited English officers to meals at his house, took the opportunity of inviting his newest customer. With a glance at Fatima, David accepted.

For her part Fatima was both excited and confused. She was a source equally of pride and concern to her parents. Her scholastic and business achievements would be assets in a son but in a daughter they were a mixed blessing. Certainly they made the local families with sons of marriageable age more wary of matchmaking and after three such approaches, all of which Fatima refused to consider, her parents despaired of ever finding her a husband, especially as she was well beyond the age when most girls married. Though her father had the right to marry her to whoever he wished, he loved her too much to make her unhappy.

Fatima looked at the family photo, taken when she was eighteen. She was beautiful then. Her mother, in a traditional long black heavily embroidered silk dress denoting she was a well-to-do woman of Kahran, was seated next to her husband in a dark, three-piece suit of Western style. Between and behind them, a hand on the back of each of their chairs, stood the young Fatima, her long dark hair swept softly back and held by tortoiseshell combs, the high-buttoned white shirt belted tightly at her slender waist, her dark, ankle-length skirt hidden by the chairs. She was fresh-faced and lovely with intelligent eyes and the hint of a smile on her lips.

The English officer visited often, sometimes to play backgammon or chess with her father, sometimes to walk with her in the olive groves surrounding the rambling two storey house. He was quiet and gentle, so respectful and unlike any Arab man she had met. He was 21, the younger son of a country gentleman, "a sort of English *sheikh*," he laughed. Reluctantly following his family's military tradition, David was more of a scholar than a soldier and something of a disappointment to his father.

It was during one such walk as they talked of Shakespeare and Omar Khayyam, of Christ and Mohammed, of England and Qmrah that he turned to her. She leaned against the gnarled and twisted trunk of an olive tree, looking up through its branches to the cloudless sky. He was close, his pale blue eyes serious for once. Fatima was both frightened and excited as she realized he would kiss her. She was confused, not knowing what to do. So she did nothing, just closed her eyes and let it happen. She trembled. The strong feelings which surged through her were entirely new to her. She wanted him to do it again but David looked around, aware that they were probably being watched. Fatima's chaperones were never far away. "Shall I talk to your father?" he asked softly, kissing her forehead.

"What?"

"Fatima, I love you. You must know that. I want to marry you."

She looked at him blankly. Yes, she wanted it too but she was surprised at her own shyness. Though she could talk to him non-stop on a thousand other subjects, her Muslim upbringing left her totally unprepared to deal with what she now felt. She wanted him more than anything. She smiled, laughed. "Yes, yes! Talk to him!" Then, realizing the impossibility of it, clapped her hands over her mouth and fled from him back to the house. She ran straight to her room, fell on the bed and sobbed loudly until her mother came running.

"Fatima, *habibi*! What happened?"

"*Umma, umma*," she gasped. "He is going to talk to *abu*. He wants to marry me. Oh *umma*, what can I do?"

Her mother, shocked at the impropriety of it all lectured Fatima on her behaviour. Normally the parents of a marriageable girl would receive a visit from the young man's relatives long before the couple met. More seriously, there was no provision in Islam for such a marriage. Though Muslim men were permitted to marry Christians or Jews, the women were not. Her parents were in a quandary as to how they should proceed but Fatima was resolute. She wanted no other and indeed it seemed no other wanted her. She couldn't eat or sleep. Her health and happiness deteriorated alarmingly until her father finally agreed to talk to the young man.

They sat on the veranda drinking coffee. Fatima crept onto the balcony above to eavesdrop. Solemnly her father outlined the law, the *Shari'a*, as laid down by the Koran and therefore indisputable. Marriage to a non-Muslim was out of the question. He would not hear of his daughter becoming Christian but if David were to convert to Islam and, in accordance with the *Shari'a*, bestow on her a dowry appropriate to her rank and status, he would agree. Fatima held her breath. Then she heard David laugh. "When do we start?" he asked.

A religion of *jihad*, with the stated intent of conquering the globe, Islam eagerly devoured converts from any quarter. They had only to uphold the first of its Five Pillars by making the *shahadah*, the declaration of faith: *La ilaha il Allah weh Mohammed rasul Allah*; there is but one God and Mohammed is from God. The other Four Pillars could wait. The *shahadah*, said aloud before Muslim witnesses established David for all time as a Believer who would never again be an infidel nor rejected by the community of Muslims.

They married in 1936. The signing of the register, witnessed by two Arab males, fulfilled the *Shari'a*, while a simple registry office ceremony satisfied the British.

Fatima took out her wedding photo. She shunned her mother's traditional wedding gown of white silk, richly embroidered in red, and wore a simple pale Western skirt and jacket. The bride and groom were a stunning couple, she as dark as he was fair; on his hand he wore a heavy scarab ring, her gift to him.

No one from David's family attended. It was years later Fatima learned that, so shocked was he by the match, his father cut him off without a penny.

A year after the marriage her parents' apprehension turned to elation when she had a son. She called him David after his father. One more year and the young lieutenant was posted to Palestine where the Arab riots had forced the British to call in all available reinforcements. Fatima and the baby went with him. They settled happily in Jerusalem, renting a house in

Musrara, an area close to the Damascus Gate to the Old City.

But Palestine was not the only place where the Arabs were giving the British trouble. In 1940 Fatima heard news from Qmrah that Sheikh Abd'allah el Khatoub, whose family had been keepers of the Holy Shrine of Kahran for generations, was giving his support to gangs of thugs who roamed the streets causing trouble for the British and terrorising those who fraternised with them.

There were riots, shops were looted and burned. Snipers shot at troops and "collaborators" were executed. It was rumoured the trouble was fuelled by funds from the Germans, intent on undermining Allied authority in the area during the Second World War.

For a period, only the most urgent military communications came out of Qmrah and it was months afterwards that Fatima learned the fate of her family. A mob looted their home before burning it to the ground. Her parents and their servants were dragged out and shot.

These were troubled times throughout the Arab world. Boundaries were redrawn, kingships created, empires dismantled. The rich and influential grabbed what they could, betraying the poor, betraying the whole Arab dream of self-determination within a united Arabia.

Sheikh Abd'allah became Sultan.

The British were making an even bigger mess of Palestine than they were of the rest of the Middle East and by 1945 sought desperately to extricate themselves from the devastation which would continue until today and God knows how far into the future.

Throughout it all, her son was growing up, playing in the street with the other boys. At first she insisted that only English be spoken at home, believing he would live ultimately in England. But with his friends the boy spoke the language of the street until Fatima was forced to intervene lest he become unacceptable to polite Arab company. Except when her husband was with them she talked to him in Arabic.

He questioned her about the streams of black coated, ringleted men in fur hats who made their way quickly through Musrara from the Jewish quarter in Mea Shearim to the Wailing Wall. The Arab boys ran after them, jeering. David, too young to understand, joined in. Fatima explained they were devout Jews going to their holy place to pray and should be left in peace to do so.

Shortly afterwards he was brought home unconscious. She sensed it was to do with the rising tension between Jews and Arabs but he never told her. He was a secretive child, just seven, old enough to learn the brutal lesson of hatred but young enough to survive it.

His father was less fortunate. On a motor bike journey to Lydda he ran into a length of piano wire stretched taut across the road at throat level. His decapitated body was found hours later, his pistol missing, newly acquired by Jewish *Irgun* terrorists.

Fatima shuddered, he had been everything to her but to them he was just a gun.

There was a vagueness in her memory about what happened in the following days. A great many people visited the house. Women stayed to console her and, at the request of his family, the body was flown back to England for burial. It was assumed that Fatima would take her son and return to Qmrah. But since the riots, she no longer knew who of her family remained or where they might be. Also anti-British feeling ran high in Qmrah and she was advised that it would not be safe for her, a British army widow, to go back.

After weeks of grief Fatima took a job in the business she knew best. A carpet merchant called Hijazi had set up recently in the Jaffa Road and needed an assistant. He was older than she but within a year he proposed. She accepted not because she loved him but because an Arab woman alone, even one so Westernised, needed the protection of a husband and Hijazi was a good man. She left the small house in Musrara and moved to his mansion at Kattomon.

David never took to Hijazi, there was always uneasiness between them. Eighteen months later Hijazi had his own son, Ahmed.

The inevitable war of 1948 between Jew and Arab came. Kattomon was overrun by the Israelis. Hijazi lost all he'd worked for. They walked for two days. She reached the refugee camp nearly dead from fatigue and in advanced labour. In filth and humiliation, crowded and confused, she brought Hijazi's second son, Ali, into the hostile world.

There they languished for two months, living in tents, queuing for meagre food rations, for ragged clothes and flea-ridden bedding. Sanitation was appalling and disease was rife. Everywhere there was noise, shouting, wailing, the cries of sick and hungry children.

When Fatima's milk dried up, the baby cried all day and night. At last Hijazi could stand no more. Better the bedouin tents than this, he told her. He made his peace with his father and took his family into the desert.

Fatima and their sons flourished in the love and closeness of the small nomadic community. Hijazi too confided that whereas before the desert had been a desolate and unrewarding waste, now it was a deep and healing ocean of peace, hard on the body but gentle on the soul.

Her husband was too clever in business to return to the pure nomadic life and soon acquired an impressive camel train to transport the fine silk carpets of Qmrah to Jerusalem, where many of his contacts, more fortunately placed than he, continued to trade in the Jordanian sector. Two decades passed. Now, since the Six Day War, even they were lost to him. "The Jews have it all," he complained bitterly. But Fatima knew carpets had long since ceased to be Hijazi's main source of income.

On his father's death, Hijazi became head of the family and moved them to the oasis of Bab'ullah. She loved him for it because it was near Kahran, where she was born and where she bore David. Hijazi found her uncle, living quietly and modestly now with relatives. He traded with them. They wove carpets of matchless quality and drove a hard bargain. Though Fatima loved the bedouin as they loved her, she was not one of them and found the life hard. After so many years of separation and uncertainty, the closeness of her family was a joy.

She was aware of another motive for Hijazi's move. The harbour at Kahran was the source of a new trade, more lucrative than carpets. From there he began secretly importing arms and ammunition for the *fedayeen.*

He refused to build a home. "Once I had a fine house and the Jews took it," he said. He vowed no one would take his home again. He would live and die in his tent.

Though David never warmed to Hijazi, he was openly affectionate to his half-brothers and when Fatima gave birth to a daughter, Nooria, behaved in a most un-Arab way and played with her at every opportunity. Fatima blamed herself. The English upbringing she allowed in earlier years proved too strong to be crushed by the ways of the bedouin. Hijazi who, like most Arab men, felt the birth of a daughter to be a matter of complete indifference, tolerable only because he already had two sons, was embarrassed by David's attention to the new baby, calling him *Umm* Nooria, Nooria's Mother, in an attempt to shame the boy.

David, still prey to the conflicting emotions of youth, grew miserable and resentful. Fatima knew he would retaliate, perhaps violently, unless she acted. Now was the ideal time for him to go to school. She had family connections in Cairo. Sadly she kissed him goodbye.

"Where is this?" Jodi interrupted her thoughts, holding up a photo of palm trees.

Fatima took the photo from her, looking at it fondly. "This," she said, "was Bab'ullah, when we first arrived."

Jodi looked around her. "Here?" Fatima nodded. The palms still stood and more had been cultivated, now laden with fruit. Clusters of dates as big as bee swarms clung to the slender trunks beneath lush green fronds, each date as long as a man's thumb and twice as fat. Beneath the palms and further out from the turquoise of the spring-fed pool were planted fields of greenery between tall hedges of prickly pear which provided not only succulent fruit but protection for the crops from animals and the blowing sand. Further still were clumps of bamboo giving added shelter as well as poles for fencing, tents and a multitude of minor uses. There grew maize, vegetables, water melons, groundnuts, aromatic balm and herbs, flowering shrubs and bushes.

Hijazi called it "Fatima's Garden." When he brought her here she was entranced. The first year she planted a few seeds, tending them carefully. Then she planted a few more.

Then Hussam returned, so different from the boy David she'd kissed six years before. The tales of his courage had reached her, nearly driving her mad with worry while Hijazi at last warmed to him, proudly informing everyone that the one they called the Sword was his son, insisting they continue to call him *el Hussam*.

She rebuked her son soundly but couldn't be angry for long. He had studied and was an engineer. She was proud of him. Yet he rarely spoke of the fighting. Hijazi enthusiastically tried to get information from him but eventually gave up, lapsing once again into grudging tolerance.

Holding up the photo, Jodi asked: "How did you do it?" She swept a hand towards the lush greenery.

"It was Hussam," Fatima replied. He built pumps and bits and pieces, and fiddled with them interminably until he made water flow in a wide arc away from the silent pool. "The desert is fertile. It only needs water," she looked around with pride. "My garden has grown large. It is hard work for the women and children, the men too when they're not with the camels. But it gives us everything we need and more. What we don't need we sell in the market at Ein Mara."

"Ein Mara?"

"It's a small village one day from here." Jodi's interest was aroused. A village, that close?

"We go there tomorrow. Leila will have her baby soon. She will see the doctor. We can take some vegetables and corn," Fatima chattered on happily. "We must walk, there's no road for vehicles."

"Can she walk so far in her condition?"

Fatima laughed. "We Arabs are much stronger than you western women."

"Will Hussam go too?"

She waved a hand dismissively: "This is women's business. Hussam would get in the way."

Jodi didn't know whether to be glad or not. Her encounter with him by the pool had changed nothing and changed everything. He had been as good as his word. She was treated as a guest and was free to move around the camp but her mind was plagued with the events which concerned her beyond Bab'ullah. That her father would send the arms she didn't doubt but it wouldn't guarantee her safety. She couldn't sit here selfishly pretending that a bunch of fanatical terrorists would do the gentlemanly thing and release her. And what of the others who would die? She knew she must do something. She owed it to them and herself to try.

"Where is the village?" she asked casually.

"What is it to you?" It was Hussam's voice. She looked up quickly. Fatima gathered her photos into the tin and went inside the tent.

Jodi hadn't spoken to him since the meeting at the pool but her senses sharpened as he confronted her. She had tried to belittle him in her mind. He was only a guard, after all. Amin's lackey. But perhaps she should befriend him, set him at ease, win his trust; it might make escape possible.

She thought quickly and smiled winningly. "I wondered if I might go. I am supposed to be a guest."

"You are a guest here and here you must stay."

Her smile faded. "Then I'm not a guest, more a prisoner."

He sat cross-legged in front of her. "We're all prisoners of a sort," he said solemnly.

"You're a philosopher," Keep smiling! Keep him talking! Make friends with the guard. "A philosopher but no one's prisoner, not you."

He laughed. "Even I."

"And who holds the key that will free you?" She was trying the Rainbow Bar technique, her eyes meeting his meaningfully.

He held her gaze, then smiled easily. "Only Allah himself," he said.

"Oh." Jodi was disappointed.

"You thought I might say you."

She was taken aback by his forthrightness but quickly recovered. "You might find it easier to escape from me than from Allah."

"Perhaps I would not wish to escape either."

She laughed, defeated for the moment, and he laughed too, standing. "If you need anything you have only to ask," he said.

She watched him go. He had a hell of a nice arse!

Life at Bab'ullah had a lot to commend it, especially if you liked simple things, like sun and sand! It also had its drawbacks, like having only one dress to wear which was too short and too baggy. Like subsisting on a diet dominated by cous-cous, pumpkin, and a dozen variations on boiled sheep. Jodi put in a mild complaint to Hussam at supper as she sat with the others around the open fire.

"Sometimes we roast gazelle," he said.

"Mmm!" She licked her lips. "When do we get gazelle?"

"There's a spring half a day from here where they drink. When I pass, I'll bring one."

Meanwhile, there was no shortage of mutton. A few sheep were kept in a wicker pen for slaughter. They were the fat-tailed variety of moth-eaten animals she'd seen in Israel, mistaken for goats, and finally christened "geep."

There was no lingering twilight in the desert. Darkness came decisively. In her tent, by the light of an oil lamp, she was fighting a losing battle to get a plastic comb through her thick matted hair. It was still early evening but the bedouin rose and slept by the sun, not the clock. Outside she heard the chatter of women as they cleared away the remnants of tonight's boiled sheep. The men sat cross-legged or on low stools by the fire, talking, smoking hubble-bubble pipes and playing chess or backgammon. There were crickets, hundreds of thousands by the sound of it. The nights were noisier than the days.

Yesterday she had scanned the desert horizon, looking for a trail, a sign of life, thinking there must be something out there apart from Mecca, the distance of which was uncertain, though she'd approximated the direction from the rather casual amount of praying which went on. Today she knew Ein Mara was out there, direction unknown but distance more certain. Tomorrow Leila would go and if a pregnant woman could get there in a day, so could she. She wouldn't even need food, perhaps a little water.

But Hussam would soon see she was missing. He would easily catch up with her. Damn! How could she do it? She needed a plan. It might be the only chance she had. She mustn't blow it. All she needed was a day, one day and she'd be free. How could she get him away from Bab'ullah for one whole day?

Jodi smiled as an idea took shape in her mind. Her breath quickened at the danger, the excitement of it. Could it work? Well, nothing beat a try but a failure. She had nothing to lose.

She looked out of the tent, at the small groups of men by the fire. Hussam played chess with Ahmed. She sat by them, looking at the board.

Ahmed shuffled uneasily. He said something to Hussam who looked at her and laughed. "He says you should be with the women."

She bristled: "Why?"

"*Laysh*?" he translated to Ahmed. Ahmed stood, gesticulated to the board, said something angrily and walked off.

"I'm sorry," she said to Hussam. "I've spoiled your game."

"He was losing," he said smiling.

"So I see," she said, appraising the situation.

"You play?" She nodded. "Well?" She nodded again. "Then play."

"Not tonight, I've got a headache!"

"Aha! You're afraid you'll lose."

"I won't lose."

He laughed. "You won't lose if you won't play."

"I'll play tomorrow."

"Tomorrow then." She walked back to her tent, aware of his eyes but did not turn.

CHAPTER 8

The blast threw Amin backwards. For a moment he lay stunned. The Israelis had his position. He'd better move out. He could re-site further along and lob a couple more over before pulling back.

It was dark and Amin felt for the mortar. The blast must have knocked it sideways. He felt further, his hands touching something warm and wet, pliable yet shapeless, to which a few rags clung. He recoiled, wiping the warm sticky substance on his shirt. Amin had seen death many times but to feel it, without seeing, turned his stomach.

He shouted urgently to the others: "Fayez, all of you, follow me."

There was no sound. In desperation he flicked on the torch, shielding its beam with his hand. Of the mortar nothing remained but a few shreds of steel. The corpse he had handled was no more human than the sides of meat in a *souk*. Beside it lay Fayez as good as dead, blood dripping slowly from his open mouth, his breath rasping in his throat. Two others were dead and a fifth sat with his head in his hands, wailing softly.

Amin grabbed him by the sleeve. "Come on," he urged, pulling him up.

Another explosion, dangerously close, brought a squeal from the lad, who fell to the ground. Amin kicked him. "Get up! Get up! Curse you!" He dragged him to his feet again, pulling him, stumbling through the darkness. They reached the Land Rover as another volley of shells shook the ground behind them. Amin hoisted the lad over the side before jumping into the driver's seat and starting the motor. The engine screamed as he crashed the gears and spun the wheels in a shower of dust and sand before racing away. For miles he didn't dare switch on the lights but when he did, drove like a madman, adrenalin still coursing through him.

Three dead and Fayez! Four! Desperately he tried to clear his mind and make sense of what happened.

It was *Shabbat*, the Jewish Sabbath, when, had they been the Godfearing race they claimed, the Jews would be in their synagogues or homes keeping this day holy. But on the eve of *Shabbat* the little border town of Kiryat Shmona bulged at the seams with truckloads of workers from the surrounding *kibbutzim* and *moshavim* going to the cinema or sitting out at pavement cafes. There was dancing. Amin heard the music, so close had he been.

They had shelled it before, enjoying the Israeli admissions of casualties, picturing the scene as frightened parents threw their children onto any moving truck leaving town, clinging to the sides themselves. The panic, the fear and, later, the mourning were sweet success to his fedayeen. Retribution was always swift. The Israelis would pursue him, violating Lebanon, her border and the small villages through which he raced. He must drive through the night to reach Sufa.

Gradually, his speed lessened. He turned to the boy. "Are you all right?" The lad nodded quickly, stifling a sob. "Your first mission, eh? They're always the worst. Next time you'll find it easier."

"I wasn't afraid!"

"Ha!" Amin slapped his leg. "No! You were brave. I saw you myself. You acted with courage. At least two of the mortars you fired would strike the very heart of the town."

He lied and knew it, but the lad would tell his friends of his success. Victory, even when manufactured, was good for recruitment. Not that recruitment in the lower ranks was a problem. *Fatah* was awash with eager young Palestinians, nearly 10,000 of them. It was weapons, experience and leadership the freedom fighters lacked. Officers bungled their way through training sessions, many of them seconded from Jordan's King Hussein's army to spy on *Fatah*. The last thing they wanted was for the *fedayeen* to increase military strength and threaten Jordan.

They had ten days, these youngsters born and raised in refugee camps, to learn from reluctant leaders all they needed to know about weapons handling and sabotage before they faced the might of Israel. Discipline was tough and, if recruitment was high, so was desertion, although punishment was severe, sometimes death. Beatings were commonplace. It was no way to build an army.

Kushi was good, when he curbed his excesses. Discipline was a side-line Amin allowed him to amuse himself. His real value lay in his ability to organise acts which caused most outrage in Israel; a rocket attack on schoolchildren, a bomb in the Tel Aviv bus station.

He had begun promoting from within his own ranks. It was difficult. So few had leadership qualities. How could they? He had thought Fayez... He shuddered as the scene of earlier returned, looking at his hands, stained with blood between the fingers. He wiped them on his shirt again.

Amin gave a cigarette to the boy and lit one himself. He couldn't continue leading raids. He was needed elsewhere. He must negotiate guns. He must make the Arabs see that supporting him was their best chance of obliterating the Jewish state. But first, he would solve the leadership problem. The pressure on Israel must never let up. One good officer could take a troop to a hundred real victories. One such as Hussam.

His meeting with Hussam had unsettled Amin. He was wasted in the desert. His fate was sealed in Palestine, the blood of his father spilt there. He looked down at his shirt, streaked with blood. He must get rid of it. They were on the main road now, patrolled by police and the UN. He pulled in, unbuttoning the shirt hastily as he jumped out of the Land Rover. Walking over to the bushes, he screwed it up and pushed it between the branches. Leaning against a tree, feeling its rough, warm bark on his back, he drew deeply on his cigarette.

The lad watched him through the open window. He was young and wide-eyed, his innocence destroyed forever tonight. Amin felt a throbbing in his groin and fought the temptation to take the lad, though he could knock him unconscious for it.

No, Sufa was the goal. There would be time enough for this one another night. Amin threw his cigarette end on the ground and walked back to the vehicle.

The day of Leila's departure wore on interminably. The heat of the day came and went before the caravan gathered. It seemed an anti-climax. Just six women and two men, a tiny grey donkey that looked as if it could barely carry itself, let alone Leila, and four camels, laden with huge bundles and bags full of lumps and decked out in bright woollen tassels, rugs and bells.

From where she sat in the shade of her tent flap, Jodi watched them go thinking: "See you there!"

Hussam, David on his shoulders, walked to the edge of the camp with them, shouting instructions to the men. Leila waved him away and the others laughed at whatever it was she said.

Jodi took careful note of their direction, westward up the nearest slope of the north-south valley in which the oasis lay. It was nearly an hour before they reached the ridge and were out of sight. Another hour went by. She was edgy, full of anticipation and fear about what she planned. She felt she would burst or at least blurt it out if she didn't do something to occupy herself until it was time.

She'd go for a swim and wash her hair. That would kill another hour or so. Going into the tent she pulled off the dress which she had the distinct impression must stink of B.O. She would wash that too. Fatima had given her a cake of yellow scented soap made from lanolin, no doubt donated by the geep before they were boiled!

Wrapping herself in the cotton sheet, she followed the bamboo-lined path to the pool. There was no one there, the silence of the great desert broken only by the soft swish of palm fronds in a gentle breeze and the incessant clop from the irrigation channel. She washed the dress first then hung it on the bamboo to dry before unwrapping the sheet and walking naked into the water. It was bliss. Cool but not cold. She plunged beneath the water, shaking her head, feeling the coolness on her scalp. As she surfaced she rubbed the scented soap into her hair then piled the tangled mass onto the top of her head and massaged it into a lather. She washed her whole body and felt clean and cool and really good about herself for the first time since she'd been here.

The day was cooler now. She swam lazy lengths of the pool before emerging. The red sun sank below the ridge which Leila's party had climbed. Her hair was nearly dry already. The cool water had freshened her perceptibly and faded the marks on her body. She pulled the cotton dress over her head. It was dry and fresh with the faint aroma of the soap on it.

As she started back along the path she could smell the smoke from the fire, hear the loud laughter of the women as they cooked. Already some were eating, sitting cross-legged sharing huge plates of cous-cous which they pressed between their fingers and dipped into the soggy mutton. Jodi wasn't hungry but she knew she must eat, tonight of all nights.

She sat alone. Hussam sat with David listening to the lad as he chattered through mouthful after mouthful until a woman led him away by the hand, protesting loudly.

Hussam stood and slowly made his way towards her, stopping to exchange a few words here and there. He reached her.

She smiled. "You still want to play?"

"Of course!"

"You don't mind playing with a woman?"

He laughed: "I am not Ahmed."

"You don't mind being beaten?"

"Ha! That won't happen."

"Would you like to bet?"

"What have you to bet with?"

She paused then said softly: "Anything you want that I can give." She watched him through lowered lashes. The words scored a direct hit.

"You mean it?" he asked, serious but suspicious. She nodded once, slowly. His breath quickened and he shouted Ahmed who brought the board and pieces, looking disdainfully at Jodi before walking away.

Hussam watched her thoughtfully as she set out the pieces. They were beautifully carved from olivewood, the board inlaid with mother of pearl like those made in Bethlehem. She took a pawn from each side but before holding out her hands for him to choose said: "It's only fair that you make a bet too: anything I want if I win."

He shook his head. "I cannot give you your freedom."

"Tut, tut. You don't sound so sure of winning anymore."

"Anything but your freedom."

"Anything?"

"If it is in my power to give it."

She held out her clenched hands. He chose white and smiled at his luck, moving king's pawn to king four; opening gambit. She went along with it until the last moment and foiled his fool's mate with a seemingly lucky move made in ignorance of what was being attempted. It was difficult not to smile. He was so disappointed.

A few interested observers gathered, making occasional comments in Arabic which were intended to be helpful but which Hussam brushed aside impatiently. She swapped queens as soon as the opportunity arose. It always disconcerted the opposition but added to the illusion that she didn't know what she was doing. It was unconventional but she played well without her queen. Most players didn't and sometimes it gave her the edge that was needed.

A sigh had gone up from the gathering when she took his queen, followed by a shout as he removed hers. The game progressed messily. He was good, better than most she'd played. Good enough to beat her. Just a little too eager. After an hour she was left with only king, castle and pawn while he retained king, castle, black bishop and four pawns. He should have checkmated easily, but the stakes were designed to distract him. With every move he checked, pinning her down, moving in for the kill. She needed respite for just one move and when ultimately it came, she moved her castle in quickly to trap him between her pawn and king.

"Checkmate," she said.

The onlookers roared. Hussam couldn't believe it. The move had come so unexpectedly. All his attention had been on checkmating her, he hadn't seen the danger to himself. He stood, throwing the board aside. Jodi clasped her hands, chuckling with glee. She looked up at his furious face which made her laugh more. He folded his arms. The others were jeering at him now. "Beaten by a woman! You'll never live it down," she laughed. She hadn't seen him look so glum but his dejection couldn't spoil her moment of triumph. She put her hand to her chin thoughtfully. "Now, let me see, anything I want that is in your power to give. Anything, you said! I am right, aren't I?" He nodded gravely, watching her closely as she walked up and down in front of him in mock contemplation. She couldn't suppress a chuckle. "Well, what I would like most in the world, next to my freedom which you cannot give, is something to eat that doesn't go 'baa' when I bite it. Tomorrow you must go to the spring and fetch me a gazelle for my supper." She added teasingly: "after which we can play some more chess if you like."

Tears of laughter streamed down her face as she watched his reaction. There must be a dozen emotions racing through him right now ranging from self-recrimination to downright murder.

She ran to her tent still laughing. It worked! It worked! Tomorrow he would be away all day. She would escape! Happily she pulled off the dress. She must try and get some sleep. She would need all her strength.

He entered and she turned in surprise, clutching the dress to her. The laughter was gone. His eyes swept down from her face. Her heart raced but she fought to stay calm. What had happened was too much for his pride and she knew now she'd lost control of what she started. He stood for a moment then slowly walked to her, reaching out one hand to touch her hair, stroking it absently until his hand closed around it, pulling her to him.

If she expected sudden passion, she was disappointed. Taking her head in both hands, he looked into her eyes and she understood what he asked; did she know what she'd done?

"Yes," she whispered almost inaudibly and he kissed her a series of full and gentle kisses. She heard his heartbeat in his breath.

Stepping back she let go of the dress. As he looked at her she felt awkward, vulnerable. She wished he would come to her, hold her, cover her body with his, anything but stand there. Then she realised it was the first time he had seen the full evidence of what they did to her at Sufa. Kushi concentrated on the sensitive areas. More than anywhere else, her breasts and inner thighs bore lasting marks of his sadism.

She looked down at the scars she bore then raised her eyes to his. "It's all right," she whispered. "It's all right now."

He came to her and, beginning with those on her throat, gently kissed every mark on her body, sinking to his knees, pulling her down with him and searching still more till he found those half inside her, kissing each in turn till she cried out for him and he answered, joining himself to her, so hard the pain was inevitable but bearable because deep inside, where they were one, and where his strong, slow movements repeatedly withdrew and replaced some vital part of her, there grew an ecstasy, spreading warmly throughout her body, inside and out till it swept her with it, overwhelmed her yet drew him on, sucked him in, refusing to release him unless he too surrendered and he did. His body convulsed, he whispered her name and she held him as if he were hers to hold.

She woke in the night. He stood by the flap of the tent, looking out.

"Hussam?" He came back to her. "Don't leave, not in the night."

"Hush." He stroked her hair and held her till the fear left and the want returned and he kissed her and made love to her till the want left and then there was only him and she slept.

At dawn he woke her. Over one shoulder she saw the barrel of a rifle, its tooled and worn leather strap diagonal across his chest. He touched her face. "I'm going for your supper."

"Oh!" She sat up, conflicting emotions crowding into her awakening mind, the decisions of yesterday meaningless now. Gently he kissed her breasts and lips then quickly he left. She looked straight ahead. His kisses had roused her. Alone she was incomplete.

Wrapping the sheet around her she ran outside. In the half-light she saw the camel striding silently away. The camp was quiet. Soon the women would be up, baking pita bread at the small open kiln. She must decide now. There wouldn't be another opportunity like this.

Returning to the tent she clutched her head with both hands, damning the turn things had taken. But she must hold on to reality. The desire for love with Hussam was an illusion. Where could it lead? At best to being wife number two and at worst to a violent death. The decision was made. Freedom was possible. It was the only choice. She reached for her dress and pulled it on feeling more absurd than ever. Numbly she went through the motions she'd planned, filling the goatskin water flask and slinging it over her shoulder. She took a blanket in case she didn't make Ein Mara by nightfall. She rarely wore the leather thonged sandals Fatima gave her. They were useful only if she went out in the middle of the day when the sand was too hot for bare feet. She slipped them on now and draped a *kaffiyeh* over her shoulders. It would be useful to protect her head and face from the sun.

The camp was still silent but she took no chances, crawling out under the canvas at the back of the tent, rather than leaving through the flap where she might be seen.

She ran along the winding path to the pool and westward to where she could still see the tracks of the caravan from the day before. The path wound slowly upwards, becoming much steeper at the top which she reached as the sun broke the eastern ridge, casting a long low shadow ahead of her. She looked back towards the camp, which the rays of the new sun had not yet touched. It slept on. She had made it. No one would follow her now. After last night they would assume she was with Hussam. No one could tell her footprints in the mass of others made yesterday.

She turned westward. Ahead there was a flat plateau. She could see the tracks continue in the sand far ahead and out of sight. It would be a cinch. Jodi followed them quickly. She was afraid a wind might blow up and obliterate the trail. There was no sign of civilisation anywhere in this barren waste.

Her shadow was ahead of her, growing shorter constantly. The sun beat on her neck and head in spite of the *kaffiyeh* and she could feel the backs of her legs below the short kaftan begin to burn. Well, there'd be time enough to get over a bit of sunburn. It was nothing compared with what Amin and his torturer might do had she stayed at the oasis meekly awaiting her fate.

As she walked her thoughts strayed back to Hussam. He was a closed chapter now. The right man at the wrong time. The story of her life. She was surprised how simple it had all been. Tonight or tomorrow she would be at Ein Mara. She would try not to meet up with Leila and Co. but it didn't really matter if she did, once there were others about.

What would Hussam do when he found out? Would he be furious? Hurt? Well, it was his own fault for getting involved with kidnapping. She had to protect herself.

How long had she walked? She looked at the sun. It still cast a shadow before her but its heat was merciless. She must have risen at four but perhaps it wasn't yet eight. That meant four more hours of worsening heat until midday. She decided to go on for two more hours then shelter from the worst of the heat until mid-afternoon. The backs of her legs were bright red. The skin felt tight and chafed. She tried to cover them by draping the blanket over her shoulders and letting it trail down to the ground behind her but streams of perspiration began running down her back and chafing there until in agony she stopped and sat down. Surely it was ten o'clock and she could rest for a few hours.

She looked around for shelter but there was nothing. Miserably she pulled the blanket up over her head and tried to fan it out around her so that she was shaded but not stifled. The thongs of the rough hide sandals had rubbed blisters on her feet. Some had burst. Flies pestered her, landing persistently on the broken skin which she tried to cover with the blanket. What the hell did flies find to eat out here when she wasn't around? Soon there were dozens of them, homing in on her as she sat, landing round her mouth and eyes.

She drank from the goatskin flask. The warm water brought little relief and it tasted dreadful, like the smell of old shoes. Yet she'd seen men at the oasis drink from identical flasks. Her eyes ached in the white-hot glare. She closed them and tried to think pleasant thoughts. Thoughts of England and how green and cool it was, thoughts of Jerusalem, the city of gold, thoughts of how she would soon be safe, if she could only bear this a little while. Four hours wasn't long and the worst would be over.

But time passed even more slowly when she sat than when she walked. The persistent flies made rest impossible. Jodi decided to practice her girl guide training, walking and stopping intermittently. At least she'd have the satisfaction of knowing she was getting somewhere, however slowly. She tried to sing but the air was hot and dusty, drying her throat. Around her the desert stretched away grey and flat, rough stones strewn on the baked ground, occasional dead bushes standing like brittle black skeletons. That vegetation could ever have lived here was a wonder.

Walking and resting she continued until her shadow was around her feet. Moving at all was an effort. When she rested she looked ahead for a target for the next move, picking out an odd-shaped stone or mark on the ground. The effort to get there was enormous, sapping her strength, needing all her dogged determination born of the stubborn streak inherited from her father. Still she followed the trail.

The sun was now on her face and shins. She felt the tops of her feet begin to swell up between the thongs that cut her deeply now. She covered her hands with the blanket which got progressively heavier, making her arms ache. The sun glared in her eyes until all colour faded. The landscape was black and white, the heat worse now than at midday. What if she didn't make it? She fought back the panic. Even in her misery she refused to give way to despair, telling herself it must now be three o'clock, she was nearly half way there, probably further. The trouble was she hadn't questioned what "a day's journey" meant to a bedouin. Did it mean from sunrise to sunset, or a full 24-hour slog? And why had Leila's party left after midday instead of first thing?

She paused, looking back. The earth was flat and desolate, indistinguishable in character from that ahead. Thank God for the tracks. How much time had passed? Her feet bled and the flies were black on thc wounds. Jodi stumbled on. It seemed a little cooler now. She concentrated with all her might on putting one aching, bleeding foot in front of the other.

The landscape became rockier. The rough stones were bigger and closer together. It was difficult to see the tracks between them. It was more difficult still to walk without catching her feet on the sharp edges or slipping off the stones.

Ahead in the far distance, she could just make out a rocky outcrop. There were no tracks now and she headed for it hopefully. But she was wearier than she could ever remember being. She knew she'd driven herself to her limit. "The body can go on longer than the mind thinks it can," she repeated for perhaps the twentieth time. But it had to stop sometime. Her sometime was now.

Jodi searched for somewhere to sleep. The day had been hot as hell but already she felt the bitter chill of the night to come. There was no shelter. With her hands she heaped a few large stones together before collapsing beside them, wincing with pain as she pulled off the sandals and examined her feet, torn by the leather straps and blistered by the sun. Her flask was half empty. She had enough water for one more day. Even crawling, she could make it; she had to!

The sun sank blood-red and Jodi took care to mark the point where it touched the horizon near the rocky outcrop. Within an hour she was shivering in the darkest, loneliest night she'd known. By day the desert seemed silent. Now it was alive with sharp little sounds, slitherings and clicks which were all the more terrifying for being lost in the great black bowl of which she was the exact centre. Above, a billion stars lent precious little light to the vast blue-black sky. There were whisperings and soft noises which swished past her as she pulled the blanket around her head to shut it all out. The night she'd hoped would bring rest and repair to her exhausted body became one more terrifying ordeal.

For the first time she cried, sobbing bitterly beneath the blanket, shaking both from cold and despair till oblivion came.

She woke as the first light was washing away the stars of the eastern horizon. At first she couldn't move, her body frozen in a numbness which slowly gave way to pain, her head splitting, her neck and back aching as if every bone had been beaten. It was still too dark to pick out the rugged landscape, so she sat huddled in the blanket watching the sky lighten and the land take on its harsh contours.

"Not far now!" she said aloud, standing hunched, unable to straighten her back immediately. She caught her breath as the skin on the tops of her feet split open with the pressure of her weight. She couldn't yet see but, bending to touch them, they were bloated and suppurating. The thongs of the sandals wouldn't fit over her toes. Well, she'd have to get going now before the ground got hot. Maybe she'd be in Ein Mara before the sun was high. She hobbled slowly forward, towards the rocky outcrop. The pain subsided as she forced her feet onwards, overtaken by numbness.

She felt a lifegiving warmth strike her back immediately the sun rose. Why couldn't it stay like that? Warm, comforting, healing. Too fast it soared high and hot, summoning the flies, the dust and a new tormentor, the knowledge that she couldn't go much further. The rocky ground burnt the soles of her feet.

The outcrop wasn't far now. She would make herself get there before stopping. There would be shade on the other side. She could rest there till the day grew cooler. She was hungry and deadly tired. Perhaps she could sleep too. Beneath the outcrop the ground was sandy. Skirting it she saw the land sloped away slowly to a distant patch of green interspersed with low buildings almost indistinguishable in colour from the desert. It was the village.

With a yell she flung the sandals and blanket in the air, threw back her head and laughed at the sun. She'd made it! She'd made it! When reason returned she saw it was still a long way off. She needed rest and a little repair if she was to get there today. Limping to the other side of the headland, she fell on her knees in the cool, sandy shadow.

With a sudden fierce hiss the snake reared. It was rigid, tensed, ready to strike, just two feet from her face. Jodi froze, mesmerised by the flicking forked tongue, the spreaded hood, the shining gold scales which blended into a pale cream stripe down its front. It seemed an eternity as she waited in horror for the fatal blow, unable even to look away.

With a crack the creature's head exploded, its slim erect body falling in coils in the sand at her knees. It writhed in its death throes and she turned in time to see a man lower his rifle.

It was Hussam.

CHAPTER 9

"He wants proof she's alive."

Amin was deep in thought, though his mind was not on the woman. To dismiss the problem he said: "Send the photo. Tell him next he'll have proof she's dead."

"You know this consignment will take twelve weeks? Six to put together, another six in shipment now that Suez is closed."

"Give him ten. It's enough." Though he spoke to Kushi, it was at Hijazi's sons he looked. Ahmed was the image of his father, the same in temperament too. Although he had not the same cunning, the shrewd business mind, he could yet learn. Ali, two years younger, was very different. He had more the look of Hussam, though not as big and nowhere near as stubborn. They sat around the bare table drinking coffee.

"We've heard from Jerusalem too," Kushi added. "The Jews are sniffing round, asking questions."

Amin expected as much but what could they learn? The trail went dead at the Haj. No one in Jerusalem knew where she was now, not even Amin's spies. He smiled wearily at the brothers. "You see the trouble this woman gives me?" he said.

Ahmed laughed. "You're not the only one. She's troubling Hussam too. This trouble!" He waggled his forefinger obscenely.

Amin was thoughtful again as Ahmed related the story of the chess and the night that followed. The brothers had left for Kahran next day, after dawn, to collect the vehicles and bring them here. Along the chassis, beneath the seats, anywhere there was space, Hijazi had secreted weapons, grenades, mortar bombs, Katyushas and AK47's. There was no sign of Hussam or the woman when they left, Ahmed grinned.

"It's good he's looking after our investment so well, eh Kushi?" Amin laughed.

Kushi grunted: "Too well. We may not get it back."

Amin leaned forward, looking from Ahmed to Ali. "What do you think?" he asked. "Is Kushi right?"

Ali shifted uncomfortably. Ahmed shrugged. "Who knows with Hussam?"

"Who knows?" Amin mimicked softly. "I know!" he roared, startling the others and standing so quickly that his chair fell backwards, clattering on the concrete. "You're his blood brothers yet you know little of Hussam." He paced the floor. "He gave his word and that's my guarantee. Would to God the word of others was as good." He stopped, noticing the fear on their faces and smiled, throwing out his arms. "If only he would fight. We need men like your brother."

Ali jumped up. "I'll join you, Ahmed too. We've talked about it. We want to be *fedayeen*."

Amin groaned inwardly. More raw recruits! But he said: "Already you do more than you know. Where would we get our weapons, our vehicles without you? When our children tell their children how we won back our country, you will be heroes."

"But we can do more," enthused Ali. "We can shoot, we..."

"No!" Amin retorted sharply. He sighed and picked up the chair, sitting on it. "Forgive me. I'm tired. Let me rest. I'll be all right tomorrow."

Ali looked at Ahmed who jerked his head towards the door. "Till tomorrow."

The door closed behind them and Amin's head sank onto his hands. So Hussam was hot for the woman. That was good. He turned to Kushi. "I have a mission for you" he said. "One you will enjoy."

✳✳✳

Uri Gershon sat with his feet on the desk, picking sunflower seeds from a bag on his lap, cracking them with his teeth and spitting the husks, none too accurately, at a basket on the floor.

The gunmen in the Haj's bedroom, the bragging in the Arab press, the peasants on the bus. Leprosy, the sergeant said. There was no leprosy on the West Bank! They'd been slow on this one. The Occupied Territories still harboured infiltrators and resistance.

So it was Amin! That much was simple. The rest was conjecture. The position of the abandoned Mercedes on the border indicated he'd headed back to Sufa, his stronghold until he vanished six months ago. Mossad agents kept a casual lookout for him but who would suspect he'd dare to operate from the West Bank? *Shin Beth* should have known. There'd be hell to pay for someone.

Amin was among the cleverer and better-informed terrorists. A wily manipulator, a good leader and a ruthless killer, given a better cause, he would have made an excellent military man. His ability to move unnoticed even in Israel showed he had wide support and his own sources of information here.

Who betrayed the woman? The Haj was a lecher but not a spy. Who did it? The bar was full of men that night. Dahoud, the owner, was helpful yet recalled few names. Uri sensed a creeping tension within the Old City. Jerusalem was clamming up on him, his friends withdrawing. Tribal ties were strong so was the fear, fed by Fatah Radio which constantly harangued the Arabs, naming those who gave Israel the slightest co-operation, making them targets for assassins and placing rewards on their heads. Amin was behind the murderous threats. Where was he? Wherever it was, the woman was probably there too.

Uri flipped through the file on his desk. Sufa sheltered a well-organised terrorist cell which Amin had divided into seven military sectors, each with its own chain of command, ammunition store and support services. The most closely guarded was the *casbah*, the old town centre of high stone buildings and dark, narrow streets, around which the sprawling refugee camp had grown. He gained a hold there by playing on the insecurity of the refugees, offering them protection from the surrounding population, corrupt government officials and over-zealous army officers.

He also offered an outlet for the repressed energy and growing resentment of their young men by recruitment to the terrorist cause. But now Amin had the occupants by the balls. His men controlled everything from food distribution and water pumping to the selection of civilian representatives and administration of justice. Getting her out of there wouldn't be easy. Israel couldn't mount another Karamah for one woman.

The battle of Karamah camp, Jordan's biggest terrorist stronghold inflicted heavy casualties on *Fatah* and the Israelis captured vast reserves of weapons and ammunition, leaving the terrorists woefully under armed even today. But Karamah also claimed the lives of 26 Israeli soldiers. Another 70 were wounded.

Uri eyed the map pinned up on the wall in front of him. Sufa was a rabbit warren and, unlike Karamah, was packed with civilians. He needed more information before he could order a strike.

The door opened and Ytzak entered, seating himself, waiting patiently, glancing at the map Uri studied as he continued cracking seeds and spitting out the husks. Finally the *kibbutznik* spoke. "I need intelligence from the inside. Can you help?"

"Maybe we can help more than you think." Ytzak leaned forward on the desk, coming as close to a smile as Uri had ever seen. "We captured a terrorist last week, more dead than alive. Thanks to our surgeons he's recovering. His name's Fayez: Amin's right-hand man."

***

If simple things like sun and sand were all Bab'ullah once offered, now it offered less: just tent and rugs! She'd barely seen the outside since Hussam killed the snake and brought her back.

"Good shot," she'd quipped with a weak smile.

He looked as if he would kill her. "It was a bad shot. I aimed at you," he said without humour. They were virtually the last words he spoke to her. To the rocking gait of the camel, she fell into an exhausted sleep in his arms, waking briefly as he carried her to the tent. She'd been more or less in solitary confinement since.

She looked on the bright side. She wouldn't be doing much walking for a week or so anyway. Her feet throbbed, red and swollen around the marks cut by the sandals, her ankles blistered and peeling from the sunburn. When she woke it was after midday the following day. Fatima was there and began bathing her feet.

"Poor Fatima," she said. "Always putting me back together."

Fatima said nothing, leaving her with a small jar of ointment. Jodi hobbled to the tent flap and was shoved roughly back inside by a man.

"Hey, watch it!" she complained, but he refused to allow her out. He didn't speak English nor could she understand the torrent of Arabic he spat at her. He sat outside in the shade of the open flap. She sat inside. She got the picture. House arrest or rather tent arrest! Conversation was impossible and the day wore on interminably. Alone with no distractions she had time to dwell on events which, insoluble for the moment, churned over and over in her mind. Fear was an even greater enemy now. She tried to dispel it with positive thoughts. She'd had a setback but it was only round one. She hadn't lost the battle yet and, to prevent the creeping terror which invaded her mind every second it was unoccupied, she began to analyse her situation.

She hadn't made Ein Mara, but she'd nearly made it. Considering the odds, that was pretty damn good. More than that, she'd learned a lot. She knew where the village was, knew the relentlessness of the heat, the terrain, knew never to cross a shadow in the desert: "You are not the only creature searching for shade," Hussam told her. All this she knew, and Hussam must realise she knew too much, hence the guard.

What she knew less of were her feelings for him and his for her. She wanted him but it was a basic want, there was no future in it. Alone and vulnerable as she was it was natural she should seek security and whatever protection she could find. That she found it with Hussam was an accident of circumstance, nothing more. Yet she found herself waiting for him, wondering when he would come, what he would say, what she would do, planning their conversation. But he didn't come, nor did she once glimpse him though others passed, stopping to shout with the guard.

In the evening Fatima reappeared. "I'm going for water. Would you like to come?"

The evening gathering of the women at the pool was as much a social event as a necessity. They filled huge pitchers and tin cans with water for the next day, carrying them back to the camp on their heads. She took the earthenware jug and hobbled alongside Fatima. The guard, different from the one who shoved her roughly back this morning, followed at a distance. Jodi glanced towards the men but could not see Hussam.

At the pool, the women chattered in groups, Leila among them. They fell silent as she approached but Fatima said something and slowly, glancing frequently towards her, they resumed their exchanges.

Jodi was wretched, assuming Leila knew everything. It was impossible to keep anything secret in this place. She filled the pitcher and sat by the pool, looking out across the darkening water. The last of the fast-fading daylight glimmered over the western ridge. Jodi felt hope slipping away with it. In the daylight she could keep her spirits up but how would she get through the night? Perhaps he would come tonight.

But he didn't. She couldn't sleep. In the early hours, her mind full of terror, she went to the tent flap and peeped out. The guard sat cross-legged by a small fire.

"*Salaam*," she said softly, smiling. He jumped slightly and turned around. It was the same one who followed her to the pool. He was young and stockily built, not tall for a man but not short. He wore a chequered *kaffiyeh* and his brown tunic and baggy pants were belted with a thick plaited leather strap through which was pushed an ugly, curved knife.

She did not try to leave the tent but lay on her stomach, head in her hands, looking at the fire. "I don't suppose you speak English?" she asked hopefully.

"*Aysh?*"

"No, I didn't think you would." She smiled again as he looked puzzled. "It doesn't matter. I just want someone to talk to. You don't have to understand, in fact it's probably better you don't." She drew idly in the sand. "You're bedouin. You belong in the desert: your home, my prison," she mused, looking around.

"*Aysh*?"

She smiled. "You," she pointed to him, "you bedouin."

He pointed to himself: "You!" he said with satisfaction.

She relaxed, laughing. "No. Me!"

He was puzzled: "Nomee?" She laughed more and crawled to him taking his hand and pointing his index finger to himself.

"Me!" she said, then turning it to her: "You!"

"Ah!" he understood. Pointing at himself he said "*Ana*!" and at her: "*Anti*!" He looked pleased.

"Yes," she said. "Yes." She was pleased too. Though it was hardly a conversation, it was better than lying alone full of fear. She taught him more words: sand, fire, tent, and learned a little Arabic. Tiredness overtook her at last. She bid him good night. "*Tasbah alla khir*." He was nice! Wrapped in her blanket she slept deeply.

The next day was pretty much the same. Fatima came to bathe her feet which, though hardly lovely, already felt and looked better. She walked more easily now. "I want to see Hussam," she said.

"Forget Hussam," came the reply. "He won't see you."

"Why not?"

"Because he's decided that's how it should be." Fatima's voice was hard but she relented immediately. "I'm sorry you must be alone."

"Can you stay with me a while?"

She shook her head. "It was because of me you escaped. You're too clever. No one may sit and talk with you."

So, she was to be alone. Alone till they got their guns. Then what? He didn't intend to help her, that was clear. Would they kill her here or would Amin come for her? The fear rose. She mustn't think like this. She must keep her mind on today, on the here and now. So far, so good. Be positive! Somehow she must talk to Hussam, make him understand. But how, if he wouldn't see her? Well, if Mohammed couldn't go to the mountain, she'd damn well make the mountain come to her.

At supper when the nice guard arrived, she stuck her head out of the tent and looked towards the men. Hussam was there, his back towards her. Tonight she refused to go to the pool, creeping outside when Fatima had gone, warming her feet by the guard's fire.

His name was Rashid and as she sat with him by the fire he was relaxed, smiling. She pointed to her bruised feet and pulled an agonised face. He looked sympathetic and she placed a foot in his lap. He rubbed it gently. His hands were big and rough and warm and soothing. He reached for the other and did the same. It was lovely. She put her head back, moaning with relief, loud enough for Hussam to hear.

From the corner of her eye she saw-him leap to his feet approaching quickly. "Rashid! *Kafi*!" Rashid dropped her foot, standing, looking guilty as Hussam rebuked him. "Why aren't you with the women?" he demanded of Jodi, his voice so cold it surprised her.

"I didn't want to go, I wanted to..." she began.

"Go to them or stay inside!" he ordered.

She bristled, her eyes meeting his defiantly. Then, turning to Rashid and winking, she said: "O.K., since you ask so nicely," and backed into the tent, silently mocking him until the flap swung closed.

There was a heated exchange outside before things were quiet and she looked out again. Rashid had gone. In his place was a stern-faced guard who waved her back. Damn Hussam! She tossed about trying to sleep. With the darkness grew despair. She sat up suddenly. She had to escape. She didn't know how but somehow she'd get away. Perhaps tomorrow would bring something.

It did. It brought back Rashid. Old sour-face was on in the morning but Rashid took the afternoon shift. So, Hussam had moved him to days to keep an eye on them. She caught Rashid's eye and smiled at him. He smiled sheepishly then looked away quickly towards Hussam's tent. She sidled up to him, remaining just inside the tent and said: "He's jealous, you know."

"*Aysh*?"

"Jealous," she rapped her fist against her chest and assumed a furious expression, pointing to Hussam's tent, "of you and I, *anta weh ana*." She waited for her words to take effect then added: "Come here tonight. *Hina, anta weh ana, el masa*." The grammar left a lot to be desired but he damn well understood it. There was no doubt he would be back tonight. Perhaps he would help her.

She felt happy again, smiling every time she caught his eye. She sang for him, folk songs which had been popular in the charts before she left England. She was no Joan Baez but supposed he could make as much tune out of it as she could out of Umm Kalthoum, the Egyptian diva whose songs moved the Arab world to tears of love, passion and despair. Anyway, he seemed to like it. He sang back to her softly in the weird, warbling descending scales which characterised Arab music. It was quite romantic really and she listened with a modest smile, occasionally fluttering her eyelashes. Whatever it was, it was almost certainly about love. All Arab songs were.

When he finished she applauded. "*Heloa, heloa*! Beautiful!" she cried. "*Anti heloa*," he said, pointing to her. She looked down shyly.

The afternoon passed pleasantly. Hussam didn't seem to be around and they weren't disturbed as they talked. As he was relieved she reminded him in a whisper: "*El masa*." He nodded.

This evening at the pool she was happier. She listened to the chatter, able now to pick out the odd phrase, make sense of an occasional question. There was still no sign of Hussam. He wasn't by the fire. The stern guard settled outside her tent as she closed the flap and waited for Rashid. An hour went by. Gradually the conversation died as the men drifted away.

"Pst!" He had pulled up the canvas at the back of her tent and beckoned to her. Quickly she slipped underneath. As she stood he lunged at her, kissing her clumsily and messily with sticky wet lips.

She pushed him away whispering: "Shh! Not here! *La hina*! Come." Silently she slipped past the tents to the far side where the camels were tethered. The moon was nearly full and she picked her way easily. He followed and she indicated the camels. "We go. *Anta, ana, meshi*!"

He grabbed her again, forcing another sticky kiss on her, his hand going to her breast.

"No. *La*!," she said sharply, struggling free. "First, go, then kiss." She pointed to the camels again. They were getting restless, stamping and complaining. She didn't want them to wake anyone.

He understood now and turned to them but a voice froze him. "Haste is from the devil, Rashid!" Her heart sank. Where the devil had he come from? He walked to them, with the patronising expression of one who'd caught two naughty children. The half-smile quickly faded and he barked an order at Rashid. Tonight, though, Rashid was not the same frightened young man who had jumped to attention when he was last in trouble with Hussam. He retorted angrily. She saw his hand go to his belt: the knife!

"No! Hussam look out!" The blade flashed in the moonlight as Rashid leapt at him. The two of them were on the ground. She couldn't see in the darkness but there was a lot of thumping and grunting going on. Hussam was the larger but Rashid held the knife. "Rashid, stop!" she shouted but the struggle continued. Oh God, what had she done? What if he were killed?

In a minute it was over. Hussam stood, the knife in his hand, pulling up a dazed Rashid by his tunic front. He turned him round and kicked his behind, shouting after him as he stumbled towards the camp. Jodi backed away as he turned on her but he grabbed her wrist, dragging her behind him back to her tent, snapping something at the surprised guard. He spun her round to face him. Blood ran down his cheek. She touched it.

"You're cut," she said.

"You want to play games?" He snatched her hand, throwing her to the floor. "There's a place we call hell, deep in the desert. You can play your games there alone. You won't need a guard because you'll never escape. You will only wish to die."

His fury was infectious. "Is it so wrong to wish to live?" she shouted, her voice trembling.

He was still breathing heavily from the fight. He wiped a hand across his cheek and looked at the blood. "*Y'allah*," he growled, turning to go.

"No, Hussam!" She flung herself at his legs, hanging around his knees, off-balancing him so he fell, then clinging to him so he couldn't get up. He fought her, trying to push her off. Still she wouldn't let go, holding him with all her strength. "You can't walk away. I won't let you. Not again!"

His grip tightened but he pulled her towards him now, kissing her roughly, pushing her knees apart. It was no act of love but a punishing of one body by another. She wrapped her arms and legs around him and clung tightly, refusing him the satisfaction of hurting her, coming again and again in waves which broke the frustration of her days without him till exhausted she released him and fell back, watching the anger in his eyes mellow feeling the firm thrust of him inside her falter, his whole being shudder and his final lunge drive her over the brink once more.

They lay for a long time. She licked the blood from his cheek, kissed his eyes, mouth and ears. He held her gently and very close, their bodies entwined, their lips brushing softly as he whispered solemn words of Arabic she couldn't understand.

"It's my oath before God that I take you as mine."

"Just like that huh?" she smiled.

"Just like that."

135

"I won't have you whoring in my camp!" Hijazi's voice broke with rage as he chased after Hussam. Hussam stopped and turned.

"She's no whore," he said coldly.

"Ha! The way she behaves, with you, with Rashid! Who next?"

"It was you who took her in."

"And you who insisted you'd protect her," Hijazi scoffed. "I didn't know you would lie between her legs to do it!" Jodi listened from the shade beneath her tent flap. There were no guards now. She didn't understand a great deal but knew from Hijazi's frequent gestures towards her that she was the subject of the quarrel.

"How I do it is my business."

"Not here! Not while I live!"

Hussam looked at Jodi and then, in exasperation, at the distant mountains. "What do you want me to do?" he asked.

"Ah!" Hijazi assumed the stance of victor. He walked around Hussam until he faced him again. "Stay away from her. Draw comfort from your wife. Be a good father. This woman will soon be gone. Forget her." Hussam looked again at Jodi. Stay away. Forget her. Easy words for an old man. "I know what you think. You think you cannot. But you think with this," he tapped his groin, "not this," his head.

"Perhaps, but she and I..." he hesitated. Hijazi would never listen. "How can I stay away?"

The question was rhetorical but Hijazi answered anyway. "Go to Kahran. There are more vehicles. You neglect your work."

Kahran, yes. A few days alone would give him time to think. The arms could not arrive for weeks. Jodi was safe meanwhile.

"Go now," Hijazi urged, "before she changes your mind." Jodi watched. She understood some agreement had been reached and Hijazi had won.

Hussam went to his tent, emerging with his rifle and camel saddle. She stood as he looked at her then walked to the enclosure where the animals were tethered. She followed. Though he must know she was there, he ignored her, throwing the tasselled woollen rug over the camel's back, securing it before lifting the bulky saddle and lashing the girth. She looked around. There were only a half dozen animals here. Somewhere there were many more but they were like haulage trucks. No sooner did they come in than they went out again. Bab'ullah was only a transit point, a watering hole. Little was loaded or unloaded here. There were two asses and a horse, a grey dappled Arab which chewed on hay, stamping its feet and tossing its head as the flies bothered it.

Hussam spoke. "After woman came the horse for the enjoyment and happiness of man, according to the Prophet. Mohammed owned fifteen mares but only eleven wives," he added provocatively.

She ignored it, asking instead: "Where are you going?"

He took her chin in his hand. "Women here do not question their men."

"Shall I see you again?"

"You don't learn very fast." He smiled: "Yes, you will see me soon."

She stepped away, shaking her head. "No. Hijazi won't allow it. I saw you."

"Hijazi won't keep me from you, you have my word."

"Your word is valueless. You think I don't know! You're not bound by a promise to a *Nazrani*, a Christian."

"My word is my word, whoever it is given to!" She was desolate in his sudden cold anger and he relented. "Look," he took the scarab ring from his finger. "This was my father's. To me it is beyond value but I give it as I give my word and shall redeem both." He slid the ring onto her middle finger. It was heavy, the green stone warm against her skin. "Now do you believe?"

"*Abu!*" David ran towards them. Behind him, Leila hesitated before walking forward. Jodi stood back as Hussam swept David up in his arms and Leila, glancing in triumph at her, handed him a large leather bag.

She was an outsider again, understanding little of what was said. He looked at her only once before mounting the camel bedouin style, as it stood. He left her standing with Leila, David running alongside him. Leila turned, eyeing her with disgust, and spat in her face before walking away.

She deserved it she knew. She stood motionless watching David run back to camp and Hussam continue out of sight.

Hijazi startled her. "*Yallah*!" he shouted, shooing her back towards her tent, keeping up a sneering tirade until she reached it and closed the flap to shut him out.

In the night she was afraid again. The Koranic penalty for adultery was death but it applied only to women. She could be stoned to death. Hussam would merely be whipped. The faces of Leila, David and Hijazi spun before her. David's laughter, Hijazi's sneer, Leila's venom. Doubt plagued her. Outside the animals were noisy and unsettled. She rubbed the scarab ring against her cheek. It was warm and solid, seeming to generate heat of its own. Still, she couldn't sleep.

She went out. The moon was full, shining so brightly she could pick out every detail of the tents and the desert beyond. The camels stamped restlessly, the Arab horse pawed the ground and snorted. Strange how a full moon affected animals. She walked over to them. The horse sniffed her hand, nuzzling the ring. She stroked his soft downy nose and scratched behind his ears. He liked it, pushing his nose back under her hand when she stopped. Beyond, where a rough wicker frame covered a small store of hay, she could see his saddle, the bridle lay over it.

It was so obvious that it took a while to register. On a horse like this it would take only a few hours to reach Ein Mara. She knew the way, she knew the snags. She could do it. Putting her cheek against the horse's muzzle, she whispered gently: "Hussam, forgive me. I have to go. Please understand."

She was almost afraid to return to her tent, worried the detour might rob her of her chance, but she needed the *kaffiyeh* and sandals. She would take a sheet to shade her legs and feet. And water, just in case.

Back at the enclosure she quickly saddled up. Thank God the animals were noisy tonight. She led the horse a long way from the camp before mounting and heading west up the slope, taking it gently. Noise travelled a long way on nights such as this. The animal was spirited and, like all horses ridden by men, had a cast-iron mouth. She had difficulty controlling him. He just wanted to run. If it was her feet that suffered last time, this time it would be her hands. Already they were sore from his constant pulling on the reins. He obviously wasn't ridden enough and certainly wasn't schooled. Still, it was no time to be picky. The struggle kept her mind from Hussam but as distance between her and the camp grew so did her confusion. Blindly she trusted her animal instinct. She could no longer make sense of her thoughts. On the ridge she paused to look back. The moon was setting but soon it would be light. Already the eastern sky glowed red.

"Red sky at morning," she mused, wondering if it held the same warning for bedouins as it did for shepherds. Tears blurred her vision as she guided the horse westward. Once the sun rose she had only to keep her shadow before her until she saw the headland. "Whoa, boy," she calmed the prancing animal. She didn't want him breaking a leg in the darkness. She'd give him his head once it was light.

At last the sun rose. Jodi was never so glad to see it. "Go on then you brute, go!" she cried, giving him rein. The horse lunged forward, galloping as if the devil were after him and, who knows, she thought, he just might be. Tears flew from her cheeks as the wind lashed her face. Not even the devil would catch her now.

CHAPTER 10

In the half-light the tents were shadows, as were the paratroopers who swept silently down the hillside towards them, fanning out through and around the fields, converging on the camp.

Timing was critical. It was just light enough to see. The troops were handpicked, working in pairs, armed with Uzis and FN-FAL rifles. All spoke Arabic. A soldier entered each tent, waking the occupants, ordering them out, while his colleague waited outside, covering those who emerged. As they cleaned out the tents, smashing rifles, dispersing ammunition, shooting the camels, the half-tracks roared down the hillside. Ten boarded the first vehicle, taking the woman with them. Another ten leapt into the second. The remainder covered the captives until the two vehicles were underway, then climbed in the third and set off in pursuit.

Uri looked at his watch. The whole operation had taken forty minutes from the top of the escarpment. The halftracks circled back to where the tents stood and the stand-ins laughed with each other, pleased at their performance.

He improvised the fields, marking out approximate boundaries. A double line of stones showed where the bamboo-lined path ran to the pool. Otherwise the terrain, the contours of the desert site he had chosen for the exercise were similar to what they would find at Bab'ullah. The approach must be from the west. They would wait on the ridge until just before sunrise and mount a swift raid, taking the woman, retreating quickly.

He wished to God he knew the identity of the man Hussam and which tent was his, but the terrorist Fayez knew only that the woman was at Bab'ullah. He had not met Hussam nor seen the camp. *Mossad* could produce nothing more than an aerial photo of the settlement and an ancient file with few and sketchy details of missions in which it was generally believed Hussam had taken part. All reference to him ended ten years ago after the massacre at Kibbutz Hashemesh. *Mossad* was informed he'd ceased terrorist activities but this whole business, together with Hijazi's gun-running, threw a different light on things.

Surprise was vital to the mission. He must be certain there were enough men to cover each tent. In spite of the treachery of its occupants, Uri wanted no killing at Bab'ullah, a tall order for his troops. The *fedayeen* were one story, the bedouin quite another. Every bedouin carried a rifle and learned to use it well from boyhood. The desert was their home. They could sense attack and would defend to the death. Bedouins dominated the Arab Legion, the only fighting force to which the Jews lost in the War of Independence. Its successor, the Jordan Arab Army, was as effective. Uri

143

knew it from personal experience and the bitter losses Israel suffered in the battle for Jerusalem last year.

His paras were more than a match for the bedouin, an elite unit with a string of military successes and more first-hand combat experience than any army in the world. Israel's paras were blooded in outright war during the Suez fiasco of '56. They took the Mitla Pass, cutting the Egyptian artery to Sinai. Then the faint-hearted British scuttled away, leaving Nasser in power and Israel to protect herself as best she could from his relentless aggression. Last year, the paras again proved themselves supreme desert fighters, spearheading the assault on Sinai, routing the Egyptian army which Nasser boasted would smash them.

He looked at the troops. They would never be readier. From England he heard Sir Roland Dimbleby had acceded totally to the terrorists' demand. There was no time to waste.

Yet Uri was uneasy. He couldn't identify it but an indefinable something, premonition perhaps, nagged that the whole thing wasn't right.

She entered Ein Mara. The horse, lathered and soaking along his neck and chest, was gasping from thirst. She stopped only once on the long ride, trying to give him water which she poured from the flask into her cupped hand. But it did no more than wet his mouth.

In the village centre, the *caravanserai* boasted a long zinc trough with a pump at one end. Two donkeys stood there lethargically, otherwise the square was empty, the small mud and stone houses shuttered. She allowed the horse to drink only a little at a time and she bathed his neck with cool water. Maybe she shouldn't, maybe it was bad for him, but he was so hot he looked as if he'd explode unless she cooled him quickly. He had galloped flat out for nearly ten minutes before slowing to a trot. She had no difficulty with him afterwards and was amazed at his stamina as he settled into a gentle canter and kept it up nearly all the way.

It was about two o'clock. Vaguely she wondered what to do next. Which door she should knock. But that was unnecessary. Turning to lead the horse from the trough, she confronted six men, two with rifles.

For a moment she was afraid, then recalled the time-honoured bedouin greeting which would tell them she meant no harm: "*Salaam aleykom.*"

An old man stepped forward: "*Weh aleykom salaam*," he returned her greeting without smiling.

"I am English. *Ana Inglisi*," she began. The men shuffled, murmuring. "I ask your help." She searched fruitlessly for some Arabic to explain. "I am a prisoner," she pointed to herself and crossed her wrists as if bound, "of the bedouin at Bab'ullah." She pointed in the direction from which she arrived. The men looked at each other and some frantic jabbering broke out. The old man raised a hand and they fell quiet. He walked to the horse and said something rapidly to Jodi. "*Aysh*?" she asked.

"Hussam," he said, pointing to the horse. "Hussam!"

How the heck did he know? She looked around in desperation. "Is there a telephone? *Telefon*?" she mimicked raising a handset to her ear. The old man started to laugh. The others laughed too. In desperation she begged: "Please help me, please!"

He motioned to the desert, towards Bab'ullah, barking an instruction and turning from her.

"No. No, you don't understand. They'll kill me." She motioned a cut-throat action. "It's the *fedayeen*: the Palestinians." She groped for any word they might recognise. They were silent, looking at each other again and she realised they were afraid. Oh, God, how could she make them help?

The old man pushed her and hailed a man who pointed his rifle at her. Dumbfounded, she backed off. They walked away, throwing occasional glances at her as they went to their homes. The old man waved her away again before entering an archway and closing the heavy wooden gate.

What now? She had assumed this would be the end of her troubles. She led the horse to the edge of the village, hoping to find a road, but there was nothing. Beyond a fringe of olive groves and palms it was as desolate on the west as the east. Didn't the bloody desert ever stop? She wouldn't go back. She couldn't go on. Jodi shielded her eyes, scanning the horizon which seemed strangely blurred, the sun hazy. For the first time she was aware of a stiff breeze which whipped up the sand at her feet, stinging her ankles. Retracing her steps to the *caravanserai*, she tied the horse and sat in the shadow of a high wall. The sleepless night, the long journey and the bitter disappointment of her reception here weighed down on her and she slept.

The horse woke her. It was fretful, stamping and rearing. The wind was stronger now and as she opened her eyes the sand stung them. Looking west she saw the sky was brown with clouds that piled up to the sun, blotting it out.

Taking the reins she dragged the horse to the old man's house, banging on the high wooden gate. "Let me in! Please let me in!" No one came but she banged and shouted louder until it opened and he angrily admonished her. She pointed west and he nodded, knowingly. From inside a woman's voice called and he shouted back. There was some dialogue and finally he stood aside, motioning impatiently for her to bring the horse.

Relieved she stepped through the gate and into a small sheltered courtyard where he tethered the animal before leading her to a low dark room. Inside were several people, two other men and three women. The men frowned disapproval and murmured. On the floor two young children played with a scraggy looking cat.

They eyed her suspiciously and she smiled and sat as she was told. The room was sparsely furnished. There was a low couch on which the old man and his wife sat with another man. Two others sat on stools while a woman was busy at a fire at the far end of the room. The smell of coffee filled the air.

A plastic vase of plastic roses stood on the square, solid table on which the woman now set small, handleless cups and filled them with thick black coffee from a brass coffee pot. She smiled at Jodi who lifted the cup thankfully and drank. The thick sweet drink reminded her how hungry she was and the woman, who seemed to know, returned with a bowl of pita bread and humus. Jodi set about it with relish, swearing it was the most delicious meal she'd tasted, thanking them all between mouthfuls. Outside it was quiet, dark, like twilight. The door to the courtyard remained open. The world waited in stillness before the advancing storm.

"*Mukhtar!*" The shout rang out clearly in the silence. Jodi went cold. It was his voice. The old man looked at her and then at the others. "*Ya mukhtar!*" It was louder now. Impatient. He stood.

"No!" she said, jumping up and standing in the doorway. "No! Don't tell him!" She put a finger on her lips but he shook his head and tried to push past her. "No!" she said again. He unleashed a stream of verbal abuse but she wouldn't move, pleading with him, kneeling and clasping her fingers as in prayer. He looked at her hands, at the ring and tapped it. In panic Jodi ripped it from her finger and pushed it into his hand. He smiled, breathing on it and polishing it on his tunic. He patted her head and nodded reassuringly. Hesitantly she let him pass.

Hussam stood alone at the *mukhtar's* gate. Across, in the shelter of the wall, his brothers couched the camels. It was a good place to sit out the storm. They met in the desert. He turned back when they gave him Amin's message and since cursed his decision to camp the night. The horse was missing. He knew immediately she took it and would go to Ein Mara.

The *mukhtar* opened his gate. "*Ahlan weh sahlan*, Hussam. You are welcome in our village."

"Where is she?"

The *mukhtar* looked puzzled. Spreading his arms, he shrugged. "I don't know what you mean."

Hussam glanced westward. He hadn't much time. He grabbed the *mukhtar's* wrist. "It's a dangerous game you play, old man."

Something fell from his hand. Hussam picked it up, looking in disbelief at the dull green stone in its heavy gold mount. The *mukhtar* panicked. "She was here," he blurted out, "but I sent her away. She went. I didn't see her go. I don't know where she is."

Hussam still looked at the ring. "You have five minutes to find her," he said. "Five minutes, old man, or I shall burn your village to the ground." He lifted his eyes to the storm. "It will burn well today."

The *mukhtar* fled inside. Hussam turned the ring over and over before replacing it on his little finger, glancing again at the menacing sand cloud and wrapping the *kaffiyeh* tightly around his nose and mouth.

She opened the gate and he looked into her eyes. The storm struck, startling the horse which reared, nearly pulling her over. She hung on as it pawed the air, terrified. Quickly he took the reins, removing his *abba* and wrapping it around the animal's head, blinding it to the storm, protecting its ears and nostrils from the lacerating sand. Jodi fought with her *kaffiyeh* as he led the horse ahead to the shelter of the wall.

She reached him at last. "Amin has sent for you," he said, "and I thank God for it."

CHAPTER 11

Khadija made life heaven or hell. She was a singer, an open supporter of the *fedayeen* who attacked the British and later the Jews, and began making large cash donations to Amin. Hussam was 17 years old. He would see her black Mercedes cruise into camp. Protected from their gaze by the tinted glass she watched the young recruits train. It didn't take her long to spot him.

Her chauffeur approached. "Hey, you! Come with me!" He held open the back door of the Mercedes and Hussam climbed in awkwardly. He was big even for a car like this. He sprawled on the seats of white fur as his eyes quickly adjusted to the dimness.

She leaned back in the corner, eyeing him appreciatively, smoking a black cigarette in a slim tortoiseshell and gold cigarette holder. Her long dark hair was swept back, her eyes painted green, her mouth bright red. He knew her immediately. Everyone knew Khadija. She sang of love and passion and struggle. She sang from the heart and her voice could move the coldest man to tears. Throughout the Arab world, she travelled giving concerts. Her records sold in hundreds of thousands. To millions, Khadija was the unattainable dream, the incomparable, the woman above all women. Hussam, calm in battle, was terrified. He couldn't bring himself to meet her gaze and looked straight ahead, feeling foolish.

"Welcome, *el Hussam*," she said in the deep mellow voice which captured men like flies. "They tell me you're so very brave. Is it true?"

Afraid his voice would break, he shrugged. She laughed a low, throaty laugh. Her perfume went to his head. She touched his hand. "What you are doing is right. You will drive the British from Egypt and return her to her people. Like all good Egyptians I am indebted to you and those who fight with you, *el Hussam*." She was in concert at the Cairo Opera House that night and pushed a ticket into his hand. "I shall sing just for you," she smiled. "We'll have supper afterwards."

It was late when she took him to her house on Gezira Island, suburb of the wealthy. Inside, a *mezze* was prepared on a low table. The damask curtains stirred gently in the soft warm breeze which blew from the Nile. She sat on silk cushions scattered on the floor and talked as they ate. She was clever. Apart from his mother, Hussam had never known an educated woman. There were no girls in his school, nor any in the student federation.

She laughed. She was happy, relaxed after her performance at the Opera House, kneeling in front of him and feeding him grapes one by one, kissing each before placing it in his mouth. She kissed him his first

152

kiss. She was his first woman. He was clumsy, hurried, out of his mind. She let him fumble and curse. It was his first time and he had to be rid of the first time. He finished quickly and lay back, breathing ecstatically. Slowly she kissed and caressed his body, whispering the words of her songs to him, rubbing her full breasts against his chest, his face, pressing the nipples into his mouth and cradling his head, teaching him with moans and sighs what it was that gave her pleasure.

He was a fast learner and a good lover, as fighters often were. Khadija loved dangerous men and the control she had over them. With men he felt secure, knew his place. In the *fedayeen* he had position. With a gun he was lethal. But with Khadija he was powerless. She was soft, small and delicate. He could crush her easily, yet it was she who crushed him time and time again. She ignored him for weeks then demanded he come immediately. She laughed and cried. Her moods confused him and he knew for the first time a power that force could not break, the power that women would forever have over men.

With Khadija he learned tolerance. He had no choice. Everything was on her terms or not at all so that even when she died, suddenly, mysteriously, he accepted it as he accepted all she gave and took. The world mourned her.

Hussam volunteered for more missions, taking his revenge on Israel. He was reckless but, unlike Khadija, his time had not come. God would not take the life he lived so carelessly. As grief diminished he became dimly aware that the purpose of his life ultimately would be revealed and that whatever it might be was the will of Allah and not he.

Leila was a good wife and a fine mother. He asked nothing more. Yet this woman from the west awakened him as only Khadija had. Like Khadija she was clever. Like Khadija she deceived him and the pain went deep. Like a caged bird, she would fly if the door were open. Fate was repeating its lesson. What was written was written, for him and for her.

As he watched Ahmed push her to Amin's door she was white with fear. Yet her eyes met his, stubbornly refusing to betray the terror she must feel. He waited outside. A crowd had followed them into the camp. There were two armed guards, thirty or more children and a dozen adults. They waved to him and laughed, touching the camel, reaching for the reins, jostling with each other.

Amin appeared. "Hussam! I didn't expect you personally."

"I've kept my word, Amin. Now I can go in peace."

"Go? But you've just arrived." Hussam tried to turn the camel but the crowd around him was growing. There were *fedayeen* cheering and women throwing flowers. "You're still a hero to our people," Amin shouted above the noise.

An old man hurried up. The crowd parted to let him through. He greeted Hussam effusively. "We're honoured to have you as our guest. What we have is yours, *ya* Hussam, and tonight we will feast." Hussam submitted. Amin he could refuse, the *mukhtar* he could not. It would be unpardonably rude. He allowed them to lead the camel to the *mukhtar's* house. The crowd still surged round but the old man dismissed the women and children as they sat outside to drink coffee. Men and young soldiers gathered. Those who had no stools squatted on their haunches or leaned against buildings.

For Hussam, the scene was painful. It was the first camp he'd entered in 20 years. Though there were buildings, not tents, the bitter air of desolation and betrayal was as oppressive as he remembered. The narrow streets, dry and dusty were strewn with piles of rubbish in which children played and skinny dogs dug with their paws. Across from the *mukhtar's* house, one of a low, flat-roofed row hurriedly built out of stark concrete blocks, was the communal building where food and clothing were dispensed daily to endless queues of those whom meagre handouts could not satisfy. Focussed on him, the eyes of the old men were hopeless, the young, proud but unsure. Amin was right, they lacked leaders, though their direction was sure, Palestine.

The *mukhtar* spoke with pride of the young *fedayeen*. Many had never seen their homeland but the older generation brought it to life for them, kept it alive with tales of orange and olive groves, the tall cedars of the Jordan, the vines and figs, the lush valleys. From this chaos it was a glimpse of Paradise. They were eager to return. The *mukhtar* prayed only to be spared to see it.

He led Hussam to where women cooked the evening meal for Amin's men. Over an open fire they roasted a whole sheep.

Amin was there already. "Even here we find something special for our guests," he laughed. "It takes a little friendly persuasion, that's all."

Hussam wondered what he'd done with Jodi. As if reading his thoughts Amin winked and said: "I hear she was giving you problems, brother. I couldn't have that. Two of my men will guard her now." Hussam was silent but Amin wouldn't let it drop. "We'll see how well her daddy does. If he's good, maybe I'll release her, maybe not."

"She's your hostage. She's nothing to me," Hussam snapped.

Amin seemed surprised but he quickly smiled and slapped Hussam's back. "Ha! That's better. At Bab'ullah I thought you'd grown old."

A woven mat was spread on the ground before them and on it were placed small bowls of pistachios, humus, groundnuts, olives, chickpeas and a dozen other appetisers with baskets of bread. The old man reminisced as more plates were brought laden with the thickly sliced roast meat and rice mixed with peppers which they ate as bedouin, with their fingers, moulding it into small spheres to be placed in the mouth without touching the lips.

"Tell us, Hussam, of your exploits," the *mukhtar* urged. "Tell us of the battles you waged for our country."

There were sweet cakes, honeyed pastries. To Hussam they tasted bitter like his memories. "It was long ago, *ya sheikh*," he said.

"Hussam is too modest," Amin declared. "I'll tell you how he saved my life. No, my friend, I will tell it," he dismissed Hussam's protest. "We struck ten miles inside the cease fire line. It was Hussam's idea to blow up the water supply to Kibbutz Hashemesh in the Negev." *Fedayeen* gathered around Amin to hear the story. "He was a great one for sabotage, *el Hussam*. He had a genius for knowing where to do most damage. Without water Hashemesh was nothing but a sand dune. There was no well, no spring. The water was pumped from many miles away. He laid his hand on Hussam's shoulder. "Our hero, the engineer, understands pumps and pipes very well."

It was a good story, colourfully told but not too accurately. Hussam would not forget the raid. Amin covered him as he wrapped plastic explosive around the pipe at three places along a half mile section. He set the fuses to blow within seconds of each other. He argued that the blasts should be delayed so the *fedayeen* could escape but the others wanted to watch the pipe go up.

Returning silently, he came up behind an Israeli guard taking careful aim at Amin's back. In an instant Hussam fired. The shot echoed in the desert silence and the guard slumped forward as the first charge blew.

"Were it not for Hussam I wouldn't be here to carry on the war effort," Amin concluded, slapping his back. "We made them pay. We killed them all."

Hussam stood. "Forgive me," he told the *mukhtar*. "We've had a long journey. I must sleep."

The old man bid him good night and Hussam nodded to the young men crowding around Amin. Walking back to the camels he was thoughtful. Behind him the feast continued. They would tell stories and sing battle songs till early morning. He passed Amin's command post. Inside there was scuffling, He stopped and listened. He could hear men laughing and a woman's stifled cry.

Hussam pushed the door open. A guard held Jodi, struggling, on the floor, his hand over her mouth, her hands tied. Another knelt in front of her, undoing his trousers. Hussam leapt at him, knocking him sideways, putting his hands round the guard's throat and crushing the windpipe with his thumbs till his breath rattled. The other guard was on him from behind, pulling on his chin, forcing him to release his grip. Hussam slammed his elbow into the man's groin and went back to throttling the first.

Jodi screamed. He let the man go. The other was already limping through the doorway. Picking up the first by his jacket collar, he slung him out, kicking the door shut in rage.

She lay sobbing. He cradled her in his arms, stroking her hair, telling her it was all right. "Don't go," she begged between sobs. "For God's sake don't leave me here." He sighed. "Take me back to Bab'ullah."

"You will run from me."

"No. No. I promise."

Hussam smiled. Now she would promise anything. Tomorrow would be different.

"You made a vow before God that I was yours."

"Ah! You laughed when I made it. You thought you were still in England. Now you see why we do such things."

"I'm sorry." She was no longer crying but an occasional sob broke through and tears hung on her lashes.

He kissed her eyes and assumed a serious expression. "Here a woman needs the protection of a man. In return she should be obedient." She tensed but nodded quickly. "She should keep her man's home, cook his food, warm him with her body, bear his sons. Would you bear me sons, *habibi*?"

Jodi looked at him blankly for a moment but recovered swiftly. Yes, she'd do anything, anything.

"Do you vow it, as I vowed?"

"Hussam, that's not fair."

"Then stay with Amin."

"No, no. I vow it."

He laughed, pleased with himself, and slipped his hands under the loose cotton kaftan, lifting her to him.

"Untie me."

He shook his head feeling her nipples respond to the gentle caress of his thumbs. "I should keep you like this until you are pregnant. Then you will never escape."

✳✳✳

She knew now how reprieved prisoners on death row must feel. She rode in front of him on the camel and sang and sang till he told her to shut up. Then she laughed and sang some more. "Hey, have you ever done it on a camel, my love?" she whispered. "We could you know."

"If you don't shut up I'll take you back."

She pulled a face at him. Getting her away from Sufa proved simpler than he'd hoped. Amin put up surprisingly little resistance. "You see what trouble a woman causes?" Amin said when he heard of the attempted rape. "It's what I feared. It's why I brought her to you."

"I'm taking her back," Hussam told him.

"Wait! Yesterday you said she was my hostage. She was nothing to you."

"That was yesterday."

"Ah!" Amin paused thoughtfully. "And if I give her to you, what will you give in return?" Hussam was silent. "Fight with us Hussam. You can have a hundred women!"

He shook his head. "Last night you boasted of our raid at Kibbutz Hashemesh. Yes, I saved you there and you owe me for it."

Amin frowned then shrugged, laughing. "You bedouin! Another wife, eh?" He thought for a moment. "All right. Take her on one condition; that you don't release her until the arms reach me. Then do what you want with her." Hussam turned to go.

"*Ma salaam*, my brother," Amin smiled. "When you change your mind about the fighting come back to me."

It was a long journey to Qmrah and they took it slowly, Ali and Ahmed going on in front, sneaking backward glances at Hussam and his noisy woman. "Hijazi will be furious," she said.

"Not if you behave."

"I'm practicing, I'm practicing." She put her arms around him, hugging his chest, concentrating on being quiet. It was difficult while she was so happy.

Suddenly the camel stopped. Hussam hailed his brothers and she saw them stop too. "What...?" she began.

"Hush!" he said sharply. She listened but heard nothing. He shouted again, pointing to the rocks left of them and urging the camel on until they were hidden. Taking his rifle he jumped down and shinned the rocks till he looked over the top. Jodi joined him, Ali and Ahmed followed, rifles in hand. She could hear it now, the low sound of diesel engines. They were in a *wadi*, a dry, winding valley. Either side steep hills rose, scarred with rocky outcrops, dotted with scrub. From their vantage point they looked down directly onto the only track through.

The vehicles swung into view, three half-tracks such as the ones she'd seen in Israel. They travelled fast. She counted ten soldiers in each, armed and helmeted, wearing full battle gear; the camouflage fatigues and olive-green combat jackets of the Israeli paras. She looked at Hussam. He was motionless but his eyes missed nothing. When he turned to her his look was unsure and she realised she had only to stand and shout to be rescued. He grabbed her, swinging her round, clamping his hand over her mouth, her head to his chest. She struggled furiously as the sound died away, the half-tracks racing up the *wadi* out of sight. He let her go.

"How dare you!" she cried. "I wouldn't have shouted. I wouldn't!"

Hussam ignored her. "*Yallah!*" he shouted to the others who raced back down the rock to the camels. He pulled her along behind him. "Get on!" he said, pushing her at the camel.

"Stop pushing." He took hold of her hair, pulling her face close to his. "Get on!"

He climbed up behind her, slapping the camel with a stick and cursing until it galloped. Jodi clung to the saddle. The thing moved as fast as a horse but with no stirrups she barely kept her balance. Hussam beat it mercilessly. She thought it must drop from fatigue but it raced onwards. Finally it slowed and he allowed it to walk. There was some frantic conversation between the three brothers.

"What is it?" she asked. "Hussam, what's happening?"

"The Israelis," he said. "Where were they returning from?"

"I don't know."

"There can be only one place." They travelled through the night. The camels kept up a punishing pace but it was late morning and the sun was high before they glimpsed the green of the little oasis in the distance.

Tired as she was, Jodi felt a growing terror. Something which was neither mind nor body warned her that whatever waited at Bab'ullah, she didn't want to see. The desert was deathly quiet and every step closer tuned her senses so that she no longer saw nor heard but rather perceived the dreadful secret that the little settlement kept.

From the height of the camel she looked down on the small fields. A few sheep strayed in them, bleating pitifully. The path which led through the tall bamboo bore marks of fighting, a rifle, a sandal, a *kaffiyeh*, then opened suddenly onto the full horror.

There were no tents, only charred remains where once they stood. Nothing moved but the relentless, encroaching sand which piled up in small mounds on the lee of scattered, broken objects. Afterwards she recalled the scene without dimension, like a badly painted landscape. The colours were wrong, the positioning wrong, the lighting, the style, subject, object; unreal. Her mind couldn't grasp its enormity and at first absorbed only details: the bread which had burnt, still clinging to the sides of the little kiln; what would they eat today? the women's clothes all ripped, she should cover them before the men saw; the broken water pitchers; the wasted food; the mess everything was in, it would take days to clear up.

Perspective grew slowly. The slashes of red, the grotesque shapes, the rags which flapped with the breeze, the stench and the flies were all that remained of every living person at Bab'ullah. In slow motion she saw Hussam wander among them. He looked lost but she followed him anyway. He bent to pull back a *kaffiyeh* obscuring an old man's face, the head all but severed. It was Hijazi. He moved quickly now, frantically turning corpses which lay face down.

Vaguely she remembered the others searching, Ali falling on his knees by a woman, clutching her hand and pressing it to his face, murmuring: "*Umma, umma.*" Hussam stared down and Ahmed wailed aloud. The sound echoed eerily. Jodi looked helplessly around, her eyes drawn to a face she knew, a face which had spat venomously at her, a body which had been round and pregnant.

She turned to see Hussam, his eyes fixed on the mutilated form that was Leila. She took his shoulders and shook him. "Don't look, Hussam. For God's sake don't look!" She tried to turn him, to pull his head to her but he stood rigid. Desperately she searched for a blanket or sheet. A charred rug lay in the burned-out remains of a tent. She grabbed it and drew it quickly over Leila as Hussam knelt, her bloodied head in his lap, stroking the dark flowing hair.

Jodi withdrew. She walked to the pool. She felt shock, she felt horror and grief. She was stunned, confused and sad. But most of all she was useless, superfluous. Like the slow clop from the irrigation channel she still functioned but what for? What was the reason? What was the point?

She sat, her arms folded on her knees, and looked at the reflections of the tall, heavy-laden palms. Who would harvest them?

In Israel the stories of atrocity were all against Arabs. Naively, she hadn't considered the Israelis capable of such things, or had she merely closed her eyes to the possibility? We were all the same after all.

The incident of the dog returned. It happened when she stayed on *kibbutz* for two days, writing about some English volunteers. Like them, she slept in a wooden hut, one of three rows which faced each other in a triangle, raised off the ground on piles of bricks.

An afternoon siesta was disturbed by shouting and a loud bang. An English boy yelled: "Kill her! Kill her!" Jodi rushed outside.

A *Nahal* boy of the army reserve stood with an Uzi sub machine gun. An English girl was in tears. Two others were on their hands and knees looking under the opposite huts. On nearby slabs was a trail of blood.

"What happened, for God's sake?" she demanded.

Someone, she couldn't remember who, said: "They've shot the dog. She's under here. Why don't you finish her off, you bastard!" The boy with the gun grinned. Jodi looked under the hut. The dog's big eyes stared out at her, glazed.

"We can't leave her there," she said.

"You shot her, you get her out," the sobbing girl yelled at the boy who turned and walked away. The little dog moved her head. She was lovely, rather like a Yorkshire terrier, but she always barked and snapped at anyone who went near her. "They made her like that and now they've shot her," wept the girl. "They kept throwing stones at her and now they've shot her."

Jodi called the dog's name. For some time she wouldn't come and when she did, the others screamed. She was covered in blood. Jodi felt around the little body, trying to find where the bullet had entered.

"She's only hit in the leg," said a girl, but it was obvious from the feel of her and the blood dripping from her mouth that she was dying. "For God's sake finish it off!"

"Wait," said Jodi as the boy with the gun came nearer. She still couldn't find the wound. The little dog lifted her head and there it was, a red gaping hole right in the middle of the chest. It hardly bled but as the beautiful brown eyes stared up, the blood gurgled in its throat.

"You'd better kill it," she said. But the dog seemed to understand. It leaped from her suddenly and one of the *Nahal* boys caught it, tying a piece of wire around its throat. She looked at the blood on her hands but couldn't bear to look at the dog again, walking back to her hut instead.

Outside the *Nahal* boys laughed, the English girls cried and the English boys swore. Jodi looked out briefly. The dog had been tied by the wire to a tractor which drove off as the little animal tried to run behind. She felt sick. The boys were still laughing. "God, what cruel people they must be!" she thought.

"What cruel people," she said aloud and became aware that she was looking up into Hussam's grief-stricken face. He fell on his knees and she held him as sobs wracked his body. She was weary, beyond tears, but he wept like a wounded animal, burying his face in her hair, her clothes, her lap until he lay still and quiet, looking, as she did, across the silent pool.

CHAPTER 12

"My son wasn't there!"

Amin listened intently. Flanked by two guards he sat at the table. Hussam sat opposite. "We searched the desert, the fields. There was no sign of his body."

"The Israelis must have him."

"Why would they take a boy?"

"Why would they do what they did?"

Hussam stood, walked to the window. "We both know why they were there."

"We should kill the woman. It would teach them a lesson."

He shook his head wearily. Amin rose, slamming his fist on the table. "We should kill her, I say!"

Hussam rounded on him: "As you killed Khadija?"

"She was a whore. They all are."

"Amin, don't touch the woman. This time I'll kill you. I swear it."

Amin backed off, scowling. "What will you do? Hold your woman while the Israelis hold your son?"

"If they have him I'll find him."

"How?" Amin was confident again. "How will you find him? Walk over the border and ask?" He paused. "My friend, we're not dealing with a bunch of disorganised zealots now. They don't care for talk, only killing. You want more proof?"

Hussam gazed through the dust-streaked window. Outside children were playing. He looked at Amin. "I want my son."

"Then trust me. I have friends on the West Bank, in Jerusalem and Haifa, even among the Druze on Mount Hermon. If anyone can find him, I will." He continued carefully: "Are you willing to fight for him?"

"Not only for him, for them all. It's why I came."

Amin's eyes glowed with satisfaction. "Good," he nodded, "good."

The next days were full. With Amin he watched the noisy training sessions, boys marching up and down, shouting ludicrous slogans, waving assault rifles, firing excitedly and missing the mark. The quickest team to assemble a mortar took two minutes. No wonder casualties were high.

"This is the army of Palestine?" he asked. "You send these against the Israelis?"

"When we were in Egypt, when we started, were we better?" asked Amin. "No! But we had Nasser who stood against the world. Who do they have? Hussein who cowers before the Jews!"

What they had was violent hatred passed on from generation to generation and shared by the youngest Palestinian children. Hussam fell victim to it as a child in Jerusalem when, out of boyish curiosity he followed the streams of black-coated, ringleted Jews in fur hats who made their way quickly through Musrara from Mea Shearim to the Wailing Wall. In a line they stood before it, one side of a narrow alley, so tall he could not see the top. At its base the stone blocks were huge, almost the height of a man, the foundations of Solomon's temple, but they grew smaller higher up. They called it Kotel Hamaravi, or *ha Kotel*, and before it the strange looking men mumbled into little books, dipping their straight-backed bodies in quick little bows, small boxes strapped to their heads and arms. Draped in white sheets with grey stripes down two sides they performed their curious ritual again and again, some mumbling, some wailing in anguish, some shoving folded slips of paper between the stones.

When they left he approached the wall, hardly daring to touch it but dying to know what was in the papers. Carefully he pulled a piece from the deep crack between two massive stones then ran quickly home. In his room he unfolded it and looked blankly at the lettering. It was neither the English writing he learned at school nor the Arabic his mother taught him. They were strange, square symbols, each carefully formed with thin and thick pen strokes.

Hussam was frightened. It was God's writing. He must put it back or something terrible would happen. He ran back through the Damascus Gate, clutching the paper in his hand. Pushing through the crowds which thronged the *souk*, he came to the narrow sleepy back streets of the Moslem Quarter. As he rounded a corner at speed he charged straight into a group of boys, knocking one of them, winded, against a wall.

"Hey. Look where you're going, ass," said one, a good deal taller than Hussam, grabbing hold of him by the front of his jumper and looking him up and down. "Who are you?"

"He dropped this," said another, picking up the paper which had fallen from Hussam's hand and unfolding it for them all to read.

"He's a Jew. He's a dirty little Jew."

"A clumsy Jew with the manners of a pig."

"With the face of a pig and he smells like a pig."

Hussam kicked the boy holding him and bolted as the grip on him loosened. But the others were on him, dragging him to the floor, kicking, punching, screaming with every blow: "Jew, Jew, Jew!"

It was the first and last time anyone knocked him unconscious. He was seven, not much older than the son he now sought.

Outside Amin's command post stood a Jeep in which lounged three *fedayeen* in fatigues and camouflage peaked caps. These were men of a different breed. They were older with the casual self-assurance of proven killers.

Amin slapped the driver's back: "These are my elite," he said, smiling with satisfaction. "Once they were like those others. We send our best to Beirut. They know how to train soldiers there."

They eyed Hussam with arrogant indifference. He walked around the Jeep, examining it, the arms, the equipment. A modified radiator condenser system was rigged up front, while jerrycans of water and petrol were lashed to the sides and bonnet. "This is a desert vehicle," he said. "Where do you go?"

The driver looked at Amin who nodded. "The Negev," he said, watching his own hand as he shoved moodily at the gearstick. "Sometimes the Golan."

Mounted up front was a Browning .50 calibre. "You shoot down aircraft?" Hussam asked good-naturedly.

The driver turned to his friends and smiled. Then he turned contemptuously on Hussam. "They don't fly Spitfires any more."

Hussam was examining the gun, sighting it. "No," he said, swinging it round, getting the feel of it. "They fly Mirages, Mysteres and now they have Skyhawks. This gun can bring them down," he had the driver in his sights now, "and men." One bullet, released with a deafening report, lifted the driver's hat. The eyes that smiled smugly now held a shocked stare.

Amin roared with laughter. "Eh Hussam, don't shoot my best soldiers. Do it to the Jews, only aim a little lower." He turned to the others. "Come," he said, leading them inside.

"These are good," he told Hussam, throwing his arms round the shoulders of the two nearest. "Young, impetuous, a little tactless, but good. They work well together. Teach them more, Hussam, make an army of them, your army. Lead it into Palestine. I want strikes deep inside Zionist territory." He released them, slapping their backs. "With these you can do it." He turned to face them, introducing each.

Mahmoud, tall and slim, who wore black gloves. He was good with explosives. Before they could get plastic he had a bomb factory which he burned down with home-made incendiaries one day by accident. With a quick movement, Amin seized his hand and pulled off the glove, pushing the sleeve up to his elbow. The hand was shiny, patchy red and white, the flesh shrivelled, with scar tissue stretched tight over the back and up his arm, the muscles wasted. "They wanted to amputate. He wouldn't let them. Good, eh?" He whipped the arm around, holding it locked behind Mahmoud's back. The soldier grimaced in pain. Amin smiled cruelly: "It's not strong but it works. Now you're more careful with your bombs, eh friend."

"Baseem," he said, releasing Mahmoud and tapping the biggest man on the chest. "He was in

Jerusalem with me, carried your woman over the border." Baseem was good with his hands, with a knife, silent, the best at reconnaissance, at improvising weaponry. He had big, strong hands which could break a man's neck like a stick, shoulders which would carry two thirds of a medium mortar and four bombs. With Baseem, a mortar crew need be only two.

Then there was Kamel, the driver. Moody, intense, sometimes short-tempered. Younger than the others but good because he hated. "To him our struggle is *jihad*. He hates Jews most of all. Skilful with a mortar and bazooka, he's the nearest we have to an artillery man and ready to die for the cause because Allah reserves a special place for martyrs."

Hussam sat silently, unmoved by the theatrics. Amin walked to him, put a hand on his shoulder and turned to the others. "Hussam will lead you. Take your orders from him. Learn from him." He went back to them, speaking to each in turn, almost in confidence except that his voice, even when low, echoed around the bare room. To Kamel: "You have not met, will not meet, a better soldier." To Baseem: "You were made, trained. Hussam was born." To Mahmoud: "He can replace any one of you, or all. If you learn one hundredth of what he knows you will have learned well."

He returned to Hussam. "You have two weeks before your first mission. So my friend, I give these men to you. Use them well."

"I want two more."

"You shall have them!"

"My brothers."

"Ahmed? Ali?" Amin laughed. "They're not soldiers."

"Send them to Beirut. When they return I want them with me."

Hussam examined the arsenal, finding what he wanted, boxes of plastic, grenades, a Dragunov sniper rifle, AK47s. He took only a passing interest in the bazookas and mortars. They were of little use for the missions he planned. "I'll hit specific targets," he told Amin, "military or civilian, those which will cause most disruption."

"and most publicity," added Amin. "Victory is nothing unless the world sees it. Cause outrage hit civilians, town centres, *kibbutzim*."

Hussam shook his head. "When I find out who was at Bab'ullah, I swear I'll hunt down and kill every man of them. Not one will escape. But bombs in supermarkets, no. I know the Jews. They're proud, they unite against terror. Outwit-them and they destroy each other. Think as they think. Strike as they strike. Two or three well-planned acts of sabotage will undermine their confidence. *Mossad* and the *Knesset* will tear out each other's throats."

Amin considered it.

"If you have spies in Israel use them. Uncover their secrets for me and I'll hit them hard. They'll regret the day they saw Bab'ullah. They'll gladly give back my son."

Amin smiled. "It's like old times."

"When you have our mission, tell no one but me," Hussam warned. "*Mossad* has spies everywhere, even here. For that reason I'll make camp elsewhere."

"We need you here."

"I'm bedouin, I can't live in this place."

"Where will you go?" Hussam shrugged. "You don't want me for two weeks. I'll be back then." He hesitated. "I'll keep watch. If there's word of my son, fly the flag the wrong way up."

It was agreed and Hussam's camp remained secret. Ali and Ahmed went to Beirut but he kept Jodi with him. They spoke little, yet they communicated. He demanded, she conceded. He took, she gave. Her guilt was total, her desire for absolution infinite, her punishment, that everything was not enough.

In the evenings she sat with her chin on her knees, watching the sunset over Israel. The flat-topped fortress of Massada cut a black silhouette in the crimson sky, reflected in the dead waters of the Dead Sea. South lay Sodom, north, Qumran, home of the Dead Sea Scrolls, ancient site of Gomorrah. It was a stage set for a one-act play. Even the colours were right.

She sensed him behind her but it was several minutes before he sat, his knees either side of her, his arms folding around her, his cheek against her hair. "What do you think, *habibi*, night after night when you sit here?"

She leaned back against him. "I wonder how terrible things happen in such a beautiful place."

"The beauty is within you for seeing as you see."

She shook her head. "Everything I see is at war. There's no beauty in war!"

"You're wrong," he said. "War is the most terrible beauty of all. We face ourselves for what we are, for the things we can do. The fine words and high ideals are stripped away. We're the animals God made at the beginning, unchanged, unchanging. In peace we pretend we're better than we are, closer to God than we were. In war we see we're not. War shows us only truth and that's its beauty."

She sighed. "This land isn't promised, it's cursed."

He turned her to him. "I have to think what to do with you."

"I'm coming with you."

"With me?" He was startled.

"I can help."

He shook his head: "It's too dangerous."

"If it's dangerous for me, it's dangerous for you. I want to be with you."

He refused even to consider it.

"Amin will kill me if you leave me behind!" There was desperation in her voice.

"Amin won't find you," he said, but knew it wasn't true. He had no friends here, no one he could trust. This was Amin's territory. He knew everyone, everything. Hussam was under no illusions about Amin. His name meant "trustworthy" yet he was treacherous. She looked accusingly at him.

He couldn't meet her eyes. "You're a woman, not a soldier. You have no training. I must think of the others. You'd get us killed."

"Your brothers have no training yet they go to Beirut! Why not me?" He looked away. "They train women, I know they do!"

"And do you also know what happens if they're captured? You know what the Israelis do to women. You saw it at Bab'ullah!" He was getting angry.

"Hussam, don't you see? I can guide you. I know Israel," she reasoned. "I know it like the back of my hand. Wherever you're going, I've been there within the last three months. Kiryat Shmona, the Golan Heights, Beit Shean, Jerusalem, Eilat. Just name it! You'd be mad to leave me behind."

He was silent as she talked on. She told him about Suez, the long drive on a desert road whose only milestones were empty villages, derailed trains, bombed mosques and churches. Then a lonely night in El Kantara, a ghost of a town where she was caught in sudden shellfire from Egypt and crouched for safety in a derelict house. She pointed across the Dead Sea, to where she climbed Massada stumbling up the Snake Path in the darkness before dawn to watch the sunrise over Jordan. She described the chalk white cliffs and arches curving into an azure sea at Rosh Hanikra by Lebanon where she swam for hours believing it was Paradise, then walked the border at dusk, counting the cairns where Jews fell to Arab snipers, and realised it was not.

The misery of Gaza, the abundance of Galilee and the beauty of Mount Hermon which towered over it crowned by an electronic spy station which monitored everything coming out of Damascus.

But Hussam remained impassive. "Amin will know much of this."

Jodi tried again. "I travelled the Bar-Lev line at Suez. You want to know what artillery they have? Seven batteries, that's all, seven along 110 miles, and only fifteen fortified posts, that's one roughly every eight miles manned by less than 500 reservists. That's how they hold back the might of Egypt!"

"We won't attack from Egypt."

"All right, how about Golan?" She refused to give up. "Sixty tanks, two battalions of Golani soldiers with eleven fortified positions running from Hermon to the Sea of Galilee. I know where they are."

"How do you know?"

"Because I'm a journalist, because I'm a woman, because they're so cock sure of themselves. They took me where I wanted to go. Sometimes I didn't even ask, just hitched rides in army trucks. A sweet smile and a good pair of legs can get you anywhere."

He was silent. "Can you kill?" he asked at length. "These people you travelled with and smiled at, who trusted you with their secrets, can you meet them face to face and kill them?"

She felt as he meant her to, traitorous, and looked away. "Not until now. Not before Bab'ullah. You said war is truth. The truth is I could kill every one of the bastards."

He shook his head, taking her by the shoulders. "The truth is more terrible than that. You can't begin to understand."

"All I ask is the chance."

"Listen to me. Amin told a story at Sufa. He didn't tell it all. We raided a *kibbutz* in the Negev and I set three charges to blow the water supply. Israel was new then, the desert *kibbutzim* scarcely manned. Hashemesh wasn't in the front line. It was inside Israel. They didn't expect attack.

"I shot the guard. It was only as she fell I saw it was a woman dressed in khaki, like a soldier. She was wounded, not badly.

"The first blast sent sand showering over us. As it cleared a child came running. The woman screamed. Another woman chased after the child. Amin went mad, fired a burst at the child and it fell. I kicked his gun away and shouted at the woman to stop. She was running to the child as the second charge blew. The water sprayed red, like a fountain, where she had been. Then the last went up and it was quiet, like this.

"I ran to the child. He was small, lifeless. Others were coming with guns, firing. We fired back. We had mortars, grenades. They had only rifles but they fought well. We killed them all."

He sat in silence, his lips moving as if trying to form the words. Then he shuddered. "I can still hear the woman scream. I thought it was for the child but Amin called me to look. Kushi had her. I'd seen him interrogate prisoners before but this was different. He didn't want information. He was killing her slowly, for pleasure." Jodi shivered. "The others gathered. I saw in their faces what I felt. Revulsion, yes, but something more: an evil fascination. No one moved though she screamed to us for help. Then she begged to die. I couldn't stand it. I put a bullet through her head.

"Kushi went wild, leapt at me with a knife still red with the woman's blood. He never forgave me but I never forgave myself. I saw the truth that night. I never wanted to see it again."

It was dark now. "Is that why you stopped fighting?"

He drew a deep breath. "That and one thing more." She thought for a moment he would tell her but he said. "You're right. I can't leave you here. If you know all you say then come with us and may God protect you."

✳✳✳

One bullet can end a war. In her mind it was she who fired it every time she looked along the sights.

She didn't go to Beirut. "You're only our guide. Remember that. All that you need to know I can teach you." He gave her a gun. It was hers to keep. No one else would use it, nor should she use another. It should never be out of her sight, never out of reach even when she slept. "When things happen they happen without warning. Your gun is no good on the other side of a room. Make it part of you."

It was a Kalashnikov, the genuine article, no Chinese copy. One weapon with two jobs, rifle and sub machine gun. They all carried them except Hussam.

"If it's so good, why don't you use it?" she asked.

He carried a Carl-Gustaf and a Dragunov. "These are the two it replaces," he told her. "They do their jobs better than the Kalashnikov but it would tire you to carry two." He zeroed it for her, adjusting the sights after firing five rounds at a target 100 metres away. "Get to know it. Trust it. Love it as you love life. It may save you when nothing else can, not even I."

Jodi felt a strange thrill as she watched him with the gun. She believed herself a pacifist. In England she sang protest songs, denounced war, read with horror of acts of terrorism. Yet despite every idealistic, civilised platitude she uttered and in which her higher morality believed with desperate sincerity, some primitive perversity drew her to the compelling sensuality of men who killed.

He used the rifle so naturally, almost as an extension of his own body. She envied him the inborn familiarity which would forever make it more accurate in his hands than in hers. "Marksmanship is a skill," he told her dispassionately. "No one is a born sniper. We all learn. So can you." He handed her the gun. "You will only shoot straight with a correctly zeroed weapon. You must learn to do it yourself. What is right for me may not be right for you." She listened patiently. "A sniper is deadly only because every time he aims his position is correct. To some it's natural, but anyone can be taught." The most important thing was to be comfortable and stable. "Aim at the target," he ordered. "Now lower the rifle. Close your eyes and raise the barrel up again to position. Now open your eyes. Are you still on target?"

"Yes," she said, catching from the corner of her eye his look of disbelief.

"Then fire," he challenged. She fired five rounds rapidly then lowered the barrel, meeting his amazed expression with a cool look.

"Where did you learn to shoot?" he demanded.

"You forget who my father is," she responded, striding to the target, pulling off the card and checking it, "and you underestimate me!" She handed him the card, the furthest punctures less than three inches apart. "I'd do better with an Armature, but if this is all you've got I suppose it'll have to do."

Hussam recovered quickly. "There's more to running missions than firing a gun," he growled.

From then on he drove her hard, initially to prove she couldn't keep up. But she proved to him she could. True she lacked the strength and stamina of a man but irregular warfare was unconventional by nature. What was important was that he learned the character and limitations of his unit. Previously she was the woman he wanted, intended to have. But fate had once more intervened, once more changed the rules. He was forced to see her now for what she could become, a weapon to be used against Israel.

Unlike the Arabs she was equable, with a clever mind from a cool climate which she used to advantage when she fought. He should know. She had fought him often enough. She was tough, she would work till she dropped. She was stubborn, she didn't give up. He knew but did not acknowledge it when he followed her through the desert to Ein Mara, watching from a distance as, in pain and despair she went on. Over short distances with light weapons she was a match for any man. She could walk all day carrying 20 kilogrammes, more than enough explosive to demolish the famous Shalom Tower in Tel Aviv, should it be necessary.

He made her use Arabic all the time now. It was important if she were to follow the commands. She spoke it badly but understood well. The only dissent came from Kamel. "I won't fight with a woman, much less a *Nazrani*."

"The choice is yours," he told him. "No one has to fight." Kamel sulked but stayed.

Hussam taught her to use a knife, the slim, straight Sykes-Fairburn commando, more versatile than the curved Arab *khanjar*. She learned unarmed combat, pressure points of the neck, under the chin, the ears, shoulders, stomach, groin, kidneys. "Hit immediately and hit to kill. Don't threaten, do it. A man is stronger than you. You have only speed and surprise. Your first chance may be your only chance. The Israelis will not trust you as I did." He demanded one thing more. "Disobedience is death to a *feda'i*. In my unit the orders I give are the law. You must obey immediately, without question."

She smiled. "Don't I always?"

He was deadly serious. "Swear it, and do so on everything sacred to you so that you remember this above all else."

She slipped her arms around him but he held her back. At last she said: "All right. I swear."

Satisfied, he nodded. His strike force was ready and now he became impatient to attack. The Jews were good, their army perhaps the best in the world. But no army was invincible, no border inviolate. A surprise attack, well planned and prepared, would always succeed were it not overambitious. Most *fedayeen* raids failed on all counts. Hussam would not fail because, unlike the *fedayeen*, he didn't underestimate the enemy. They were well-equipped, well-trained, well-motivated. But above all they believed in what they fought for. They had to win. For Israel there was no alternative. Acts of sabotage would not destroy Israel. In themselves they must be damaging but, more than this, they must provoke discontent and the inevitable retaliation which would ultimately trigger another Middle East war. One day it would happen again as it happened at Massada; through sheer weight of numbers, Israel would lose.

With such thoughts he kept away the horror of Bab'ullah and the fear of what might happen to David. His mind crystallised the belief that his son was alive in Israel and that Amin would locate him. Then no power on earth would keep him from the boy.

CHAPTER 13

On Amin's orders they moved up to the ceasefire line, waiting for an artillery battle to give cover. After three nights it came. It was massive.

They moved swiftly, Hussam leading. It was as Jodi had said, tank trenches, fortified infantry positions backed up by tanks. The minefields she wasn't so certain of but while the Syrians unintentionally distracted the Israelis it was worth the risk of sticking to the dirt tracks. The tank battle raged. It seemed to Jodi they were in more danger from the Syrians than the Israelis, their shells falling erratically, though the Israeli tanks were easily pinpointed from the blazing barrels of the guns. To the south a wayward shell had started a grass fire and the smoke cloud drifted ahead of them, Hussam making for it as extra cover. She followed closely. Twice they jumped from the track as vehicles raced to the front line. The first was a near miss, the deafening tank battle drowning out the noise of approaching engines.

Hussam motioned for her to join him. "Ahead. What is it?"

She strained her eyes in the darkness, picking out a line of flat-roofed dwellings inside a high wire fence. "It's a new *kibbutz*. They call it Golan. Down the road that way is an army post. Beyond there's a checkpoint, but after that it's clear."

He waved the others to follow, heading south. They walked upright, keeping on the farm tracks to the land the *kibbutzniks* had cleared and beyond it along the old tracks until they reached a deserted Arab village dynamited by the Israelis, the flat concrete roofs lying smashed amid the rubble of the walls on the ground.

"Wait here." Hussam scouted ahead while they rested. Behind them, Baseem patrolled like a restless dog.

The tank battle ceased, though the sky to the east was alight with flames from grass fires, or was it the dawn, she couldn't be sure. Hussam returned, wanting to know if the other villages were like this. She said they were. The Golan Heights were littered with them. Not one had survived

They went on, the paths narrow, rocky. Hussam seemed to pick his way by instinct, his footing sure. She stumbled and was weary but kept up, refusing to be first to stop. He motioned them down. As they dropped, a searchlight swept the thistle tops above. A vehicle drove past, quite close, the noise of its engine fading slowly to the north. Hussam turned westward.

"There are old minefields, left by the Syrians," she warned him. "The Israelis fenced them with barbed wire but a lot of it's broken down." He nodded, keeping to the narrow paths until the land fell away in front of them and they looked down on a scene familiar to Jodi, Galilee. She felt a pinprick of nostalgia at the sight of the little settlements picked out in pale green lights. To the north Metullah, southwest Rosh Pina and between them the dozen or so *kibbutzim* and tiny settlements which farmed the fertile area.

An audible sigh went up from the group. Beyond Rosh Pina rose the high ridge to Zafat. The ridge ran northwards to where a ring of flame marked another grass fire.

"They shell Lebanon," she explained unnecessarily. It was easy to get a bearing on the bridge from here. It was almost directly between them and Rosh Pina. She glanced back east. Soon it would be dawn. Soon the *kibbutz* trucks would roar to life as sleepy farmworkers tumbled aboard, bound for the orchards and cotton fields and a relentless day of hard physical labour.

At dawn they reached another dynamited village. The western ridge glowed pink, reflecting the early daylight. Below them the clumps of lights faded and the blackness between gave way to a patchwork of green speckled with the dark silver rectangles of carp ponds.

In the shelter of a small walled courtyard they rested again. Hussam sent Baseem ahead while he searched the remains of the small village, returning with a dozen oranges stuffed down his camouflaged shirt. "There's an orchard," he smiled. Jodi bit into one

189

gratefully. For the first time she realised she was thirsty as well as exhausted.

Baseem returned, talking in a low voice with Hussam and pointing southwest down the hill. Hussam followed him but before they returned Jodi curled up in a corner, head on her pack, and slept.

Mahmoud shook her awake. The sun was high and for a moment she thought she was back at Bab'ullah, except for the battle fatigues and her hand on a Kalashnikov. He taught her to sleep like that and quickly she remembered where they were. The others crouched, looking over the crumbling south wall of the little yard. She joined them, pushing next to Hussam.

There were men's voices, relaxed, laughing. On the outskirts of the village was a clump of eucalyptus trees in which stood a large, flat-roofed house, remarkable because it was the only one which appeared not to have been blown up. Around it and the trees was a low turquoise wall beside which were parked two Jeeps, khaki in colour, heavy square Hebrew letters painted in black down their sides, machine guns mounted up front.

From their vantage point they looked down on the scene. She counted twelve soldiers filing from the Jeeps through the narrow gateway, Uzis slung casually under their arms, pushing each other, staging mock fist fights, jumping down the steps into the shade of the trees towards the house, their voices growing fainter but still audible. After several minutes the muted laughter turned to shouts interspersed with a series of splashes. She looked quizzically at Hussam.

"There's a swimming pool," he said.

"Let's kill them!" It was Kamel.

Hussam sat silently, deep in thought. Jodi watched him anxiously. This wasn't what they planned. She discovered with horror that, now it was imminent, the prospect of killing terrified her. Mahmoud crouched, fiddling with the fingers of his gloves, a habit he had when nervous. Baseem looked disinterestedly over the wall.

"We can surround them and kill them all!" Kamel urged again.

Hussam nodded slowly. "First we must do what we came for. If they're still here then, we'll have to kill them anyway." He beckoned Mahmoud. "Take Baseem. He'll get you to the bridge. Remember it's a Bailey Bridge. Place the charges exactly as I showed you or it will not break. Give them a full hour. It will give you time to get back." He turned to Kamel. "Then we can attack the house."

Once across the track the two of them vanished into the high thistles which coated the western flank of the Golan right down to the line of eucalyptus trees planted by the Israelis to give cover to the road, protecting travellers from Syrian snipers before the war last year pushed the Syrians back out of sight of the valley. The trees ended at the bridge where the road swung east to link up with the main road through Rosh Pina. It was a good junction to hitch a lift Jodi recalled.

Time dragged by. Kamel fidgeted, prowling around the courtyard, a caged animal. Hussam was like an animal too, but wild, free, maddeningly calm, every reaction honed to perfection. He heard, saw, anticipated, long before her own senses alerted her. Each time he reacted swiftly and silently. A lull in the laughter at the pool and he was by the wall, rifle ready; once he left the courtyard, skirting to the east and she caught the vague sounds of distant gunfire; once, signalled her to be still, as he brought the rifle butt hard down, she thought on her hand, but instead crushing a scorpion an inch away.

At lunchtime a delicious smell of cooking came from the house. The Jeeps stood deserted. There seemed to be no guard. Hussam vanished for a while. She felt vulnerable alone with Kamel and watched intently until he returned. Inwardly she begged the soldiers to go, to finish their lunch, to get the hell out before Baseem and Mahmoud returned. But they showed no sign of going. According to Hussam they lounged in the sun, eating, drinking beer and smoking.

To the north a herd of mangy cattle picked nonchalantly through the poor grazing. They drifted closer, spread over a wide area.

It seemed a lifetime before Baseem and Mahmoud returned. Hussam sprang up silently, looking over the wall. She joined him as the returning pair broke cover on the far side of the track and raced for the courtyard. He questioned them tersely, looking at his watch and then towards the house. Numbly she heard him outline the plan. Baseem to skirt round to the south,

Mahmoud and Kamel to take the house. He would take the north side. She must stay here.

"No!" she said but, as he turned on her, recalled how she swore to obey.

His voice was colder, harder than she could remember. "You think I don't know? It's too soon for you!"

Baseem went first, vanishing behind the Jeeps, reappearing further along the wall until he was out of sight. Hussam was next, taking up position to the right, downhill from the gateway. He motioned to Mahmoud and Kamel who ran for the wall, climbing it in the shade of the trees. She watched Hussam, her heart racing.

He turned suddenly to face north, from where she now heard a lilting cry: "*Boi, boi, boi*" A cattleman on horseback cantered idly towards the widely dispersed herd. "*Boi, boi!*" He was calling them in. A few turned their heads languidly as he rode closer.

Several things happened at once. Hussam raised the rifle. With a crack the cattleman fell, the horse rearing and galloping on up the hillside. Before the rider hit the ground, Hussam fired the opening shots towards the house. Simultaneously a puff of black smoke rose from the southern end of the long line of eucalyptus. Snake-like black trellises arced languidly through the air, heralding the huge explosion which rolled up the valley, echoing from the far ridge. The bridge had blown.

When she looked back, Hussam was gone. She thought the blood would burst out through her ears it pounded so hard. From the house came a series of thuds, grenades exploding within confined spaces. There were bursts of machine gun fire, shouts, screams. It was a long time before there was silence again. Even then, she couldn't be sure that the battle which still raged was only inside her head. Now what? Should she go to them or stay back?

As she hesitated, a figure crawled over the wall towards the Jeeps. He was bare-chested, wearing only khaki trousers, no shoes. Around his neck was the leather thong and metal identity tag of an Israeli soldier. She watched in horror as he boarded the first Jeep, cocking the big machine gun and swinging it towards the house.

His back was to her, exploding along a red line, arching in agony as he slumped forward. After a minute she realised her gun wasn't firing any more, though her finger still pressed the trigger and she still peered blindly along the sights at the body she had broken.

Hussam raced from the gateway. She was fiddling with the empty magazine, removing it, trying to fit a new one but her hands shook so much she dropped it and was too weak to pick it up.

Then he was with her, holding her against him as her legs buckled.

At first she apologised. "I had to," she said. "He was going to fire."

"Jodi, we're taking the Jeeps. You must drive." He held her head in both hands, looking at her, making sure she understood. "Do you hear me?" It was an effort to concentrate but she heard him. "Listen! Kamel is hurt. Not badly but you must drive."

"Yes."

He lifted her to her feet and steered her by the elbow to the first Jeep. She shrank back as he pulled the body of the Israeli soldier clear then pushed her into the driver's seat. Glancing over the wall, for the first time she caught sight of the swimming pool, the water scarlet in the bright sunshine.

"Don't look!" His voice was calm, firm. He turned her head to him. "You did well. But for you we might all be dead. Jodi!" Her eyes seemed to drift of their own accord back to the red pool. He turned her to him again. "Jodi! It's not over yet. Start the engine!"

Mechanically she did as ordered. He left her, returning a minute later with Kamel, limping as Hussam held his arm firmly around his shoulders, the right thigh of his fatigues glistening maroon. He lifted him into the back seat and climbed in beside her. The engine behind them sprung to life, Mahmoud driving, Baseem beside him.

"Follow the track to the road. We'll crash the checkpoint and head straight for the cease fire line. You know the best way, take it. Baseem and I will deal with the Israelis."

She was back in time now. The concentration of driving held her mind firmly in the conscious. After all, it was an Israeli army Jeep. They were all in fatigues and she was damned if she could tell an Arab from a Jew in khaki. No one would stop them until the checkpoint, she reasoned. The Jeep bumped over the rough track until it joined the black strip road. She swung onto it, tyres squealing, foot to the floor, gathering speed. Even flat out, the Jeep didn't seem fast enough.

On either side were burned-out, rusting tanks and halftracks, grim reminders of the Six Day War, shoved to the roadside and left to rot. For five miles they met no vehicles then, ahead, she saw army trucks approach. Hussam steadied the gun with one hand. She slowed, pulling the nearside wheels onto the hard dirt shoulder, allowing the convoy to pass. Hussam patted her shoulder, glancing behind to check on Mahmoud and Baseem. Then they were upon the checkpoint.

"Slow down but don't stop," he said. "Smile and wave as you pass."

The barrier was raised, probably to let the convoy through. Two soldiers armed with Uzis stood beside a halftrack. Four others sat in a line on the ground, relaxing near a pink-painted wall, their guns beside them or laid casually across their laps. Hussam raised a hand to the two on guard and she felt her fixed smile begin to shake at the corners of her mouth. One of the guards stepped forward into the road, flagging them down.

"They're not letting us through," she said.

"Keep going!" His voice was steady. She saw the guard swing the Uzi forward. The Jeep lurched, either because her hands on the wheel shook with terror or because of the deafening burst from the machine gun. The guards flew backwards, flung to the ground like rag dolls. The soldiers by the wall sprang up but to one side of them the peeling pink paint disintegrated in a line which continued through all four, throwing them back against it one at a time with tremendous force.

The road ahead closed in like a tunnel. It was all she saw now, crouched forward over the wheel, foot hard down, concentrating because her life depended on it, all of their lives, for what they were worth.

Sufa had not seen such a celebration. It went on all day and all night. The heroes were lifted shoulder high, including Jodi, including Kamel who, though barely conscious, smiled feebly between grimaces of pain before they bore him off to the medical centre.

Amin was delirious with joy. Immediately he radioed Beirut and before the night was out Voice of the Arabs was claiming 100 Israeli casualties and a dozen bridges destroyed.

Jodi allowed herself to be swept along. Even Hussam seemed moderately flattered by the jubilation. They carried him to the *mukhtar's* house where the old man embraced him and wept. The gunfire was incessant as the elated *fedayeen* waved rifles in the air. From the sidelines, the women kept up a shrill, triumphant ululation. Hands reached to touch them, voices to thank them. If Jodi doubted what she did, it vaporised before the happiness of the people, a people who had long cried out for justice, for revenge. Hussam brought them victory and they loved him.

They feasted but she couldn't eat, dancing instead in the crowd for hours, jumping high in the air, throwing her head back, shouting, laughing, allowing the men to lift her up, spin her round.

It was dawn when they carried her to a house, pushing her through the door and closing it behind her. A dozen candles lit the small room, festooned with palm leaves, flowers, coloured paper cut-outs and some Arabic writing on a banner she couldn't read.

He was waiting but she remained by the door, the space between them too wide to cross because of who they were, of what they had done. They stood as on opposite edges of an abyss until she stepped forward and, finding the ground solid, flung herself at him, tearing at his clothes and hers, demanding him with every ounce of her limitless strength, laughing hysterically until he hit her and she retaliated, wanting more pain, more pleasure, more release, more, more, more than the killing of a man, the bloody pool, the ripped bodies at the checkpoint. Then she was crying softly, her tears wetting his chest. They lay quietly, at peace again.

"There is no more," he said, his fingers touching her hair. "Now do you begin to see the truth?"

She sat up feeling alone and confused. The crowd which had bolstered her, kept her from herself, still sang and danced in the streets. Why should the agony of one people be the ecstasy of another? It didn't make sense.

"How do I live?" she asked helplessly.

He stroked her face. "As a Muslim you would live only for now. The next moment is not yet created. It is a void. Perhaps it will be filled but only *insh Allah*, by the will of God. As yet it is not and you needn't worry about what is not."

She looked away and the banner with the Arabic writing caught her eye. "What does it say?"

"*Dam butlub dam*. Blood demands blood."

Her eyes went back to his. "I can't stop thinking about the man I killed."

Gently he pulled her to him, kissing her lightly. "What we did, what was done to us, is done. Right or wrong, nothing will change it. You cannot wish it away. To relive it will hurt only you, no one else."

"Don't you have any conscience? Don't you feel for the families, the children of the men you killed?"

He sighed. "If I do, does it help them?"

"Answer me!" she demanded, pulling back from him.

"They were soldiers. They knew the dangers yet they were careless. They paid the penalty. No one among us is ever deceived. We allow ourselves to be deceived. So the fault was theirs. The victim is responsible for his suffering."

"Even at Bab'ullah?"

He drew a shuddering breath and immediately she was ashamed but he answered calmly: "Even at Bab'ullah. Over the years we grew soft. There were no blood feuds, no threat until Amin brought you. We should have foreseen danger but did not. Yet even to take blame is not necessary. What happened was written."

"Is that what you believe?"

"All Muslims believe this. Our lives are pre-ordained. Whether we kill or are killed it is God's will. We accept it by Islam, submission; that is the meaning of the word Islam. We submit to the will of Allah. So should you. Your life and mine are predestined. We can only follow the course set for us."

"*Kismet*?"

He nodded. "*Kismet*."

"That's a cop out."

"It's how I live. You wanted to know."

"And Israel. Isn't that *kismet*?"

He nodded. "As is our fight to destroy it."

"But why? What's the reason behind it all? What's the purpose? Why are we here if everything we do is predestined?"

"Why is a question we do not ask. If it is written in the Koran it is accepted as God's word which came to us through Mohammed. God will not send another prophet, Mohammed was His last so the Koran can never be challenged. Nor can we know God's purpose. We can only submit to His plan."

Jodi thought about it in silence. It was a seductive idea. It absolved one from all blame, all conscience, the torture she even now inflicted on herself for what she did. Hussam suffered no such remorse. The violence, atrocity, the carnage excused over the ages as *jihad*, was all permissible, all O.K. It was all the will of Allah no matter how appalling, how inhuman. It seemed eminently sensible to believe. Allah was obviously better equipped to deal with the self-recrimination which plagued her than she herself so why worry? How exquisite to be a Believer. No wonder the Muslims despised as weakness the conscience of the infidel, the unbeliever.

She wanted to ask him about Kibbutz Hashemesh, why he stopped fighting and where it all fitted in with Islam but somehow knew the answer to that too would be *kismet*. It wasn't worth waking him. It occurred to her that this was the first time she had seen him asleep. He had a gentle face, older, troubled in repose and she realised how vital a light his eyes held for its absence to work such change. Yet even as he slept she felt safe. He took long deep breaths through his nostrils. His senses seemed awake, still testing for danger.

She laid her head on his shoulder convinced she would never sleep again.

CHAPTER 14

"They call it the National Water Carrier," Amin was saying. "The main section runs from here in the north to here." His finger traced the route on the map spread in front of him.

Hussam looked closely at the contours. "Do you have pictures?"

"Only this." He picked up a black and white photo. It showed two rows of oblong concrete slabs laid at 45 degrees in facing rows across a half-filled channel snaking through the arid landscape, seemingly unfenced, unguarded.

Hussam had heard of it. Five years earlier when Israel announced the project to irrigate the Negev Desert with water from the Sea of Galilee, it became a major international issue with Syria and Jordan claiming it would rob them of water. For Israel it was an ingenious solution. Rain fell almost entirely in the winter and the annual average decreased sharply from north to south. Water from the swamps of the Hula Valley drained into the Sea of Galilee where it evaporated or flowed into the Jordan and became uselessly saline in the brackish waters of the Dead Sea. This channel fed sweet water down to the coastal plain as far south as Beer Sheba.

Without it the land would return to desert, the crops shrivel.

"What happens here and here?" Hussam pointed to places where the contours fell but the blue line continued across.

Amin shrugged. It must be pumped or carried by aqueduct. They were the points to attack. "We tried to blow it up before, in 1965," Amin said. "It was the opening shot in our new Palestinian Revolution. Then we failed. We must not fail again."

A unit had crossed the Jordan, laying ten sticks of gelignite in the concrete channel at Beit Netopha but the charge was discovered and disarmed as the unit made its escape back across the river only to be captured by a Jordanian patrol who shot and killed its leader. Amin was bitter that his first casualty had been at the hands of his Arab brothers. Even now he bristled at the slightest hint of government interference in, or threat to, Fatah missions.

Back at camp Jodi sat breaking down a rifle. Hussam insisted the weapons were cleaned, oiled and zeroed daily.

He pushed the photograph at her. "In Israel did you ever see this?"

She picked it up. "No. What is it?"

"Our next mission."

She put the gun down and looked at the map, racking her brains, trying to remember anything remotely like the photo at the points where it crossed roads she'd travelled a dozen times. "Here," she said, pointing. "There's a new white concrete structure. I thought it was a bridge but maybe it carries water." She paused, following the line south. "Here, there's a pool and a pumping station." The whole channel was deep inside Israel. Even at its nearest point, where the canal left the Sea of Galilee on the west, it must be 20 miles from the ceasefire line. Getting to it undetected would be a problem.

"Could we pass for tourists?"

"I could." She looked thoughtfully at him. "You could pass for an Israeli."

They crossed the border with bedouins at night. Ahmed and Ali, freshly returned from Beirut seemingly more skilled in political claptrap than military prowess, came with them. But it was the tall, silent, heavily-veiled lady who attracted the attention of the bedouin *sheikh*.

"My sister," she heard Hussam say.

"Your father must be a giant," said the old man.

By morning they were at Beer Sheba, mingling with the early crowds at the camel market. The camel handlers badgered American tourists who straggled between the moth-eaten animals, taking photos, climbing on their backs, bargaining badly and rather rudely. On the north side, closest to the town, two army trucks were parked. Two soldiers, Uzis slung from their shoulders, leaned against a truck door, smoking and talking to the driver.

At a signal from Hussam, Ali and Ahmed started quarrelling noisily. A crowd gathered and the camel handlers began interfering in the dispute, taking sides. Soon the soldiers took notice and, walking to the crowd, pushed a way through.

Balancing a bundle none too expertly on her head and steadying it with one hand, Jodi went behind a stone wall and took off the dress. Beneath it she wore jeans and T-shirt. She emerged, her hair pushed into a *kibbutz* hat, a rucksack on her back. Hussam was waiting. He'd removed the long *thobe* and *abba*. In denims and an open-necked shirt he was just a big, gangling *kibbutznik*. He was uncomfortable, awkward and self-conscious, the way men on the collective farms looked when they dressed for Shabbat. Even so he would never escape notice. As an Arab he was distinctive. In this get-up he was sensational. Thank God Israel was such a mixture of nations, cultures and physical types. Thank God the Jews were so *laissez-faire* and his ambling, arrogant manner could pass for the upper extreme of fairly typical. Those jeans did wonders for his behind. She threw an arm around him, kissing his cheek. The act was pure bravado but it helped stop her shaking. On him, its effect was different. He recoiled, looking around nervously.

She reassured him quickly. "It's OK. They do it all the time here. You're in the west now!"

"Don't draw attention to us."

"Are you kidding? Have you seen the women swoon as you pass?" She stopped a man. "*Slee'ha. Ayfo taxi*?" she asked in Hebrew. The man pointed to a row of dusty brown Peugeots parked in the shade of a eucalyptus tree and she thanked him: "*Todah rabah.*"

They climbed into the front one. "Tel Aviv," she told the driver. She looked at her watch. Baseem and Mahmoud would be crossing the Allenby Bridge into the West Bank. Baseem crossed that way before. Thanks to Moshe Dayan's "open door" policy, Arabs with relatives on the West Bank could enter legitimately for a visit. Soldiers stopped the buses to check passports and interrogate passengers. Tales of a magic ray which could detect lies came from the Arabs who travelled that route and, though it seemed unlikely, with the Israelis you could never be sure. Certainly it wasn't safe for them to carry plastic. Jodi's rucksack held enough for both jobs.

The taxi driver kept up a steady flow of conversation in broken English. She drawled that she was American, and Hussam was a new immigrant, both working on the same *sephardi kibbutz*. Thankfully, the driver was, *ashkenazi*, a western immigrant, and spoke no Arabic. It wasn't remarkable that an immigrant knew no Hebrew. Most Israelis were foreigners in their own country and few spoke the language well.

Hussam stayed quiet, his eyes fixed on the passing landscape.

In Tel Aviv, as Mrs. Rosa Blaumfeld from the Bronx, Jodi rented a car. The real Mrs. Blaumfeld mislaid her handbag in the *souk* of Jerusalem. Apart from cash and travellers' cheques, which never reached Amin, it contained her driving licence and passport, which did. The new Rosa Blaumfeld and her *kibbutz* boyfriend attracted no suspicion.

At a preselected spot near the pumping station which was close to the old border with the West Bank, they hid a package, explosives and detonators, for Mahmoud. Then they drove north to the aqueduct, reaching it as the brief Middle East twilight clung to the western sky.

It was exactly as he hoped. Tall, slender columns supported the white concrete channel across the *wadi*. Each column might contain perhaps 15 tonnes of reinforcement. As darkness came, the sound of the crickets all but drowned the soft swishing of water flowing gently above. The columns at either side were shorter. Standing high up the banks of the *wadi* he could reach the tops where the moulded slabs rested on the columns.

He unwrapped a two-kilo block of explosive. A quarter should be sufficient for each column but he cut the block into three in case he'd underestimated the reinforcing. On the smooth white slabs beneath he rolled the first piece into a long sausage shape, pressing it into the expansion gap until it encircled the top of the column, then carefully inserted detonators either side. He repeated the process on the furthest column and for good measure wrapped the remaining plastic around the foot of the one in the centre. Quickly he covered the distance to where Jodi kept watch, reaching inside the rucksack, feeling for the remote control.

"Get in the car. Start it up ready," he said. "Wait!" He caught hold of her wrist. A vehicle was coming. He heard the engine. The lights broke a hilltop, shining on the two of them.

He pushed the control back in the rucksack and put his arms around her, drawing her to him. "Kiss me!" He pushed her down, lying half across her, putting his hand under her T shirt, kissing her. She could see in the headlights his eyes were open and he looked towards the oncoming vehicle. It drew level with the car, slowing almost to a stop. Then it hooted and men cheered, laughing and calling out as it drove on. She tried to sit up but he held her down until the noise of the engine and the laughter died away.

"What the hell do you think you're doing," she said when he released her.

He shrugged. "They do it all the time in the west. You said so at Beer Sheba."

"Can I get in the car now?" He listened and nodded, taking the remote control again. As she started the engine he adjusted the dial and pressed the button. The flashes lit the night like lightning, followed by a roar.

He leapt into the car and she accelerated away. Behind them white smoke drifted upwards to the starry sky.

✳✳✳

Hussam's successes breathed life into the flagging *fedayeen*. On the borders of Israel incidents increased. There was a new enthusiasm at Sufa but Amin was not pleased. "The Jews don't admit them," he grumbled. "No mention in their newspapers of Golan, nothing about the Water Carrier."

It had gone well. Mahmoud reported the pumping station destroyed. He and Baseem returned separately over the Allenby Bridge. The Israeli guard told him to take off his gloves. Asked about the burns he said simply: "Napalm. Your pilots did it." Jodi and Hussam rejoined Ali and Ahmed at Beer Sheba crossing back to Jordan as bedouin.

Amin paced the room. "They censor the news," said Jodi. "*Aman* have people at the press centre. Nothing gets through which they consider a breach of military or national security."

"It's a small country. How do they hide nineteen deaths?" asked Hussam.

Jodi shrugged. "Israel has one of the worst road safety records in the world. People say the statistics are adjusted to cover up military deaths. I never saw a road accident all the time I was there."

"We need something they can't hide," Amin continued, his eyes on her. Jodi felt her flesh creep. Without Hussam she couldn't be in the same room as Amin. Once he had caught her alone. "What are you?" he asked. "You fight like a man. You're tall as a man and you think like a man. Yet you are a woman." He touched her breast as if to make sure then laughed as she pulled back, shuddering.

His elation over Golan was due more to the massacre of soldiers than the destruction of the bridge while he barely disguised his disappointment that there were no casualties at the Water Carrier.

As Amin pondered the problem, Hussam sat quietly. At length he asked: "What of my son?"

Amin looked puzzled then shook his head. "No news yet, my friend, but there will be, I assure you."

The weapons Amin demanded as ransom were underway. Soon they would be at Qmrah but Jodi knew she would not be free then. She could never be free. What would become of her she couldn't say and she tried to live as they, as if her life were predetermined and she must submit to fate, whatever befell. It brought a surprising inner peace.

For a week they waited. Kamel returned, limping but adamant he was ready to fight again. He told and retold tales of his part at Golan. Each time the detail grew more sickening, each time his eyes glowed brighter. He could not wait to get back to his holy work. Though his shrill voice annoyed Jodi, she was fascinated by his total lack of fear. He took Islam at its most literal. Even death held no terror. His reward would be Paradise, that most perfect of places open only to those who fought for Allah, closed to unbelievers, he said with pitying look at the *Nazrani*. He described to her the Paradise of the Koran, the "Abode of Peace" where the worthy dwell forever by flowing rivers in gardens of unimaginable beauty, shaded by sidrahs and palms, abundant and unforbidden fruit trees. Here he would recline on a jewelled silken couch, praising Allah for evermore, conversing with other virtuous men who, like him, had suffered on earth for Allah's sake and were charitable, humble and forgiving.

"What about women?" Jodi asked.

Whether or not women reached Paradise by their own efforts remained inconclusive and Kamel dismissed it as unimportant. Certainly there were plenty of virtuous dark-eyed maidens already there who it seemed, were largely for the pleasure of the virtuous men. She let it drop.

"He is *Shi'a*," Mahmoud explained quietly. "We are *Sunni*. We are not as he, but he is a good soldier."

Kamel held religious court with tireless regularity. He could recite the entire Koran from memory and at least once a day gave a loud and excited monologue which the others for the most part ignored. Only Ahmed challenged him and then there were noisy exchanges, hands placed on daggers and guns.

"Surely they wouldn't kill each other?" she asked Mahmoud, concerned over one violent quarrel.

"Perhaps they would."

"But they're on the same side."

He smiled wistfully and told her the story of the frog and the scorpion, how the scorpion asked the frog to bear him across the Jordan on his back. "No, you will sting me," said the frog. "Why would I sting you? We would both drown," replied the scorpion. So the frog agreed. Halfway across the scorpion stung him. "Why did you do it?" the frog asked in agony. "Now we shall both die." "Oh well," mused the scorpion, "that's the Middle East!"

She liked the story. If ever she got back to being a journalist she'd use it somewhere.

Then one day Baseem drove into camp. "The flag," he said to Hussam, "the one at Sufa. It's upside down."

CHAPTER 15

In the ghostly light the oranges shone out from between the rich green leaves like so many tiny suns. A group of peasant workers followed the elderly Druze as he walked agitatedly between the trees, snapping instructions to those with the hoses. Soon the sun would rise and the watering must cease.

It was Friday, *yom-el-jumah*, the holy day. He looked east. It was nearly time. His workers would soon return to their homes, except for those who took the truck to Haifa. Friday was a good day for selling his produce in the market. The Jews paid a high price before the Sabbath for unblemished fruit. The truck would return empty after nightfall and he would be the richer for it, much richer after this particular journey.

His orchards ranged right up to the ceasefire line. The Israelis didn't keep too close a watch. After all, the Druze and the Jews were friends; hadn't he told them so a thousand times? Hadn't he told, with tears in his old eyes, of the oppression, the harassment, the discrimination of Arab against Druze, the history of atrocity before the Israelis liberated him and his people?

The Jews, of all races, understood. They sympathised and left him in peace.

He stopped beside the new red Mercedes, its cab decorated with dozens of coloured plastic flowers, silken tassels and embroidered velvet panels with holy inscriptions for good fortune. On the back the wooden crates were nearly all loaded. He urged them on faster until the last one was stacked. The baggy black Druze trousers billowed in the light breeze as he waved the peasants aboard.

There were seven, six men and a woman. He looked appreciatively at the two big men. He could use workers like that. Shouting final instructions to the driver, he slammed the door shut and watched the vehicle trundle slowly down the dirt track towards the road.

Hussam looked across the crates at Jodi. He hadn't intended bringing her on this one. It was too personal. He would regain his son, have in his power the man who took him, the butcher of Bab'ullah. The prospect made his whole concept of the mission a great deal less detached than it should be. For the first time since Kibbutz Hashemesh he didn't trust himself. Once more the arena was a *kibbutz*, Gana, a small, remote settlement of native-born Israelis, first generation of the Promised Land, who proudly called themselves *sabras*, the Hebrew name for the spiky tender-hearted prickly pear to which they likened their national character.

For Jodi, each mission was easier. She still felt fear but not the terror of that first episode on Golan. "If they capture you the Israelis may be lenient," Hussam had told her. "For me it would be different." She knew he would never let them take him.

Jodi was with them because she knew the *kibbutz*. It was where they shot the dog. She suggested an attack on Friday evening, *Erev Shabbat*, when every *kibbutznik* would be gathered into the communal dining room to welcome the Bride of the Sabbath, sing praise, break bread and drink with mild distaste the sticky sweet *Shabbat* wine from small, clear plastic beakers. Alcohol was not a Jewish vice. It was almost never to be found on *kibbutz* with the sacred exception of *Shabbat*.

"Wait until the singing finishes. There's a prayer, then those on kitchen duty bring the food. Almost everyone will be in the dining room then," she said.

She drew them a plan of the *kibbutz* and a more detailed sketch of the dining room. There was only one entrance through double doors. At the other end was the kitchen with two entrances. She showed them the position of the hut which served as the administration office, the central parking area where the tractors and trucks stood, the layout of the living accommodation and the huts where the overseas volunteers slept.

"They won't keep this one quiet," Amin had crowed.

The Druze truck slowed, coming to a stop at a dusty, shaded spot beneath some tall trees. Either side of the quiet, narrow country road were thick reeds and green bushes.

They formed a human chain while Baseem swung down half a dozen orange crates which were passed along silently to the thicket. The truck drove off as the reeds closed behind them. Ahead stretched a long day. Pulling off the peasant clothes to reveal fatigues, they armed immediately from the arsenal within the crates. Mahmoud carried the bag of explosives. Tonight he would blow Kibbutz Gana from the face of the earth.

They moved slowly. There was plenty of time. Hussam and Baseem took turns to scout ahead, the others following in single file, five paces apart. The lush green Galilee vegetation gave ample cover and a light breeze kept up a continuous rustling of leaves, covering the soft sounds of their advance. Only occasionally was the birdsong and chirping of crickets broken by engine noise from a tractor or truck on the road. Once they heard the chatter of workers in an apple orchard, climbing rickety aluminium ladders, baskets strapped to their fronts into which they carefully loaded the ripe fruit, emptying the baskets into huge square bins between the rows.

Hussam pushed on until they sighted the *kibbutz*. It nestled at the foot of the gentle eastern slope of the wide valley, overlooking its own orchards and cotton fields. He stared at it for a long time, watching for signs of life, as if any moment his son might appear within reach so he could snatch him to safety.

Amin had assured him he was alive, a hostage for Jodi's safe return. There had been a difficult moment when Amin told them. Jodi immediately offered to give herself up but Amin refused. The Jews were treacherous. They might still kill the boy once they had her. Also, he wouldn't get his guns. He wouldn't hear of it.

"David is more important now," she said.

Amin's eyes narrowed as he rounded on her. "I will say what is important," he hissed. She shrank back from him. He seemed to reserve a special look for her, one which never failed to strike her down with fear.

In return for his information on David, Amin demanded destruction of the *kibbutz*. He wanted casualties. "When you are there, remember your family. Remember Bab'ullah. You will meet the man who ordered it. His fate, the fates of all, will be in your hands. Don't betray your people. Nothing will be too bad."

Hussam sized up the little settlement. He beckoned Mahmoud, pointing out the small red-roofed concrete bungalows amid the green lawns and pink-blossomed bushes. "You won't have much time, half an hour perhaps, no more," he told him. "Ahmed will help you. Take Ali to keep watch." Mahmoud nodded. To Kamel he indicated the thin wire, Gana's only telephone link with the outside. It should be cut before the attack, but not too early. There must be no alert, no suspicion that anything was amiss.

From a large packing shed came the sound of music on a radio and the hum of machinery. Otherwise the *kibbutz* was quiet.

At mid-afternoon work ceased. The scene was suddenly alive with people spilling from the big shed.

Tractors and trucks began returning from the fields, children hurried from schoolrooms to waiting parents, going home to prepare for Shabbat. Jodi heard their laughter and again felt the prick of a traitor's conscience. For an hour the *kibbutzniks* straggled back from the fields and orchards, wandering wearily to their homes, emerging showered, refreshed and decked out in their best clothes. Families were together, walking through the gardens, pausing to chat with others. Young volunteers filed from the huts which clustered at the very base of the hill, slightly apart from the concrete bungalows.

Jodi had warned of the *Nahal*, the army reserve boys who lived as volunteers at Gana as part of their national service. They wouldn't be armed but still, any foolish heroics would come from the *Nahal*.

The *kibbutz* had two guards. They patrolled after dark and would do so until dawn, armed with Uzis, safety catches on because of civilian proximity, especially children. *Kibbutz* children were sacrosanct and horribly spoiled, the soldiers of tomorrow.

At dusk the lights shone out from the windows of the big dining room. Hussam moved the unit up to the *kibbutz* boundary. They could hear the clatter of cutlery, the chatter of women bossing each other about. To the north of the dining room was the administration hut from which two men emerged carrying guns. They stood talking for a few minutes and walked off together along the main track from the centre of the settlement to the road, wishing "*Shabbat shalom*," to the latecomers hurrying past them to the dining room.

Hussam gestured urgently to Baseem and Kamel who followed them, melting into the undergrowth, heading for the road.

In the dining room the piano struck up like the piano of doom. It had a thunderous seriousness, demanding accompaniment from the unwilling voices which quickly gained strength and confidence.

"*Erev shel shoshanim*," they sang, "evening of roses." Hussam headed for the group of vehicles parked in the open space. He motioned for them to follow. "*Le al Shabbat ble ta'am oo ble re'ah...*" the song rose up through the warm air. Jodi and he were to take the kitchen, Baseem and Kamel the main door, once they disposed of the guards and cut the wire. Mahmoud would lay charges at the cornerstones of each bungalow. The Israelis weren't the only ones who could blow up villages.

"*Shabbat shalom, Shabbat shalom...*" Jodi tensed. It was the last hymn. Across the yard Baseem signalled. They were ready. The piano of doom echoed into silence and a man's voice solemnly began the blessing. Hussam turned to Mahmoud, who beckoned Ahmed and Ali, moving between the trucks and running towards the lawns and shrubberies, softly illuminated by the porch lights of the neat little dwellings. The droning voice ended. There was a scraping of chairs and an eager clatter began. Voices rose happily. Another Sabbath had started.

They took their signal from Hussam. Jodi ran for the south door as he raced for the other. She entered with a burst of fire at the ceiling, the cue for Baseem and Kamel to enter the main door.

"Move!" she yelled in Hebrew at the startled women in the kitchen. "Into the dining room!" One screamed, another dropped a tray of meat, then slipped and fell on it as she tried to run. Hussam was already at the door of the big room. Jodi followed, driving the four women ahead of her.

Inside there was panic. Then the crowd seemed to shrink together as they realised what was happening. Hussam let go a burst above their heads and ordered them onto the floor.

"Get down!" she translated.

There was a sound of breaking glass. Hussam swore and shouted to Kamel at the far end of the room. He ran outside from where came a volley of machine gun fire. Kamel returned smiling. "*Nahal*!" he shouted. "A dead hero!"

Hussam waited for the room to calm down. His eyes scanned the crowd, seated now on the floor between the two long rows of tables, their white cloths stained with spilled wine and food. He ordered them to lie flat on their stomachs.

"You have a boy here called David. He's my son," he yelled. "I've come for him. Where is he?"

Women clutched children to them, terrified for the most part. The men needed watching. Every one was a trained soldier. Every one had fought a war last year. Those who understood Arabic looked up blankly.

"Where is he?" Hussam bellowed so loudly that children screamed and a woman began crying. Still no one spoke.

"Who is secretary?" Jodi demanded in Hebrew. Faces turned to a man who slowly stood. He was tall and slender and hesitated momentarily before approaching.

"Where is my son?" Hussam demanded of him.

The man replied in Arabic: "I don't know what you mean." Jodi sensed something going terribly wrong. Hussam was shaking. She was afraid. "Where is Uri Gershon?" Hussam asked, his voice low, trembling.

The secretary hesitated. "Uri is not here."

"Liar!" Hussam's anger exploded. With the butt of his rifle he hit the man in the face. He fell heavily, blood spurting from his nose. Hussam turned to the others. "Who is Uri Gershon?" he asked, surveying them dangerously.

No one spoke. He levelled his rifle at the secretary and asked again. There was a deathly hush. The rifle ended it with an ear-splitting crack which faded into horrified screams as the man slumped back on the floor. This time he didn't get up.

Jodi felt sick. She kept her eyes on the crowd. Men had lurched forward. "Get back!" she shouted but to herself sounded less than convincing. She no longer recognised the voice as his.

"I'll ask again, after which I shall shoot another, then another, until I get an answer. You!" he pointed his rifle at a dark, moustachioed man, "Are you the brave Colonel Gershon?" The man stammered and shook his head. Hussam dragged him forward by his collar then pushed the barrel of the rifle into the back of his neck.

"I am Gershon!" a voice from the far end interrupted him. Hussam relaxed slowly, raised his head almost with disbelief to face the one he travelled from Qmrah to kill. Around the room there was a murmur as the man stood. Hussam watched him step between the prostrate forms. The murmurs grew. Kamel screamed at them to shut up.

"*Sheket*!" Jodi yelled in Hebrew.

The man reached Hussam who looked into his face, searching for a clue, a reason, an identity to the evil which lurked within. "So!" he said, nodding slowly. "It's you!" For another moment he stood motionless then, before she knew how it happened, slammed the rifle butt into his stomach, smashing it up into his face as he bent double. The man teetered, almost falling. Hussam waited calmly for him to stand upright again which he did slowly, agonisingly. Bleeding from a broken nose and front teeth, he tried gallantly to focus on Hussam's face which still held an expression of disbelief.

"There's nothing I can do so bad as what you did," he said coldly, his eyes still searching deeply. "I'll kill you quickly. Otherwise I might regret forever what I will do." He paused, the face no longer that of Hussam, seeming to absorb the evil it found in his victim. "Don't make me change my mind. Tell me what you've done with my son."

For a moment she thought it was Amin. There was a terrible calmness about him, a hatred which transcended emotion. No human hatred had such power. It seemed he drew on the hidden reserves of eternal damnation, absorbing all hope, all warmth, all life. In their absence she shivered with cold horror. Not even Amin had frightened her like this, not even Kushi. They were of the flesh, of the body. Hussam was possessed and whatever terrible thing had him reached out for more.

"He's not Gershon," a woman shouted. The spell broke. The room seemed to sigh with relief. Hussam blinked like a man hypnotised who had just woken. "Is it true?"

"He's not Gershon," the woman shouted again. "He doesn't know anything about your son. None of us do. Perhaps Uri knows but he's in Jerusalem."

Jodi looked nervously at Hussam. "Why did you lie?" he asked the man.

He could barely speak: "To stop you shooting them." Hussam levelled his rifle.

She couldn't stand it. "Hussam, no! David's not here. Let's go!" It seemed an eternity before he lowered the gun, surveying again those who lay on the floor.

"Make the children stand up," he said. One at a time the children stood, some with their mothers kneeling alongside, eyes turned imploringly on Hussam. There were about fifty of them, all ages, but Jodi was right, David wasn't there. Hussam strode forward, reaching for a child near the front. With one arm he lifted the lad, carrying him back to where Jodi stood.

"This boy reminds me of my son," he said loudly so they all heard. "The same age, same height, same build. Tell Uri Gershon I shall keep him until I have my son. He will be returned as my son returns. Dead or alive, the choice is his."

A woman shouted "No," rising to her knees, the man next to her pulling her back.

Hussam continued: "Ask Uri Gershon about Bab'ullah. Ask him how he left my home, then thank your God I left any of you alive." He signalled to Kamel who went out. In a minute they heard him shooting up the vehicles. There was a moment's silence before an engine sprang to life. "Don't try to follow. The smallest excuse to kill you would give me the greatest pleasure."

Hussam thrust the child into Jodi's arms and she ran out to the vehicle, an open pick-up. Mahmoud and the others were already in the back. She pushed in beside Kamel in the front. The child was crying and wriggling to escape but she held him firm. Baseem raced from the double doors, lobbing a grenade into the office hut as he passed. It went off as Hussam ran from the kitchen, pausing to throw another back through the door. He and Baseem made the truck as the tyres started squealing and a second explosion shattered the kitchen.

They were half a mile away before the first of Mahmoud's charges blew, flaring bright orange in the sky above the treetops.

✳✳✳

In the Rainbow Bar, Dahoud read the latest report of *fedayeen* success at Gana. The news was a poor compromise of what little the Israelis admitted and the wild exaggerations of *El Fatah*. Somewhere between lay the truth.

A full bottle of Coca Cola was put down heavily on the bar beside him. Dahoud's nerves weren't good. He jumped. Uri Gershon eased himself onto the next barstool like a horseman in a saddle.

"Peace!" said Uri. "That's what I bring you friend. Peace!" He smiled but Dahoud did not relax. Uri continued: "Peace, between Arab and Jew! Let's drink to it. *Le chayim*, to life!" He put the bottle to his lips and drank. From down the bar Mustapha watched nervously. It was early, the place empty. The Israeli soldier would keep it that way. He had seen him many times in the Old City. He came asking questions when the English woman disappeared. People liked him but kept at arm's length. It was the first time he'd been in uniform. No one would come while he sat there.

Uri turned the newspaper towards him. "Ah!" he acknowledged, "Kibbutz Gana. It's my home you know." He drank again, then slapped Dahoud on the back. "But of course you know! I told you, remember?" Dahoud gave the briefest of nods. Uri's voice lost its warmth, the comradery gone. He leaned close to Dahoud: "You are the only one who knew!"

His home loomed large in his thoughts today, blotting out all else. This morning he had sat, head in hands, grief matched by guilt and outrage as Ezer and Weissman debated.

"It must cease," Avrom Ezer said gravely. "Twenty-three dead in just two attacks. How can it happen?"

"The man is good," said Weissman. "We always knew it was poor leadership which held the *fedayeen* back."

Ezer was angry which he rarely was. "One man?" he demanded. "One man makes fools of us, makes nonsense of our borders, hits targets deep within our homeland, murders our young men..?"

For the first time it made sense. Until Gana no one linked the spate of terrorist successes with the carnage at Bab'ullah. "One man and a woman," he told

Ezer. Jodi was the seal on Hussam's success. She knew Israel better than most Israelis. Without her he could never move so swiftly with such certainty.

"It's a mess!" Ezer concluded. "I send you after one hostage. Now there are two!"

Uri rose in anger. "There's still one. She's no hostage. They've worked on her, indoctrinated her with their brand of hatred. She held a gun at Gana. She's a terrorist like the rest."

Ezer waited in silence for the atmosphere to calm. "We can't keep such incidents quiet," he said at last. "Look at the papers." He pushed a copy of *Ma'ariv*, the daily paper, across the desk. "Four Die in Kibbutz Attack," it read.

"There'll be an outcry. The cabinet demands reprisal," Ezer continued. "Where are they now?"

Weissman shook his head. "They're clever. They move camp after each raid. They don't tell anyone, not even Amin. We don't know where they are. How do we retaliate?"

Ezer's parting commands were: "Find them. I want the one responsible. I want him dead."

It took a while for Uri's thoughts to clear. Hussam had known Gana was his home. Not many knew, only one in the Old City. Facing Dahoud he recalled how the surly bar owner had warmed to him as he warmed to very few. "We talked of Galilee, your home too before '48. No one in Jerusalem has spoken to me of Galilee," Uri was saying now. "Why did you betray me? Did I steal your home? Drive you out? Are you paying me back? Is it that or is it the money? How much did Amin pay for the woman?" Dahoud tried to stand but Uri laid a hand on his shoulder, his eyes holding him rigid. "Get a message to Hussam." It was an order. "Tell him to meet me at Jericho. There's an olive grove by the Jordan, south of the bridge. Tell him to bring the boy hostage and tell him I have news of his son." He lowered his voice. "This is for Hussam's ears. If Amin learns of it I'll close your bar. But that will be the very, very least of your worries, I swear it on the new graves at Gana."

He patted Dahoud's shoulder twice and left quietly.

✳✳✳

"*Layla layla, haruach lochreshet, Layla layla, bochra hatsomeret...*" As Jodi sang the haunting Hebrew lullaby she looked down at the child. He had clung to her all day, crying if the others came close. Now, as she cradled him, he fought sleep.

Hussam watched her from a distance. The strange lullaby calmed him as well as the child, dispelling the last traces of his earlier rage.

He'd leapt from the Jeep before it stopped, clearing the distance to the command post with one stride before bursting in on the surprised Amin who was in conference with three others. Overturning the table, he lunged at Amin, dragging him from his chair, throwing him against the wall with such force he was winded. It took all three men to tear him away from his victim. He cursed Amin to hell before storming out, pushing his way roughly through a crowd of *fedayeen* gathered at the door, jumping back into the Jeep and ordering Kamel to drive.

"*Layla layla, sayi el enayich…*" The child's eyes closed. She continued softly for a minute then stopped, lying him down gently on a blanket and wrapping it around him.

It took a woman and child to bring peace in the midst of this nightmare. No man could work such magic. Hussam thought of David, of Leila. His head fell to his hands, he would go mad. When he looked up she was watching him but looked away quickly. He went to her.

"Don't touch me!" she said. "Don't touch me!" as he reached for her, for some comfort, for the understanding a woman should show. She shrank from him, the fear as he'd seen it in her eyes at Bab'ullah when, delirious, she mistook him for Kushi.

"Jodi…"

"Don't ever touch me again!"

"Because of the *kibbutz*?"

"You shot him in cold blood after I called him out. He was unarmed and he was telling the truth!"

"You forget Bab'ullah."

"I shall never forget Bab'ullah," she shouted. "But someone has to stop." She hesitated, her eyes wild. "They kill you so you kill them. Blood demands blood! You take me, they take David and you take him," she indicated the sleeping child. "When does it all end?"

"It ends when it ends!"

"Don't give me any more of that *kismet* crap!"

She thought he would hit her and recoiled as he grabbed her shoulders, shaking her, his voice low and menacing. "Then tell me! You tell me, *Nazrani,* you of the love and compassion, you of the forgiveness of sins, you who turn the other cheek, tell me what they did to your Christ!"

The silence was broken by their laboured breathing. "Let go!" she said, her voice hoarse. "I told you, don't touch me again."

He brought her closer, his fingers digging into her flesh. "When I want you I will take you. But for now I don't want you." His look was one of contempt as he released her abruptly and strode away.

CHAPTER 16

A rare rainstorm had broken that afternoon. The air, warmly moist, smelled of earth, fruit and flowers and the good things yielded by the soil under the kindness of the sky.

"Giving and receiving," thought Uri. Tomorrow the sun would beat down, taking back what it gave. The earth would shrivel in response, withholding its bounty.

He sat, his back to the grey bark of an ancient olive trunk. It seemed as old as time this place, where the armies of Joshua and the returning Israelites sounded the trumpets which breached the massive stone ramparts of Jericho. The sounds of the night were all he heard now. There was no warning of approach but he was aware quite suddenly that he wasn't alone. "Welcome to Israel," he said.

Hussam stood before him, rifle trained on him. "Where are your men?"

"Around." Uri gestured vaguely.

As soldiers they met, equal in strength and truth. The reasons and the justifications belonged elsewhere, in the dusty rooms of politicians, the heady incense clouds of the men of God. They dealt a truce as impersonal as battle, a means to an end. Only the outcome mattered.

"You have the boy?"

"If you have my son."

"I don't. But what I know will lead you to him." Hussam's eyes narrowed with suspicion. "Hear me out," Uri continued. "It's a long story. It took a great deal of time to fit the pieces together." He paused but Hussam was silent, waiting. "We didn't kill your family."

"You're lying!" Hussam said without emotion. "I saw your convoy return. I almost walked into you."

"Yes, we were there. We planned to rescue the woman and on my explicit orders there were to be no casualties if they could be avoided. But when we got there we found it as you did. In all my fighting I never saw so terrible a thing. We could never have done it."

"Only the guilty leave unburied dead."

"You should know that!" Uri retorted angrily, then checked. He drew a deep breath. "I allowed forty minutes only for the complete operation. What could we do; a small strike force in enemy territory? We couldn't spare time to bury them." He looked directly at Hussam. "Ask yourself, would you have done otherwise?"

"You killed them." Uri shook his head. "Then who?"

"Who had most to gain?" Hussam did not answer. "Two men benefited from the killing. One, your Sultan, Sheikh Abd'allah. For years he took bribes from Hijazi. When Israel found out Palestinian arms came in through Qmrah, naturally we took steps to put an end to it. We threatened the Sultan with reprisals. He had to stop Hijazi."

"Hijazi was just one man."

Uri showed mild surprise. "You undervalue yourself. If my information is correct, the Sultan doesn't share your popularity. He was afraid of you, of what would happen if he murdered Hijazi and you found out." He waited, giving Hussam time to assimilate the information.

"You said two men would gain."

Uri nodded then asked: "Why weren't you at Bab'ullah when it happened?"

"What is it to you?"

"Let me answer for you. Because you were at Sufa, and on whose invitation?" Hussam was silent. "Let me answer again. It was Amin."

"Ha! Do you think I don't know you're trying to set me against Amin. He didn't invite me. He sent for the woman."

"Knowing you would go with her."

Hussam thought back, recalling Amin's eagerness that he should stay for the night, the feast. "It was the *mukhtar*," he began, then stopped, knowing Amin could make the old man do it. Amin had sent for Jodi but let her go: too easily.

"No!" Hussam still refused to believe it.

"You've been tricked," Uri said brutally. "Don't deceive yourself further."

"Why would Amin want them dead? Hijazi gave him guns!"

"Hijazi was a crook! He charged high prices which Amin had to pay. He needed guns at any price. But that wasn't enough for Hijazi. He got greedy, began buying up stocks of outdated ammunition, cheap, dangerous stuff which no arms dealer in his right mind would touch."

"How do you know this?"

"Amin launched a mortar attack on Kiryat Shmona. A bomb pre-ignited, blew the mortar to shreds, killed three of his men and badly wounded a fourth. When our troops got there they found six unexploded shells. The original dates had been painted over, new ones painted on."

Hijazi would be capable of such a thing. Hussam must acknowledge it to himself if not to Gershon. Uri saw the doubt in his eyes. "Amin no longer needed Hijazi. Since the Six Day War our Arab neighbours are coming round to the *fedayeen* as their best solution to the Jewish problem." He was philosophical, spreading his hands. "For us it's just another in a long line of final solutions. In any case, Amin and those like him pleaded their case well. Quite recently the arsenals have begun filling with communist arms. Guns are no longer such a desperate issue." He paused to give his next words special emphasis. "The same cannot be said for officers. Guns can be bought. Leaders, ones he can trust, cannot. Poor leadership, high casualties, little success, flagging moral; guns alone couldn't stop the rot. But a returning hero, one who would bring quick results! Ah, such a man could change the course of his war." His eyes glowed as he warmed to the plot. "Let us return for a moment to your Sultan. Here is a man with a hero he didn't want yet couldn't kill for fear of a popular revolt. Supposing Amin approached him with a plan which would rid him of this menace, solving at the same time the dangerous problem of Hijazi.

"Supposing he guaranteed that following a massacre by Qmrahi troops the blame would fall squarely on Israel. What better way to winkle a reluctant hero out of his land forever? You would return to the *fedayeen*, hell-bent on revenge. And so you have!"

Cleverly Uri had gathered together the tangle of threads which trapped Hussam. Now he began drawing them in. "Amin heard we captured his man at Kiryat Shmona. He assumed he would talk, they always do, but by then it suited his purpose. When he knew an Israeli strike was imminent he sent for the hostage to lure you away. Then the real killers moved in. They weren't far ahead of us. The timing was perfect. By leaving Sufa that morning you had to meet up with us at some point. The rest was left to your imagination."

The story mesmerised Hussam. Memories raced through his mind: Suez, Kibbutz Hashemesh, Khadija, Jodi, Bab'ullah. Amin! All his life it had been Amin! He'd thought himself free. Now he saw Amin's voracious hatred allowed no escape. There was a long silence before he turned angrily on Uri, demanding hoarsely: "Why should I believe you?"

"You don't have to. I have a witness." Uri walked a short distance and whistled a signal. He returned to Hussam and waited.

At a footfall on the soft earth they turned to see a young woman step from the shadows.

"Nooria!" She ran to him, jumping into his arms, hugging him and weeping.

"They left her for dead. God knows what they did to her. The wounds have healed, superficially anyway."

Hussam gently disentangled her arms, looking into her face with disbelief and then at Uri. "We counted the dead. Some were beyond identification but we counted."

Nooria spoke. "Leila's sister was there. She came to help with the baby. They killed her too," she burst into tears again, clinging to him while he stroked her head.

Uri waited before saying: "We want the boy back."

"Where is my son?"

Nooria answered: "The soldiers took him. They carried him away..." her voice trailed off under Hussam's horrified expression. The Sultan's affinity for young boys was a poorly guarded secret.

"The boy!" Uri insisted again. Hussam gave a shout and in a minute Jodi came forward. In her arms, wrapped in a blanket, the young boy was asleep. An Israeli soldier appeared, taking him from her, Uri briefly checking him as he was carried past and back into the darkness.

To Jodi he said: "The guns have arrived at Qmrah. We've guaranteed your safe return to your father if you come with us now."

For a moment her eyes and Hussam's locked in some sad, silent conversation. Then he looked away. She hesitated and finally shook her head. "I have to see this through. Tell my father...he'll understand."

He nodded and turned to Hussam. "You've given us much grief. Tonight we have a truce. When it's over what will you do?"

Hussam was not about to tell him. "I'll do what needs to be done."

"You'll go to Qmrah, of course. It's fortunate for you that a shipment of arms awaits collection. You'll need it. But can you afford to turn your back on Amin?"

Hussam knew he could not. Though the thought of further delay filled him with fear for David, his time of reckoning with Amin had come. "Let us help," Uri urged. "You'll need arms and military support. There's only a handful of you. You'll never break the *casbah* without artillery." Hussam shook his head but Uri persisted: "You'll find that in spite of our differences Israel can be a good friend. We have a common interest in wishing Amin dead."

"No!" Hussam recoiled. "Your war is Amin's war, not mine. There can be no common interest. I'll settle my score in my own way. I won't be used again, not by Amin and not by Israel."

"Good luck then. May God bring us both the peace for which we search."

They left him, a lone trumpeter at the walls of race hatred which stubbornly refused to tumble. Uri sighed. It wasn't all milk and honey having your own land.

There was another clandestine encounter that night, darkness wrapping itself protectively around the figures huddled in the narrow alleyway. Nowhere was safe from the Sultan's spies.

"We're with you," the younger of the two men was saying. He was tall with a military bearing and pulled the dark brown *abba* together at the front, covering the military uniform and the epaulettes denoting his captaincy.

"All of you?"

"All junior ranks."

"What about the men?"

"They'll follow. They're as disillusioned as we."

Aref smiled though there was no pleasure in it. The words spoke death for them both should they be reported back to the palace. The power and the wealth of Qmrah rested with a handful of corrupt individuals, mainly relatives of Sheikh Abd'allah. There was less freedom now than when the British ruled more than 20 years ago.

General Aref Ayud owed much to the British. Through the military skills they taught he was able to oust them from his country. Himself the son of wealthy parents, he had never wanted to be anything but a soldier and his father, who enjoyed the trust of the occupying force, won him a place at the Royal Military Academy, Sandhurst.

Aref was nineteen when he saw Britain and hated it immediately. The climate, the country, the weather, were cold and unwelcoming, the skies grey, the air damp and foggy. The first six weeks of square bashing in drizzle under the hawk-eyes of uncultured

NCO's who called him "sir" in tones they might reserve for some contemptible animal, were so alien to the warmth and friendliness instilled by his Arab upbringing that he all but gave up his military aspirations right then.

People were aloof in this island of remote individuals who never touched and rarely spoke. They behaved almost as badly to each other as they did to his own people in Qmrah. He realised in later years that his loathing of all that surrounded him then was a blessing. It concentrated his attention on his purpose and after a year he passed out of the academy with honours.

Back home his allegiance was courted by Sheikh Abd'allah whose infant army he raised in just a few years from a shambles to an efficient fighting force, and whose irregulars he coached in explosives handling and rifle marksmanship. On the Sheikh's elevation to Sultan, Aref's reward was a position of military power, though not that of supreme head. The new Sultan owed many favours and in any case, Aref's allegiance was born not of fear but of belief in the cause, love of his land. Fear was constant, more manageable than love. Men of belief, of conviction, could act unpredictably and not always in the best interest of their patrons. Aref always suspected that while his less talented superiors gave him free reign in matters of military management, they kept a watchful eye open and so, as it proved, with good cause.

Over the years Aref watched corruption spread. His dream of a free, self-governed, independent Qmrah was mercilessly shredded while his job became less one of national security than of policing the streets, quelling civil unrest, arresting and interrogating the ringleaders or those whom the Sultan had the slightest suspicion might harbour uncharitable thoughts towards him.

Recently his position had become precarious, his loyalty seriously questioned when he queried the alarming number of suicides among political detainees. Bab'ullah was the last straw. The Sultan sent a new man, an Arab but a foreigner, to hand pick a task force ostensibly to frighten the bedouins and persuade Hijazi to cease arms trading. Aref's foreboding turned to horror when, too late, he learned the true purpose of the mission. He since blamed himself. He should have known from the men selected that it would be a bloodbath.

"I too am most upset," Sheikh Abd'allah wheezed, with little attempt at sincerity. "I understand the bedouins put up fierce resistance and our troops had no alternative but to open fire."

"My sources say the bedouins were attacked without warning."

The Sultan looked shocked but: "I shall look into it immediately," was the only response he gave. "Incidentally," he added by way of afterthought as Aref turned to go, "I understand a boy was taken captive, the son of the one they call the Sword."

Aref froze. He had sought to hide the boy. "That is so," he reluctantly admitted.

"He's a hostage against reprisal but that's no reason why he shouldn't be shown every courtesy, every comfort. He is after all an innocent child."

"I shall see to it."

"Perhaps I should see to it personally," the Sultan said in a voice which had no perhaps about it. "Bring him to me."

Aref stalled. "The boy was filthy, louse infested, your Highness," he lied, enjoying the look of distaste, the recoil his words created. "He's been quarantined. It would be wrong to expose your Majesty to possible disease until we're certain there's no risk."

"Yes, quite," the Sultan wheezed. "Make sure I'm kept informed of his progress."

Aref's position was more dangerous than ever. He would not be able to protect himself for much longer, let alone the child. Even so he hesitated. Rebellion was not in him. He was a loyal soldier to whom the idea of mutiny was repellent, unworthy, even when those in authority, right to the very pinnacle, proved themselves so unworthy.

His army was built on the principles of loyalty and patriotism. How could he contradict it now, setting comrade against comrade, countryman against countryman, brother against brother?

"We are with you," his accomplice was urging, looking first one way then the other along the narrow passageway. "Give the order. Tell us when!"

Aref felt suddenly weary. Perhaps he was too old. Perhaps he should leave it to the younger ones. They looked only to the coup, the victory, the glory, the liberation of the people. Aref looked beyond. Supposing his revolution succeeded. Who would rule? Would the new regime be better than what existed now, the one for which he fought, in which he once so passionately believed when he too was young? What of the people? Would they rally to the army? They had little reason. The Sultan's continual use of the army as a weapon against his own people made his military men as unpopular as himself. Aref's plan for a swift, contained military operation against a corrupt few could spread like a plague into full blown civil war.

The young captain was too eager. Aref put a restraining hand on his arm. "Patience, young man," he said soothingly. "Be prepared. Be ready to move at any moment. I'll give the order when the time is right."

CHAPTER 17

From his vantage point in the surrounding hills, Hussam trained the binoculars on Sufa. The place was dangerously quiet. In the streets, no children; on the rifle range and assault course, no *fedayeen*. On the westernmost hill, overlooking the road, two snipers waited but he had already skirted them.

He focussed on the *casbah*. A machine gun nest topped the tall flat-roofed building over the old gateway. The barrel of another heavy MG protruded from the top of the mosque's slender octagonal minaret. In the shadows he caught occasional glimpses of khaki and camouflage battledress. He lowered the glasses. He was expected and Gershon's conclusion was correct. Thus armed, the *casbah* was invincible.

Hussam had hoped for the element of surprise, a slim hope. No message, however secret, came out of Jerusalem without reaching Amin. He surveyed the scene for a long time. Amin couldn't hide forever. His soldiers couldn't remain on alert, the camp this dead. Sooner or later daily life would resume. Knowing the refugees it would be sooner. Their wretched, hopeless existence, their proximity to constant danger made them casual, even fatalistic about the chances of walking into bullet or bomb. But Hussam's anxiety about David gave him little time for a siege. Perhaps the element of surprise could be reconstructed.

Amin knew of the meeting at Jericho. He surmised, correctly, that Hussam would return to kill him but he could have headed directly for Qmrah. Amin couldn't be certain whether he was safe or not. The more time that elapsed, the safer he would feel. Amin was a skilled leader but fighting armies of equal force wasn't his style. He was a raider, a skirmisher who hit and ran, moving fast and freely. Now he committed the cardinal sin of the guerrilla. He was holding ground. But the *casbah* was a good friend even to an unskilled defender. Its narrow winding streets, its high windowless outer walls, could be held by a handful of men.

The day progressed, the camp began to live again. First a child would run out, an adult pursuing and sweeping it back to safety. Then figures began scuttling out of one building into another. The hours went by. Women appeared with water cans, at first hurrying but then casually strolling to the communal taps. On the hill the snipers were relieved, so was the machine gun nest and, he assumed, though he couldn't see, the minaret. A Jeep casually patrolled the camp perimeter.

Hussam watched intently, the Dragunov cocked and ready. Amin had only to appear to be dead. But there was no sign of him. By nightfall *fedayeen* openly patrolled the streets. Men sat in groups drinking coffee and children played around doorways where women, arms folded or hands on hips, stood talking. Hussam slipped quietly down the hillside. He waited beyond the camp perimeter for a minute before sprinting silently into the shadows of the outer rotted corrugated iron and wood shanties. A dog barked and a man shouted at it. He kept his distance from people but strolled casually, looking like any other guard. The last few yards along the main street into the *mukhtar's* house were the most hazardous. Hussam closed the door quietly behind him. The old man looked up in surprise. Hussam motioned him to be silent, reopening the door a crack to check he had not been seen, then seating himself at the big, square table in the centre of the room.

"Hussam!" By lamplight it was only now at close quarters that the old man's eyes focussed clearly on his visitor's face, but he smiled and reached for Hussam's hand, kissing it.

Embarrassed, Hussam withdrew it, clasping the old man around the shoulders. "I've come for Amin," he said.

The *mukhtar* shook his head. "Amin says you betrayed us. That you went to the Zionists and would bring them here to kill us."

"Do you believe him?"

He shook his head. "Many of our young men do. The *fedayeen* rally to him. They hold the *casbah*."

"Where is Amin?" The old man shrugged. Hussam got up and went to the window. Floral curtains hung from a piece of wire. They were closed. He lifted one slightly and checked the scene outside. It was as before. "Can you get him to come here?"

"You would kill him in my house?"

"It would save much bloodshed, *ya sheikh*, the blood of your sons."

He shook his head again. "He won't come. I asked once today. He sent the Syrian."

"What Syrian?"

"He is called Nuri Tassah. He came from Damascus a week ago."

Tassah! Hussam smiled. Nuri Tassah! Nuri the Syrian! He hadn't seen Nuri since Egypt. He patted the *mukhtar's* shoulder reassuringly. "Send for him again."

The *mukhtar* went out and hailed a young boy, giving him the summons for Amin. Then they waited in silence for a long time, the old man returning to the table, shifting uneasily in his seat. Hussam moved to the window holding the Carl-Gustaf, the sniper rifle slung over his shoulder. From the direction of the *casbah* a young boy came running. He was followed at a more leisurely pace by a man whose face Hussam could not make out. He moved back by the door. A heavy boot sounded on the stone step and the door swung open as the figure entered.

Hussam kicked it shut and the soldier turned to face him. His hand went to the Kalashnikov but stopped short. "Are you with Amin or me, Nuri?" Hussam challenged him.

Nuri hesitated then smiled broadly. "It depends who's holding the gun!" he said.

Lowering the Carl-Gustaf, Hussam slapped his friend's back, clasping his hand in a greeting reserved for old friends. "Why are you here?"

"Amin wants officers. Syria sent me."

"Syria or Dablan?"

Nuri grinned. "So you know?"

"I know Colonel Taher Dablan hates *Fatah* and has set up his own rival group. Are you his spy?"

"He wants Amin watched, that's all."

"He wants Amin destroyed. So do I!" Seating his friend at the table he spoke quickly in a low voice, revealing all the dreadful truth he learned at Jericho. "Amin killed my family and blamed it on the Israelis," he concluded. "That's why I must kill him. Now to protect himself he lies to you as he lied to me."

They heard him out in shocked silence. The *mukhtar* became agitated. "I believe you *el Hussam*. You are honourable. Amin is evil, God blacken his face! At first he was our friend but now he rules here." He started to shake, his voice quivering with rage. "He has no respect for the old who are closer to Allah than he. He spits on me and tells me what to do. He threatens my family if I refuse." His voice was getting louder. Hussam hushed him, going to the window again.

Nuri's answer was more measured. "You have many friends here Hussam but Amin is greatly feared. Few have the courage to cross him and to divide the *fedayeen* would mean brother killing brother."

"The choice is theirs," Hussam replied. "I cannot make men fight." He turned back to the table. "But the time has come for Amin and me. One of us must die."

"Pray Allah it's Amin," the old man interjected.

For a moment Nuri sat silently, then said: "What do you want me to do?"

"How many *fedayeen* are with Amin?"

"Two hundred but only fifty mount guard."

Hussam was thoughtful. Idle, the men would grow restless in the confined space of the old town with its dark buildings of small rooms divided by narrow streets. Already tension would be high. The comradery which preceded battle did not endure, especially if the likelihood of fighting were in doubt. Arab temperament being what it was, as time passed there would be disputes, trouble.

Putting an arm round Nuri's shoulders, he outlined a plan.

"He's nothing to me," Khadija had said, her repulsive red mouth pouting up at him, her painted fingers spread across his chest. "You are the one I want."

He stood impassive as she rubbed her fat little body against him, taking his hand and placing it over her breast. His hand closed cruelly and she gasped. He clutched it tighter, taking her face with his other hand, pinching her mouth till it distorted between his finger and thumb.

"Who do you think I am? Your pet dog Hussam who slobbers after you?"

She broke free, holding the injured breast, backing away as he advanced. She banged into a table and put her hands back to steady her. They closed on a silver-framed photo which she hurled at him. The corner caught him above the eye before splintering into fragments on the marble floor. He cursed, halting momentarily, rubbing his head, smudging the blood. She found a paper knife and held it aloft like a dagger. "Don't come any nearer!"

Amin laughed, grabbing her wrist and twisting the knife away, pressing the point into her throat, then rethinking and tossing it aside. It fell with a clatter. "No," he said. "No, we won't mark this pretty body. It mustn't look like murder." He spun her round till she faced herself in a large gilt-framed mirror. "Say goodbye, *habibi*. You will never sing again."

She struggled, clawing at his hands with long red nails. He let go and she ran, stumbling through the open windows onto the terrace. But he was after her and much faster, throwing her down and gagging her with one bleeding hand to silence her cries for help.

"I should show you the marks on my back where they beat me. No one abuses Amin. No whore betrays Palestine and lives!"

They found her body downstream a week later, decomposed and partially devoured by the creatures of the Nile. The coroner returned an open verdict. She had drowned but who could tell under what circumstances? A photo of herself in concert was discovered smashed at her home. She was well-known for artistic temperament, manic depression. It could have been suicide. Rumours abounded. To her distraught public, Khadija's death was as romantic, mysterious and passionate as the unattainable woman herself.

She deserved it. The woman's craving for danger had finally gone too far. His *fedayeen* spies had seen her enter the Gezira Club with a British officer after which Amin was arrested and questioned. They held him for a week wanting names, places, dates, but what they did was child's play compared with the violence he'd withstood from his dead benefactor. He told them nothing but when released confronted her alone. She offered him money and, when that failed, her disgusting body.

"Morale is failing fast." Nuri's voice roused Amin from his memories. Amin only half heard him. He remained silent. "Two hundred men, idle here inside the *casbah*. There'll be trouble."

"Why hasn't he come?" was all Amin said.

"Perhaps he won't," Nuri replied.

He shook his head. "He will. He will."

Hussam knew of Khadija's affairs with other men, of her betrayal of Amin to the British officer, but he did not learn the truth of her death until three years later at Kibbutz Hashemesh when the enraged Kushi taunted him: "You weren't brave enough to kill your own whore. It took Amin to do it." Then Hussam simply walked away from Amin and from Palestine. He would not walk away this time.

"Our reports say he's going to Qmrah to rescue his son." It was Nuri again.

"He'll be back."

"It could be weeks! We'll be better prepared if we continue to train. Let me take half of them out. When they return, the other half can go. There's a lookout on the hill. They'll warn if he comes."

Amin was ahead of time, living now in the moment of attack, in the moment of action when things would be done and not dwelt upon. He waved Nuri away and Nuri took it as a sign of approval.

Under cover of the next night Hussam moved his unit into Sufa. Silently Mahmoud and Ahmed took the minaret. The mosque was outside the old *casbah* with an unrivalled command of the whole camp. Kamel and Ali took the house by the gate. They slipped in while

Nuri distracted Amin's sentries with some detailed orders. By midnight both positions were Hussam's.

The *mukhtar's* family were to care for Nooria. Then came the long wait. It was the waiting which Jodi hated most. He told her to get some sleep and perhaps a couple of times she did doze off only to snap wide awake to the sound of imagined gunfire. In the end she contented herself with lying curled up, eyes closed, listening to the sounds of the night; dogs barking, the occasional cry of a child, a raised voice, scuttlings and scamperings and the ghostly cooing of pigeons from the rooftops, continually interrupted by the loud rhythmic snoring of Baseem who lay next to her on the floor.

When the cocks crowed it was still dark but the camp slowly heaved itself to life. From the minaret, the amplifier crackled. The dawn prayer must nearly have deafened Mahmoud and Ahmed. As the streets filled, occasional curious glances were cast towards the *casbah*. Groups gathered here and there to discuss the state of things. Lines of women with children formed before the supplementary feeding centre. They waited patiently in the growing heat before a man arrived with a key and, going inside, shut the door again. It was another hour and the queue stretched along the street and out of sight around a corner before the doors opened and the front of the queue dissolved into chaos, surging forward to push inside.

What impressed her most was the seemingly indestructible dignity of the women. Even the clamour at the front was tolerated with a quiet acceptance that the strong and the determined would take what they wanted first.

Two soldiers emerged from the *casbah*, jumping into a Jeep and driving out towards the hill to the west. Hussam watched through the field glasses, passing them occasionally to Baseem. It returned within ten minutes. The snipers had been relieved by Nuri's men. Another hour elapsed.

Then, at a shout, the sound of marching feet came from the *casbah* and a column of *fedayeen* emerged, arms swinging, shouldering guns, heads high. She saw in them a new sense of self-importance. Today they were real soldiers facing real danger, many for the first time. It made a curious and compelling change in them. Shouting "*wahad, sneen, fedayeen*; one, two, *fedayeen*" in time to the marching rhythm, they came up along the street, towards the endless queue. The column took a while to file past but the women who would normally have cheered them on were silent, closing ranks into groups, one group arguing openly with the next, a camp divided.

At the dusty training ground Nuri, from a raised stone platform, lined up the ranks. He shouted: "At ease!" as a few glimpsed Hussam and shifted, showing surprise or reaching for their rifles.

Hussam leapt up to the platform, raising his hand for silence. He surveyed them as if assessing each man. "Bring me the best," he had told Nuri. Few eyes met his as they travelled from face to face. Jodi and Baseem took up position on either side of the street, keeping watch towards the old town while Hussam made his move.

At last he spoke. "*Fedayeen*, I have fought with you. We fought well, scored successes, won victories, brought honour to the Palestinian cause. Now Amin tells you to kill me. Why?" A murmur rose. Hussam allowed it to die. "Because he is afraid. Afraid because at last I know the truth. I came believing it was Israel who destroyed my family, my mother, my wife, my unborn child; Israel that stole my son. I came for revenge believing like you that the Jews took everything that was mine. For you it's true but for me it's a lie. Amin's lie!"

Jodi glanced towards the soldiers, their attention focussed on Hussam. It was stirring stuff.

"The fight is between Amin and me. I wanted it no other way. If I had him in my sights, if I had him within reach, there'd be no need for this." His eyes swept the ranks again. "I ask no favours. Those who don't want to fight, stay behind. But those who have a grievance, those to whom Amin has lied, who he has cheated and deceived like me, come with me now! I need your help. Get me to him or bring him to me...alive!" He paused, then gave a great shout: "Are you with me?"

For one terrible moment there was silence. No one moved. Then a voice cried out: "I'm with you *el Hussam*!" and a babble grew until they surged forward in a jumbled crowd on a rising crescendo of shouts which united in a rhythmic chant: "Hussam! Hussam!"

Jodi turned nervously towards the old town. The sound must reach there. The sentries at the gate had vanished. She looked across at Baseem and he smiled at her, drawing a finger across his throat. When she glanced back at the soldiers they were carrying Hussam aloft, cheering, waving their guns.

Foraging parties rifled Amin's hastily concealed arsenals throughout the camp. They returned lugging boxes of ammunition and grenades, and a dozen mortars and rocket launchers, enough to arm a battalion. Only now did Jodi notice that the street was empty, the queue, the groups, the children, all gone. Everything was moving towards an inexorable climax. Hussam and Amin held the arena.

Hussam beckoned her. He crouched beside what looked like a tube with sights and a trigger. "It's an RPG-7, a rocket launcher," he said. Standing he snapped a length of webbing to front and rear mountings and hung it around her neck, pulling one arm through so her elbow rested on the weapon. It was surprisingly light. "You must come with the advance units. Take it to Kamel. I need him with me. Then stay with Ali. Your job is to feed the gun, also protect the gunner with this," he tapped her Kalashnikov. He armed the RPG and suddenly it was heavy. "In case you need to use it," he explained, hoisting it onto her shoulder, placing her left hand on the front grip, her right on the pistol grip.

She handled it awkwardly. "Be careful," he warned. "It can stop a tank, demolish a building." She fiddled with it some more. "Keep clear of the back and

257

always check behind before firing. The back-blast can kill." The thing scared her to death but she nodded confidently at Hussam. Still he caught something in her look. "You'll be all right," he said in a way which convinced her she would. "Stay close when we move. Do everything I say."

Within a half hour four units deployed around the *casbah* to cover each entrance and trap Amin inside. The thrust was to be through the near gate where the two machine guns were already captured. The attack imminent, Hussam asked the *mukhtar* for his blessing.

"First give our sons inside a chance to come out," he said. "Let me speak to them."

Hussam reluctantly conceded. "Take great care," he cautioned, assigning two guards to go too, training his own rifle on the empty gateway. The guards kept to the walls but the old man, unafraid, walked centrally down the street. Jodi closed her eyes and prayed. When she opened them he stood before the gate, his frail figure small, alone.

He spread his arms entreatingly. "Soldiers of Palestine," he shouted in a thin, trembling voice, "do not fight your brothers. Our enemy lies westward, not here. Why spill your blood and kill your comrades? Take no part in this quarrel. Lay down your guns and come out." His words echoed. He looked up, surveying the ancient empty walls. He tried again. "Sons of Liberation, do not betray our dream. You vowed to die in Palestine, not in the camps. Let Hussam and Amin settle their difference without us. Come out."

Jodi's eyes were fixed on the gate. For a full minute nothing happened. Then three soldiers appeared, hesitated, threw their rifles aside and walked towards the *mukhtar*, hands raised. He moved to welcome them, his arms outstretched.

Without warning two more appeared in the gateway, guns raised, firing bursts which sent bullets ricocheting up the street. Jodi flattened herself against the wall as they zinged past. She saw the soldiers fall, hit in the back. The old man checked but stumbled forward again until another burst flung him to the ground. She cried out.

One assassin was already dead, struck by Hussam's bullet even before the *mukhtar* fell. The other was brought down by a burst from one of the guards sent with old man. Jodi ran forward. Hussam's command stopped her. She heard the whine. The blast knocked her to the ground. A second whine streaked overhead and she rolled sideways, pressing into a recess in the wall as the missile struck a house further along, throwing back a half dozen building blocks which came bouncing past her down the street like rubber balls from a gaping hole in the wall.

From the minaret and the gatehouse bursts of heavy machine gun fire began while mortar crews gave cover to Hussam's units as they raced for the gate. She ran with them. From the *casbah* rose the sounds of furious gunfire. Mortar bombs rained into it while the machine guns rang out above. She pressed against the warm stones. With each blast the walls sighed, the bombs blowing up a dust storm, sending wave after wave of debris belching back. At Hussam's signal the mortars ceased.

She caught his eye for what seemed a long time and mouthed the words: "I love you," not knowing if he caught them because next moment he was through the gateway and into the shadows. The men around her moved forward and she was aware of Baseem's hand on her arm, pushing her through the gate.

Already the painted houses in the dark street bore the scars of battle. Everywhere were the pockmarks of bullets, fallen slates and debris from the mortar assault. The small windows were black, their panes strewn as silver showers across the stones, frames splintered, clinging casually to the walls or lying broken on the ground. The fight raged, raining down from windows and rooftops. A grenade was tossed in through a window and she saw them duck. A second later the blast blew the glass out with such force it shattered on the opposite wall. Black smoke billowed out in a cloud and drifted along the street. A burst of fire smashed the door and three of them raced through. Muffled sounds of guns and grenades came from inside.

A bullet ricocheted from the wall beside her and she ducked into a doorway. Directly above the machine gun still screamed. She raced up the narrow twisting stairs to where Kamel and Ali crouched amid sandbags and a pile of spent cartridges.

"Hussam wants you!" she yelled at Kamel, releasing the webbing and pushing the RPG at him. He rocked the weapon as if weighing it, then smiled broadly, snatched up his rifle and disappeared down the stairs.

As a vantage point it was superb. It looked down on the whole *casbah* and out along the length of the main street. Already the big gun had silenced all sniper fire from the high windows and rooftops on the other side of the alley. The windows were peppered all round with bullet holes. From the camp, more units sprinted for the gate beneath. She crouched beside Ali, checking the belt as it snaked from the metal box through the breech, her hearing numb from the deafening rattle of the gun. Mortars pounded the centre of the town and from the other gates came sporadic fire as Amin's men tried to escape or simply gave themselves up.

Though the fighting was fierce, progress was slow. Each building had to be cleared. From a block ahead rose puffs of smoke and the flashes of rocket fire. It was out of sight of the big gun, shielded by the rooftops in front, though Ali continued to pound away hopefully in its direction. Suddenly the face of the building disintegrated under a direct hit from Hussam's artillery, perhaps fired by Kamel. She heard the shout from the street and saw men surge forward. The next instant they fell, swept by a machine gun which started up from the ruins of the building. Casualties must be heavy on both sides.

Outside, the injured were helped towards the camp, the scene there surreal. Inside the walls all hell was loose, but outside it was quiet. It could almost have been a normal day. Here and there, groups of brightly dressed refugees stood talking, though they stayed close to their houses.

Then there was a new sound. At first she didn't realise what had happened, ducking as if it came from another shell. A tremendous explosion shook the town to its foundations. Ahead a whole building blew apart. Ali stopped firing in surprise. They looked at each other in stunned silence.

The jets came in again. This time she dropped flat on the rooftop. The sandbags tottered and one fell under the impact of another massive blast. Now she saw them turn. There were two, both bearing the white Star of David. Israeli planes.

"Come on!" She shook Ali who reached to dismantle the gun. "Leave it!" she yelled, racing for the stairs, almost falling several times as she took them two and three at a time. In the dust-filled street, men coughed, choking as they carried or dragged the wounded, hurrying for the gateway and the relative calm of the camp outside.

She searched every face. "Where's Hussam?" she demanded. The shadows screamed over and another blast rocked the town. Ali grabbed her wrist, dragging her with him. "Where's Hussam?" she demanded again. Then she was in the bright sunshine, mingling with the others as they ran for cover. She wrenched free from Ali and was about to turn back when she noticed a movement from the group Amin's men massacred before the assault began. The *mukhtar* was alive! She went to him, turning him gently. His chest was red with gaping wounds where two bullets had entered but he looked up at her with patient, confused eyes.

Kneeling, she laid his head in her lap, smiling down, oblivious in her bereavement as the jets shrieked and the people panicked and the old town was blown to bits.

✳✳✳

Through binoculars Uri Gershon observed the devastation. By radio link with the pilots he precision-directed the bombing. One more run would finish the job. He took the handset from the radio operator, then lowered it as his eyes met those of Hussam watching him from behind the sights of the Dragunov.

"Call them off." The jets screamed low directly overhead but Hussam did not flinch. "Call them off!" he bellowed.

Uri looked beyond him. "That won't be necessary," he said.

Momentarily Hussam glanced back to where a thin smoke trail cut the blue sky. Words spoken urgently in Hebrew crackled from the radio. Uri raised the handset, saying simply: "*Persedah*! OK!" He looked up at Hussam. "They're going. One of your machine gunners will be a hero."

Beside him the young radio operator shifted nervously, his hand on the Uzi slung from his shoulder.

"Drop it!" Hussam ordered.

"How did you know we were here?" Uri asked.

"There had to be spotters. They couldn't be so precise."

Uri smiled, looking towards the smoking ruin which, minutes earlier, towered at the centre of the camp. He had destroyed it without a single bomb falling beyond the walls. "If Amin was in there, he's dead now."

Hussam lowered the rifle though he still levelled it threateningly at the two men. "Amin was there, so was I, so was Jodi and nearly a hundred of my men."

"You got out, so did they."

"You would kill us all!"

"No! You'd have killed yourselves. It was madness to go in. I told you at Jericho you'd never take it. I watched you begin. If you stood the slightest chance we'd have stayed out of it. We saved you."

Hussam barked a laugh of disbelief. "You came to save me?"

"I wanted Amin dead."

"So did I."

"Then be content." From the west grew the faint repetitive thud of rotor blades.

"You took Amin from me. I could kill you for that."

"He's dead. It's all that matters."

The hill where they stood was the same from which Hussam viewed the camp two days earlier when the *casbah* looked invincible. Now his soldiers picked their way through the rubble in a hopeless search for survivors.

A black speck broke the horizon, the pounding of the rotors growing in the eerie silence which hung over the camp.

"You think I'll let you fly away unavenged?" he said.

"The vengeance is ours," Uri reminded him. "You killed twenty-three of our people because of Amin and his lies."

Dam butlub dam! "When does it end?" Jodi had asked. Hussam decided. It ended now. He swung the gun in his right hand, motioning them away with it. "Make sure we don't meet again. Next time you interfere it'll be the last thing you do."

The gunship was racing closer. Hussam turned to run, leaping aside as a volley of bullets raked the ground. Uri radioed frantically for the gunner to cease.

His eyes met Hussam's in a last, silent salute as the helicopter wheels brushed the hilltop. The two Israelis raced aboard, ducking the blades. Then they were gone, the thud of the rotors diminishing. Hussam knelt watching the helicopter. It hugged the ground, flying fast beneath radar cover.

Slowly he stood and walked back down the hill, reaching the camp perimeter, oblivious to the clusters of people who followed for short distances, complaining loudly and animatedly before regrouping to chatter excitedly among themselves.

She was alone in the main street. It was where he last saw her before he scanned the hilltops to pinpoint the Israeli spotters. Rifle dangling from one hand, eyes cast down dejectedly, she stood beside the body of the *mukhtar*. Utterly calm and beautiful, she was stillness after the storm, water in the desert, and the sight of her replenished the strength and hope that weeks of anguish, hatred and fighting had wrung from his impoverished soul.

"I love you too," he said, recalling the silent message she mouthed at the gateway.

She did not move but said simply: "Hussam," and he walked to her, enfolding her in his arms as she let the gun fall, pressing her face to his chest. "I thought you were dead." She could not lift her head.

Hussam looked down at the *mukhtar*. "He prayed to be spared to see Palestine," he said.

"He saw it," she said. "He saw his home. He died happy."

He nodded. "Come. We're going to Qmrah, to get David." He bent to pick up her gun but she kept her arms by her sides, looking at it blankly as he held it out to her.

"I can't fight any more. I'm beaten."

He lowered the gun and smiled. "I never asked you to fight. I don't ask it now. Women were not made to fight."

She searched his face, lost for a moment. Then, decisively, she straightened her hunched shoulders, breathed deeply and took the gun.

Hussam rolled his eyes upwards. How could a woman be so stubborn? Once this was over he would have to do something about her, remind her who made the decisions, before she got completely out of hand.

"To Qmrah!" she said, turning and marching back up the street.

CHAPTER 18

It was rare for the Sultan to be seen standing. Now his great bulk almost filled the open French windows, his agitation obvious as he stared out unseeingly across the formal Persian-style gardens. His small, soft, manicured hands fiddled with a string of onyx worry beads.

A staccato of marching feet sounded outside and the door was flung open. Abd'allah, servant of God, turned to see a man pushed forward, handcuffed, flanked by two guards and pursued by the ever-perspiring Minister.

"Highness, this is the leader," he stammered, forgetting the formal address. The Sultan's astonishment was registered by an almost imperceptible raising of his eyebrows. He shuffled to where the group stood, the prisoner's eyes meeting his levelly, unashamed.

"General Aref Ayud!" he said, wheezing a sigh of disappointment. "My most trusted officer."

"The General has abused his position of trust, Highness," the Minister put in quickly and unnecessarily.

"A *coup d'etat*, Aref?" mused the Sultan, raising a silk handkerchief to his lips as if too mortified to utter more.

"He sought to turn your own army against you, most gracious Majesty."

The Sultan moved slowly to a large ornate chair, lowering himself with some difficulty until the last moment when he flopped heavily on the overstuffed seat, breathing hard with the effort and raising the handkerchief once more, this time to his forehead. "It's fortunate you were betrayed." He paused, looking away as if some disagreeable thing were about to happen. "Of course you're relieved both of position and rank." He signalled to the Minister who, with trembling hands and not without difficulty, ripped the epaulettes and insignia of General from Aref's uniform. "Who are your accomplices?" the Sultan demanded.

"There is no one else. I alone bear the guilt," Aref lied.

"Your loyalty is touching," said his Highness, "but your loyalty is misplaced."

"The boy, Highness. Do not forget the boy!"

The Sultan cast a patient look at his Minister. The man was a fool. How could he forget the boy, the son of Hussam the Traitor? "Ah, yes," he said, as if recalling something unimportant. "Where is the boy, Aref? You said you would bring him to me, yet you have not. Must we add kidnapping to your long list of crimes?"

269

Aref said nothing. The servant of God looked tired. "Aref, you were my friend. Don't make matters worse. I have a man who will make you talk. I surely don't need to tell you, of all people, how efficient he is."

"You're wasting your time."

"Oh, I think not. He so enjoys his work and, in your particular case, will earn an exceptionally attractive bonus if he succeeds. I don't doubt he will."

Aref was unyielding.

"Very well!" wheezed the Sultan, raising a pale hand to examine the nails. "Take him away."

***

The road to the docks was new and wide and generally under-used. It was just one of many recent monuments to the wealth of the little country whose ruler preferred to invest its income in grandiose, well publicised, frequently photographed public works, named mostly after himself. They included a massive international conference complex, municipal building, private hospital, various concrete bridges and tarmacadam dual carriageways such as this, appreciated only by the very rich and, in passing, by a few easily-impressed foreign visitors whose conducted tours carefully avoided the corrugated shanty towns devoid of sewers, fresh water or basic health care.

This particular foreign visitor was impressed only by the view on the seaward side. A bright, harsh sunlight sparkled on the azure water where massive tankers and cargo ships lay at anchorage, dotted at random about the deep, palm-fringed natural lagoon of Kahran harbour.

Jodi rode in the passenger seat next to Baseem. Their battered Peugeot was followed by a convoy of four trucks in an assortment of colours, sizes and makes. The first carried six *fedayeen*. The others were empty. Ahead, a low square concrete building, outside which a red and white double barrier barred the road, marked the entrance to the docks. The Peugeot slowed and stopped. Baseem got out and went to the window. Inside two men kept up an animated conversation, apparently oblivious of the convoy's arrival until one, still shouting towards his comrade, slid the window aside. Greetings of peace were exchanged and Baseem produced an official-looking piece of paper. The man leaned out of the window, looking back along the line of trucks and began jabbering out the usual hindrances which preceded an exchange of *baksheesh*. From his shirt pocket Baseem took a thick bundle of American dollars. The man stopped speaking in mid-sentence. His eyes widened. It was a very large sum.

"No questions," she heard Baseem say, "and no obstacles." The man shook his head and, hesitatingly, held out one hand. Baseem split the bundle of notes into two, giving one bundle to the man. "You get the other half when we leave."

The window slid shut. A few moments later the man appeared from the doorway and climbed into the back of the car while his friend raised one half of the barrier and waved the convoy through. Now looking very official, peaked cap atop his pale khaki uniform embellished with gold braid, the man directed Baseem across a wide expanse of concrete towards a cluster of clean, new corrugated sheds. He threw a passing glance at Jodi, veiled and shrouded in a black shapeless garment which gave away nothing but the colour of her eyes. These she lowered demurely as the Koran instructed. The official would not speak to her or inquire about her. To show the slightest interest in another man's woman provoked suspicion, jealousy, anger and, often, violence.

A locomotive pulled a lazy line of freight trucks along tracks set into the concrete, dwarfing the half dozen camels, heavily laden with wooden crates, waiting patiently for it to pass. Otherwise the dockyard was empty. It was the time of the noon prayer.

"There!" The sharp voice of the official startled her. He pointed towards a warehouse with large double doors painted amateurishly in the brilliant turquoise blue so beloved of the Arabs. The splash of brightness and the Arabic number 12 painted messily in the same colour on the concrete beside the door betrayed Arab disregard for both drab geometric simplicity and the perfect finishing touch. Baseem stopped in front of the doors and the official leapt out. With a key on a large ring he opened the big padlock and slid the door aside.

Slightly to his surprise, Jodi pushed past him and was first in. Only then did he notice how tall she was and how scandalously short the garment she wore, revealing her ankles and several inches of leg. The warehouse was cool and dark after the blistering sun but Jodi's eyes gradually adjusted to the light filtering in through small square corrugated skylights. On either side, wooden crates were stacked from floor to ceiling. She recognised them and for a second was back in the warehouse at Armature, where the weapons were crated to order for export.

Hussam had told her what to get; mortars, rocket launchers, assault rifles, heavy machine guns, grenades, ammunition. It was too risky for him to come. He was well-known here, too easily recognised. He didn't want his unexpected presence in Qmrah revealed before he was fully armed and ready.

Jodi was the logical choice for the mission. He had taken her first to Jamal. The mechanic was busy shouting at someone on the telephone over the din of a truck engine when Hussam cut the ignition, grinning broadly as Jamal turned to see why the noise had stopped. He stood speechless, the handset still in his raised hand, though not at his ear, before slamming down the phone and rushing to embrace his friend.

The workshop filled Hussam with nostalgia for the days before his life changed, those days when he had thought his work dreary, his life unfulfilled, when he and Jamal, stripped to the waist, worked like *kaffirs* on Hijazi's broken-down Jeeps and trucks.

Jamal insisted on serving coffee, pressing the customary three cups on him before Hussam was able to decline and get down to business.

He punctuated Hussam's story with cries of outrage and anguish. Jamal believed his friend without question. "The people know you went to fight Israel, Hussam. There was great excitement. They said you would soon defeat the Zionists. But we thought it was they who did this terrible thing at Bab'ullah, not the Sultan."

"I thought so too. We were all wrong."

"Many would fight with you Hussam. Let me spread the word."

"No!" Hussam was adamant. He had fifty of Nuri's men, sufficient to storm the palace. Surprise was vital, more so here than at Sufa. "The Sultan has an army, tanks, aircraft. And he has my son."

"The Sheikh is the servant of Satan," Jamal muttered. "Allah will help you Hussam and so will I. Take what you want. Take everything I have. Take it for the bread and salt that is between us."

When Hussam had stayed in Kahran it was as Jamal's guest. There was indeed much bread and salt between them and a man could refuse nothing to one with whom he broke bread and shared salt. Hussam laughed, slapping Jamal's hand. He needed transport for arms and for men. Jodi sat quietly in the background. Hussam called her forward. Jamal was shy. He had stolen several quick glances at her. Who wouldn't?

"She'll go with the trucks but mustn't attract attention. Your wife will have some suitable clothes."

"Yes, but she is tall," remarked Jamal. "My wife is little."

"When she's sitting in the car no one will see."

Now, as she strode purposefully up and down the warehouse, examining the English labels, Jodi became aware of the dock official's eyes on her legs. She threw him a withering glance but realised the veil obscured most of it and, to his astonishment, pulled it aside. Now he stared at her face. She decided to ignore him.

"These two!" she called to Baseem. The first truck was backed up to the door, its passengers jumping down to form a human chain and load the crates. "And these!" She indicated another pile. The crates were too big to lift. The port official offered to call a fork lift truck but Baseem wouldn't risk it, smashing open the boxes, unloading the contents directly into the waiting trucks. Within an hour the vehicles were loaded. Splintered planks and packaging, all that remained of the broken crates, littered the floor.

"Go with the convoy," she told Baseem. "I'll follow in the car after I've hidden this mess. It'll give us away if anyone finds it."

Baseem was reluctant. "We'll wait. Hussam would kill me if anything happened to you."

The tension made her snap: "Baseem, I'm a big girl. I can look after myself! If you don't know that by now..." She stopped, relenting because of his genuine concern. "Look, we can't afford the time. Hussam needs the guns. And he needs you. Nothing will happen to me." She smiled. "Give me the money. I'll give it him when I leave." She cocked her head towards the official who for a long time had sat on a crate chain-smoking.

Baseem beckoned him. "We're going. The woman will stay to clear up. Help her." He took hold of the man's lapel and pulled him close. "You know we are *fedayeen*? Palestinians?" The man nodded rapidly. "If anything happens to her we will return to kill you!" His eyes still on the man, he released him and reached into his own shirt pocket, drawing out the wad of notes and passing them to Jodi. Then he turned and marched out.

Jodi found a space from which crates had been removed, where they could hide the packaging. She heard the trucks drive off as she scooped up armfuls of debris, dumping it behind the crates and instructing the official to do the same. He was reluctant to let a woman tell him what to do but this was obviously no ordinary woman. From her accent she was English, like the guns. He grunted. There were women and there were Western women! The Arabs called them "the third sex" and certainly this one was strange. Even when veiled like an Arab she gave orders to *fedayeen* and was obeyed.

They shovelled the last splinters of evidence into the space and heaved crates in front and above it. Jodi stood back to examine their work. It would do. Unless the crates were moved, no one would notice anything amiss. She smiled at the official, who stared back at her, and handed him the money which seemed to burn his fingers, so quickly did he pocket it.

"*Salaam aleykom*!" The greeting came from the open doorway and Jodi spun round to see the figure of a man silhouetted against the brilliant daylight. "What's going on?"

She froze, knowing the voice but unable to identify it. Inside her, horror and revulsion stirred and an unreasonable panic rose. She turned her back to him and, with hands which shook violently for no reason she could immediately identify, fixed the veil tightly across her face. Hearing his footsteps approach, she lowered her eyes and assumed the humble attitude of an Arab woman in male company. She tried to walk aside and around him to the door but he took her arm. Now she knew! Even before she raised her eyes she knew! He must hear her heart. He must feel her shake.

"Blue eyes!" he said thoughtfully. "How unusual for a Qmrahi, or even a Palestinian." He pulled the veil slowly from her face, smiling with genuine and terrifying pleasure as he, in turn, recognised her.

She broke free, running for the door. He shouted and a shot rang out. Then she was in the hot sunshine, blinded by the whiteness of the concrete as she stumbled into the arms of a man. It was a Qmrahi soldier.

"Hit immediately! Hit to kill! A man is stronger than you. You may not get a second chance." Hussam's words spilled out from her memory. She brought her knee up hard in his groin. He let go but another was on her and she slammed her straightened fingers into his eye, racing for the Peugeot before three more fell on her, pinning her arms, holding her feet as she kicked and bit and struggled and screamed, howling as they carried her back to him.

He waited until she was silent, till the futile struggle tired her and they had to hold her erect because her own legs somehow wouldn't stand.

"No!" she whispered. "No!"

"Oh yes, *habibi*, yes!" Kushi grinned.

***

Aref barely felt the blows. His body throbbed, his face burned.

"That's enough for now. No point in wearing ourselves out." The hands which held him flung him to the floor. He heard a rustle of paper then a match strike. There was the smell of brimstone and a newly lit cigarette. For a time it was quiet except for his own rasping breath.

The heavy metal door swung open and excited voices shouted before it banged shut. People seemed suddenly to crowd the room.

"Get out, all of you!" It was Kushi. "Who's this?" Aref tensed. The black hood was torn from his head. Though the cell was lit by only one bulb, the sudden light seemed bright and he blinked painful swollen eyelids. "Ah, General! I'm afraid you'll have to wait. Something more pressing has come up."

Kushi turned and Aref saw the woman, tall and blonde and terrified, though she held her chin high. The Palestinian had formed an elite corps of terror from the thugs who were with him at the Bab'ullah massacre. It was between two of these that she stood. Two more, those who had so methodically beaten him, hovered uncertainly. "Get out and take him with you," Kushi ordered, then changed his mind. "Wait!" He paced the length of the cell thoughtfully, shrugging off his jacket, rolling up the sleeves of his khaki shirt, unhooking the holster which held his Beretta, making himself comfortable in a swivel chair. "Do you know this woman?" Aref shook his head. "She's the woman of *el Hussam*, the one whose son you hold." He appraised Jodi. "She's young, beautiful, yes?" Aref was silent and Kushi laughed. "She won't look like this when we finish with her." He turned to the guard. "He can stay but make sure he keeps quiet." The soldier gagged Aref. "And out of deference to the lady's modesty, it's only right you wear this." Kushi replaced the black hood. "Use your imagination, General. You have a lovely wife. Imagine it is she I have here. I have a way with women, don't I, *habibi*?"

Jodi felt dizzy. She swayed and felt the grip of the two men tighten. He was like a child with a toy whose lack of response in no way spoiled the game.

"Remember Sufa? Remember what I did with these?" he held up his hands, "and this?" he reached into his pocket and produced a cigar, lighting it with a gold lighter and inhaling with deep satisfaction. "You told me everything then. Everything I wanted to hear." He smiled as if recalling some pleasant, faraway memory. "But at Sufa I was only playing. Today I am working: working for Sheikh Abd'allah until Amin recalls me."

He approached her, almost whispering, his lips close to her ear. "Why are you here, *habibi*? Why? Huh? My men were watching the port you know. They saw Amin's soldiers come for the guns. Why were you with them? Did Amin send you?"

Jodi's mind raced. He didn't know Amin was dead. "Yes," she said.

He turned her face to him, looking searchingly into her eyes before grinning and shaking his head. "You think I don't know Amin? You think I believe the kidnapper sends his hostage to collect the ransom?" He roared with laughter though it was cold and mirthless and ceased abruptly. "Amin would not even let you live. Your salvation is Hussam. Isn't that so?" His face became expressionless. The game ended. "Where is he?"

She didn't answer. He clamped the cigar between his teeth, reaching with one hand to touch her throat where a small round scar showed above the dress.

He pulled the neckline down to reveal another, then with both hands ripped the dress apart, pushing it back over her shoulders to look with detached interest at her naked body.

"They've healed well. But you will always carry memories of me, *habibi*." He walked to a metal cupboard, opening it, still talking as he reached inside, removing a long, flat box and placing it on a table. "No more scars, not outside anyway. Here we are sophisticated. We have drugs such as the Syrians use on Israeli pilots. They take away your sight, your speech and your hearing, just temporarily. Then we work on you. You can't scream, you can't even tell your secret to stop us, it's locked inside with all your terror until the drug wears off. Many are mad by then, but they talk."

He returned to her, smiling obscenely. "But those are not for you, *habibi*. They're for the Jews who are cold and unfeeling. Your body is warm, responsive." His hand softly stroked the skin from her shoulder to her breast. She shuddered and with a massive effort fought to get free. "Tie her down!"

In the corner Aref struggled frantically, giving strangled cries as he tried to break the handcuffs. Kushi kicked him hard in the stomach. "Patience, General. Your turn will come. Then we shall have both father and son."

Kushi turned from him, speaking softly now to the woman, in a tone which terrorised his victims. But to Aref, the Palestinian sounded less dispassionate than usual. "I'd like so much to please you. Yet you make me hurt you." He sighed. "Why? Come, talk to me. I only want your memories. Oh, and I want Hussam. I want him to see me finish something he interrupted a long time ago at Kibbutz Hashemesh."

✳✳✳

On the ridge Hussam and Baseem faced each other. Baseem was desolate. "I shouldn't have left her." Hussam watched him in silence, looking away at last towards Kahran. Where was she? "I'll go back," Baseem said. "I'll kill that miserable dog. I said I would."

Hussam put a hand on his arm. "I've sent Kamel. We must wait." He returned to the camp where the weaponry was already unpacked, assembled and distributed. The men sat in groups, talking excitedly, laughing, ready for action, armed to the teeth with the best the world could offer. Jodi had done well.

He didn't notice Nooria especially, until Mahmoud rose from one group, taking her hand and pulling her behind him to Hussam. She was dressed in khaki fatigues which, though small, were baggy on her. The others turned to watch, nudging each other and grinning.

"Hussam! See our little soldier?" Mahmoud smiled delightedly.

He looked her up and down. "What are you doing?"

Nooria blushed, lowering her eyes.

"She's *feda'i* now. She wants to come with us." Mahmoud looked pleased with himself.

"Is this true?" Hussam spoke to Nooria. She nodded enthusiastically, still blushing. "You're my sister."

Mahmoud pointed to where Ali and Ahmed sat. "They're your brothers. They are *fedayeen*."

"She's still a child."

Nooria walked to him, gently taking both his hands and looking up shyly into his eyes. "I am old enough to marry."

"Old enough to shoot too. Watch." Mahmoud strode purposefully to a heap of discarded tins, emptied at lunch. He piled them into a neat pyramid and returned with an assault rifle, giving it to Nooria. "Show him," he said.

With three short bursts she demolished the tins which flew away in a cloud of dust. A cheer went up from the men. When the dust cleared one tin remained. Raising the stock to her shoulder and aiming professionally, Nooria fired once, striking it near its base. It zinged upwards and back. The men cheered again.

Hussam looked in astonishment at his sister. Her long black hair was drawn back in a single plait. She breathed excitedly, flashing gazelle-like eyes beneath long black lashes. Her smile was as captivating as it had been when she was a baby. He had watched her grow and she was right. She was no longer a child. One glance at any man in this camp could tell him that. She flicked the safety catch and held the gun out to him.

"Keep it," he said. Why not? After all, one of his best soldiers was a woman and the whole world was mad anyway.

She leapt at him, flinging her free arm around his neck and stretching to kiss his cheek. Mahmoud beamed, giving Nooria a congratulatory slap on the back. "I'll look after her," he promised.

Nooria pushed him playfully. "I shall look after you." The soldiers roared with approval.

"Women!" Mahmoud shrugged. Women! thought Hussam, turning to look back toward Kahran. God of Compassion where was she? He had not planned to attack until nightfall but if Jodi were captured: if she were interrogated. He closed his eyes at the thought. He had to prepare for the worst or was it the best: that she would talk. At least if she talked she might be spared. But if she talked the palace would be defended. The Sultan might flee. He must bring the attack forward.

Baseem, who still stared intently towards the city, called him. A vehicle was coming, throwing up clouds of dust from the rough track winding up to the ridge. Hussam raised the field glasses. It was Kamel. Beside him, the passenger seat of the pick-up was empty. When the vehicle drew up Kamel shrugged. "I couldn't get close. The port is crawling with soldiers."

Hussam decided. "Get in the trucks!" he shouted. "We're going in now."

✳✳✳

God, don't let him turn me into an animal! Not this time! Keep me sane but most of all keep me quiet! She lay suspended between consciousness and shock-induced sleep, the brain's anaesthesia for pain. But Kushi never quite let her sleep. She dozed, relaxing, her mind drifting away across interlocking hills of green fields before pain summoned, beginning a long way away, drawing her to it with increasing speed until it struck her with such force her whole body shook wide awake under the impact.

The scene changed to Bab'ullah: the black bedouin tents. Hussam was smiling down at her, his rough, warm hands caressing her face. "Where is he?" he said. She blinked, the face blurred. Behind it the blinding sun became a bare light bulb then blurred again. "Is he here? In Qmrah?" She didn't understand. Who? Who? "Hussam." There was a trace of impatience in the voice. "We know he is here. You have only to nod. The pain will stop." She smelled cigar smoke. That was bad, though she couldn't remember why. The rough hands still held her face. "Just nod your head if he is here. Like this. It's easy to do."

No! No! No what? No thank you! No chance! No god but Allah! No place like home! Or just plain no, if you like, or even if you don't like! No! It was a sound without sense. She didn't know what it meant, didn't understand why she had to say it, only knew she must. She clung to the sound, the shape of her lips, the way her tongue touched the roof of her mouth when she said it and said it and said it. Our lives are predestined. The next second is a void. She fell into it, floating, falling, but the pain pulled her back, bore her up through the blackness till she broke consciousness once more.

Above the ceiling was stark concrete. She turned her head from side to side. Was she still in this cell where she was an age ago? He sat beside her, his head level with hers, resting on his arms which were folded on the table. She began to drift into sleep again but he took hold of her chin, shaking her head till her eyes opened. "You've changed, *habibi*." He looked disappointed. "Where is the bird that sang to me at Sufa?"

"No." It was all she knew how to say.

He stood. "Hussam is in Qmrah. That I know, whether you say it or not. Already the search for him is on. It's only a matter of time before he's found. But he's armed, is he not? Armed with Amin's guns! If you leave it to the Sultan's army, he will fight and be killed. If, on

286

the other hand, you speak, we may take him by surprise, alive. Don't you want him alive?"

Jodi regarded him dully through half closed eyes. Then she began to laugh, quickly forgetting what was funny but continuing to laugh because it was a new sound and pleasant.

He hit her across the face with his open hand. But she knew now he wouldn't break her. He might kill her, *insh Allah*, but that was different. It was merely loss of life, not loss of soul. That was hers to keep, whatever he did, wherever in eternity he sent her.

Kushi saw the change in her immediately. She couldn't take any more today. He cursed. The prospect of failure enraged him, particularly with a woman, this woman. Had he misjudged? She was stronger, much stronger, both physically and mentally than she was before. He could kill her, but not yet, not yet! He would wait till they brought him Hussam. Meanwhile, she had other uses.

Furiously he turned on Aref, kicking him violently, without warning, so the body convulsed, jerking into a protective foetal position. "Well, General, have you heard enough? What I do next is not for your ears." He spoke to the guards. "Take him out. Get his wife." He turned back to Jodi, "Now leave me with her and whatever you hear, whatever happens, I want no interruptions."

Jodi felt the ropes tighten, then fall away as he cut them with a knife. She was free but she could not move. He jerked her up violently. "Time for play," he grinned, drawing her to him. His breath was vile. "Woman of Hussam," he sneered, "since you won't tell me where he is, show me how you please him."

He pressed his open mouth on hers, forcing his tongue down her throat. She could feel his erect penis. He was holding her against it, rubbing it with her body, his pelvis thrusting in short little movements to heighten his pleasure, strengthen the urge. Though she wanted to fight him, to cry out, her defences wouldn't work. As he released her she fell to the floor. He unbuttoned his trousers and pulled her up by the hair, thrusting his penis into her mouth. She couldn't breathe. The panic charged her reflexes and her hands grabbed his wrists, struggling to push him away. But the weakness of her resistance excited him, his thrusts accelerating till, gathering every ounce of strength and determination she bit hard, tearing flesh, tasting blood.

He recoiled violently, shrieking in agony, throwing her away from him as he doubled up, pressing both hands to his groin. Jodi stared around dazed. On the table was the knife he used to free her. Hanging on with one hand; she felt about on top with the other, praying for strength, praying for consciousness.

Her hand closed on the hilt and she plunged the blade into his stomach, ripping upwards as Hussam taught her. He sank to his knees, silent, his eyes meeting hers in surprise, one hand moving to clutch the gaping wound which spilled red entrails. And now she couldn't stop herself, slamming the knife into his chest, his throat, his back as he fell forwards, attacking again and again and again long after he was still, yelling and crying with every blow. When she stopped she was kneeling, both hands on the knife which protruded from his back.

She shrank away suddenly as if the crime were not hers and she had stumbled unsuspecting on some scene of carnage. But her hands and body were wet with his blood. She couldn't stand and only now felt the agony of each move, of the effort required and the tiredness, the nausea which swept her. She could sleep for ever, but she mustn't! Why mustn't she? She just mustn't!

Holding onto the table, Jodi pulled herself to her feet. She leaned against it for a long time, not trusting her legs, rocking slowly from one to the other, testing the strength in each. She forced her feet to move, grimacing at each step.

Reason began to return. Kushi's jacket still hung on the wall but there was nothing else to wear. She looked down at his body. She would have to strip it. Methodically, devoid of feeling, she unlaced his boots, pulled off the socks and trousers. There was little blood on his trousers. Mostly it was on the shirt and this she couldn't touch. Everything was too big. She belted the trousers tightly then reached for the jacket and holster which held the Beretta. She must look like nothing on earth. But she was more dangerous than she had ever been in her life. The pain of her bruised body, the effort of staying awake, the deep subconscious hurt, fused into a silent and unassailable rage. Every trick of escape and killing she knew, she would use to get out of this hell.

Opening the door a fraction she looked along the dim corridor. It was deserted but muted voices and occasional laughter came from an open door. She stumbled along, trying to run, stopping just short of the door, flattening herself against the wall and peering into the room. There were two of them, the two Kushi dismissed. She couldn't get past the door without them seeing. Jodi made a commitment and, raising the Beretta, strolled almost casually into the room, killing the nearest outright, then turning the pistol on the other, who had risen. He fell wounded, screaming. Coldly she put the gun to his head and fired again. Then she was aware of a third, sitting against the wall by the door. She spun round.

Aref, still handcuffed, was struggling to stand. She stared at him blankly before slowly raising the gun. Aref saw she was deathly pale, eyes dull, movements sluggish, deliberate. He knew the look, like soldiers who in battle temporarily lost reason, judgement. The mind stuck like a needle on a damaged record. Mechanically, it could kill and kill again, friend or foe, until the trauma ended. But though her finger squeezed the trigger, she did not fire.

"Where's the boy?" she asked so calmly she might be asking the time.

He was ashamed. "It's too late. I already told them," he said. "What he did to you; I couldn't let my wife..."

Weariness swept her again. She lowered the gun and walked to the door, looking out along the corridor. It was still empty. No one ran to investigate screams and shots in this place.

"Take me with you," he said.

She looked genuinely surprised. "Why?"

"I can help you escape," he said. "Until today I ran this army. Few know of my arrest."

Absently she touched the torn shoulders of his shirt where the epaulettes had been, then looked down at the handcuffs. "He has the key!" He nodded to the soldier whose brains she'd blown out. She turned the corpse, feeling in the pockets, finding a small key on a ring and returning to Aref to release him. His wrists and face were swollen and bleeding.

"You're a mess," she observed. "No one will believe you're still a General."

"It's our best chance," he said. "Just walk with me, one pace behind, like an aide." He took a peaked cap from a peg, pulling it forward to shade his face. Then, wincing with pain, gently laid a jacket across his shoulders, pocketing a gun and handing her a chequered *kaffiyeh*, such as the ordinary soldiers wore. As she covered her hair he took a cane from the table, placing it under his arm, straightening his back in the best military manner. She wanted to laugh. They were like pantomime soldiers, a comic, pathetic sight. But he was right. It was their best chance.

"They brought me in by the main entrance. There is another but it's guarded. It opens onto a courtyard where my vehicle is parked. When we reach it get in the passenger seat. I'll drive."

She followed him along the corridor, through a door. He turned left and she saw daylight beyond a high metal gate. Outside a soldier lounged on a straight-backed wooden chair. He looked out towards the sunshine and didn't see them approach.

"Open up!" Aref barked, rapping the bars with his cane and turning to face Jodi, as if impatient. The soldier jumped, reaching for his keys, hastily opening the door. He gaped in amazement as he glimpsed Aref's face. "Sir.."

"Silence. Don't report this to anyone. I don't want it known a prisoner struck me."

"No, sir!" The soldier was at attention, his eyes directly ahead. Jodi slipped past quickly. The sudden shock of the late afternoon heat and glare made her head spin. They marched purposefully to a hard-top Land Rover. She almost fell in, slamming the door with relief. At least the glass would help obscure the view to outsiders of the odd couple inside. Beside her, the General was having difficulty just turning the wheel but that was his problem, she could barely hold herself upright as the vehicle lurched forward. One obstacle remained, the barrier at the entrance to the army post. A soldier, assault rifle slung on webbing over his shoulder, stepped out, motioning them to stop.

Aref leaned out of the window, shouting: "Idiot. Can't you see I'm hurt. I must get to the hospital." The soldier hesitated. "Quick! Or I'll have you on a charge!" Turning, the soldier shouted to another who raised the barrier. Both saluted as the Land Rover sped beneath it and out onto the shimmering black road.

***

The heat of the workshop was oppressive. They stood or sat wherever there was room, silent, waiting: awaiting the order he could not give. To come so far! To be so close!

Hussam's worst fears were confirmed. Around the palace there was intense military activity. Tanks and sandbagged gun emplacements were thick outside the high wall encircling the palace grounds. On the battlements armed sentries patrolled while a helicopter hovered overhead. Reconnoitring earlier he viewed the gate through which he'd intended taking the delivery truck with his soldiers hidden inside. The Qmrahis searched every vehicle before turning it away. Nothing was allowed through. He handed the field glasses to Baseem who cursed under his breath. There was no chance now of snatching the boy with a mere 50 men, however well-armed. They couldn't take on the whole Qmrahi army. Even in the streets the search was on. Armoured cars cruised the highways while troops from armed personnel carriers searched buildings and mounted road blocks.

Back at Jamal's, Hussam looked around in frustration. Soon the Qmrahis would search here too. They must retreat, if only temporarily. He would have to rethink the attack.

Kamel distracted him. He stood by the door, on guard. Now he called urgently to Hussam. An army Land Rover was pulling into the yard, driven erratically, scraping a low stone wall as it turned and juddcred and stalled. Inside were two soldiers. Hussam took up position with his rifle, motioning the others back. The vehicle stopped.

"Take the driver," he told Kamel. "I'll take the other." Through the sights he saw only the chequered *kaffiyeh*. His finger tightened on the trigger but the soldier stumbled, falling as the vehicle door opened, and momentarily Hussam lost his mark. Quickly he resighted, steadying his aim. Now the face turned to him and with a cry he lowered the gun, putting out a restraining hand to Kamel.

"It may be a trick," Kamel warned.

"Hold your fire!" Hussam ordered. "Let them come. Keep the man covered." He was in torment watching her. Plainly she needed support. The man seemed little better. Though he tried to help her, she staggered, falling against a truck, steadying herself against a wall. Hussam's eyes scanned the road, the skyline, every building. It seemed a long time before she reached him.

He grabbed her, pulling her away from Aref who was shoved aside, pinned against the wall by Kamel's rifle. There was no resistance in her, nor any response to his embrace. She lay against him, held by him, stroked by him. When he looked down at her, she barely showed recognition. He pulled off the *kaffiyeh*, examining her pale face, the empty eyes. "What have they done to you?"

Jodi blinked. She knew there was something, something she had to tell him. One thing she had fought oblivion to say. But it wasn't what he wanted to know. "Who did this?"

She must remember. It was vital she remember. He had to know. She felt his arms around her and tried to pull free. "Hussam..."

"Tell me!"

"Hussam, the radio station, you must..."

"Jodi..."

"Listen, please listen," she gasped. Listen carefully because I don't know if I can make it make sense, she added silently. "Take the television and radio stations. They won't be guarded." He looked puzzled. "Hussam, it's not just David any more. It's this whole damned rotten country. Hussam, the people love you. Jamal said they'd follow you. Take over radio and television. Tell the people!" Her eyes closed. Did he understand? She opened them again, clutching his shirt. "Hussam, I'm a journalist. Believe me, words will win this war." Did she say it or did she dream it? So much hurt, so much hate, the smell of Kushi still on her, his blood, the blood of the two soldiers, no three, don't forget the Israeli! Please, no more fighting. No blood. The world is bleeding to death. She waved vaguely towards Aref. "General, the coup. Tell him!" Now, now she could let go. Now she could sleep.

Her head fell back as he lifted her and looked at last at Aref, his bruised face resolute as he spoke. "We have little time, *el Hussam*."

CHAPTER 19

Muhammed bin Kabina drew deeply on the water pipe, half squatting, half reclining on the rush seat, his attention on the backgammon board. It was early evening. Throughout the Arab world the coffee houses were filling with men. It was a time for relaxing, socialising, meeting friends, arguing and generally putting the world to rights. From the radio, Umm Kalthoum's impassioned song all but drowned the vigorous shouted conversations. The air was heavy with smoke and the aroma of fresh roasted coffee mingled with cardamom.

Tonight the talk was all of the army, the scandalous behaviour of soldiers who, throughout the afternoon had stopped traffic, searched houses, patrolled the streets and interrogated citizens. The excitement reached new heights as rumours circulated of the return of Hussam to Qmrah.

Bin Kabina was more accustomed to listen than to talk and it was he who first noticed the abrupt halt of Umm Kalthoum's progress through the entire Rubaiyat of Omar Khayyam. For the first time in twenty years the radio was silent. He raised a hand to those around him and the hush which fell on them gradually spread across the room and out onto the narrow dark street. Passers-by gathered at the door.

In the plush officers' mess the same hush was evident. All day, since word of Aref's arrest began to spread, a fatalistic gloominess had prevailed at army headquarters. There was intense activity at the top. Several young officers were questioned. Then came the whisper of Aref's escape. Now, here he was, speaking to them from the television. A gasp went up at the sight of his injured face. Haltingly, glancing occasionally at a single sheet of paper, Aref told the story: the massacre, the young hostage, the planned coup, the brutality and torture. "Even as I speak Hussam waits to launch the assault which will free his son from the tyrant Abd'allah. Many support him. Many want justice and freedom for our land. Many suffer because of the Sultan's corruption and greed. I call on them now to rally to Hussam!"

In the coffee house the hush was broken by a cry of "*Allah akbah*! God is great!"

"What will you do bin Kabina?" his colleague asked nervously from the other side of the backgammon board. He was jostled as men pushed past, hurrying out onto the street, shouting and laughing. He knew his friend to be moderate, a careful man who measured the consequences of any action carefully before making a move. If men like bin Kabina rebelled, the Sultan's rule was over.

"Do?" Bin Kabina considered it calmly. "I shall go for my rifle."

* * *

"Highness, Highness!" the Minister shrieked, bursting through the double doors unannounced and followed at a discreet distance by the beautiful youth.

The Sultan was seated at supper. Before him the table bore plates of sumptuous sweet and savoury delights and, though Islam forbade it, a tall glass of Madeira nestled in his raised hand, barely moistening his lips. He lowered it, shocked at the Minister's outrageous intrusion.

"Highness. Hussam has called on the people to join him. The traitor Aref Ayud, speaks even now on our broadcast network. He's calling for the army to mutiny, to turn their guns on the palace!"

The tall glass shattered on the floor. The Sultan rose and moved faster than the Minister had ever known to the tall windows opening onto the balcony. In the darkness there were shouts. Just a few. But, unmistakably, things were not as they should be. The sound of running feet on the gravel beneath, a door slamming, the disturbed screech of birds from the aviary, small sounds, here and there converged on him, feeding his fear.

He hurried back into the room, to the bright lights, the loyal and familiar faces, now anxious, eyes shifting. "Where is the boy?"

"We have him, Highness." The Minister gave a shout and a guard entered, carrying a boy who squirmed and kicked, demanding to be put down. The soldier lowered him to his feet, holding him firmly by his jacket. The lad stared around. There was fear in his eyes but there was courage and pride, qualities the Sultan admired. He looked at him and loved him. Under different circumstances the child would be a sensuous diversion to the dreary palace routine. What was the old saying? A woman for children, a goat for satisfaction and a young boy for pleasure! Crude but succinct!

Outside the noises were increasing, fusing into a growing dissent. The shouts were loud now, coming from far away, beyond the high walls. There was a sound of motor engines and cars hooting, then suddenly the night was brilliant with flares which burst over the grounds, drifting lazily in the gentle breeze. The Minister, his tunic damp, his face running with sweat, rushed to the window.

Your Highness!" He turned in horror to the Sultan. "The tanks! Their guns are aimed at the palace."

Hussam stayed hidden until the tank turrets began turning. Then under a flag of truce, flanked by Kamel and Mahmoud, he approached the officer. The officer saluted. He knew Hussam by reputation only but instinct told him this was he.

"Hussam, we are loyal to General Aref Ayud. He's called on us to support you which we do gladly. Allah be with you."

As the flares died, groups of people were gathering, converging on the palace walls, nervously silent at first, then beginning to shout excitedly. Torches and hastily-scrawled banners were waved. The small groups merged into larger ones. There was whistling, music and banging from anything that would make noise, wild gunfire from the occasional rifle.

Within the walls, through the dark stillness of the Persian gardens, Hussam moved noiselessly. The palace was quiet, though it glowed with lights. Upstairs, beyond a wide balcony, there was intense activity. He signalled the advance to halt. Shapes appeared in the balcony doorway. Raising the Dragunov, Hussam took aim. There were two of them, soldiers of the Household Guard, one of whom swung a child onto the marble balustrade, holding a pistol to his head. Hussam lowered the rifle. Slowly, a massive figure shuffled onto the balcony, remaining behind the child. Using him as a shield.

"Hussam! Traitor of Qmrah. I know you're there."

Below, Hussam was silent, watching David, watching the soldiers.

"Hussam, I say!" The wheezing voice was impatient. "Must your son know you are a coward, afraid to show yourself?" Still Hussam did not move. Beyond the walls the clamour of the crowd grew. "Listen carefully," the Sultan's voice was shrill. "I offer you an exchange. My life for the boy's. Is it agreed?"

Now Hussam showed himself. In his son's eyes he saw shock, then recognition, then desperation. He lurched forwards as if he would leap into Hussam's arms.

"*Abu! Abu!*" David struggled, slipping on the balustrade, dragged back by the soldiers. "*Abu!*" he screamed. The horror of Bab'ullah, the confusion of the ensuing weeks and the relief of seeing at last the father he had never ceased believing would return, burst from him.

His child's grief nearly broke Hussam. He would agree to anything. The boy's lonely cries rent the darkness and no one reached to comfort him. He sobbed unrestrained, his little arms stretching out hopelessly towards his father, way beyond reach. The guard carried him, still screaming, inside. Sheikh Abd'allah's face assumed a smugness born of the assurance that Hussam could do nothing. "Your answer!" he demanded.

"It's agreed. Release the boy."

The Sultan smiled. "When my safety is assured."

"I assure it." Within the palace his son's cries diminished.

"Perhaps you do," the Sultan concurred, "but what about them?" He pointed to the clamouring mob beyond the gates.

Hussam was impatient, his only concern for David. "Tell me what you want."

"A helicopter to transport me to the airport, and my plane ready to fly me from Qmrah. Your son will be my security until I land safely at my destination. Then, and only then, will he be released." A rifle bullet from the crowd struck the balustrade, shattering the marble. The Sultan cried out, hit in the hand by a fragment sent flying. He turned quickly and hurried back inside.

Hussam beckoned Kamel. "You heard?" Kamel nodded. "Then make the arrangements quickly. Tell the officer. The crowd must be held back at least until the helicopter is safely away."

"You'll let him escape?"

"Do it!" Then he summoned Mahmoud. Nooria was with him as she had been since they broke camp. "We're going to the airport," Hussam told them.

"How?" Mahmoud indicated the surging crowd now battering the gate.

"There's more than one gate."

The control tower was the obvious vantage point. It looked down on the smooth tarmac runway, long enough to accommodate the largest jets, though rarely bearing anything bigger than cargo Constellations or the daily Boeing 707 flights of the Air Qmrah passenger airline. One such craft, furnished as a travelling palace, was permanently reserved for the infrequent use of the Sultan and manned by a crew whose loyalty to him was unswerving. It stood away from the buildings, though well within range of the Dragunov which now bore high powered infra-red sights.

From over the city came the thud of the approaching helicopter. It showed no lights. Even with David aboard the Sultan wanted the risk of attack minimised.

Beneath one wing of the Boeing, a tanker of the airport's aviation service fleet pulled away. Refuelling was complete. The generator lead fell away from the fuselage and through the cockpit window Hussam caught sight of the Sultan's crew checking instrumentation. The servant of God wanted all haste once he arrived at the airport. Everything was ready. In the cab of the vehicle-mounted boarding steps, the driver sat waiting to speed clear at a signal immediately the passengers were aboard. Above, in the open doorway a young woman, her long, dark hair swept back tidily beneath an Air Qmrah stewardess's cap, adjusted her neat uniform.

Cautiously the helicopter circled once, touching down just a short distance from the Boeing.

From the stairs to the control tower came a scuffling and Mahmoud appeared, breathless, a bag in one hand, his gun in the other. Hussam looked at him quizzically and he nodded, smiling. Behind them Baseem trained his gun on the three air traffic controllers, just in case they should think of communicating a warning to the aircraft.

Hussam raised the rifle, steadying it on the sill of the open window. The sight found the helicopter, rotor blades beating as the door opened and steps were lowered.

First to emerge were two Household Guards. Rifles ready, they took up defensive positions at the foot of the boarding steps. For a moment they surveyed the scene then signalled to the helicopter. A third emerged, carrying David. He stood with the others by the steps as a group filed hesitantly from the helicopter, looking around nervously and hurrying towards the Boeing. Among them Hussam spotted the massive figure of Sheikh Abd'allah flanked and supported by two guards. His finger tightened on the trigger as he begged Allah for strength not to fire yet! Yet!

Quickly the party mounted the steps. The Sheikh stumbled once and was unceremoniously bundled upwards as those behind him rushed for the safety of the plane. At the top they ignored the young stewardess who welcomed them. Now only the three guards and David remained. The soldier with the boy backed up the steps, keeping himself between the aircraft and the child. Hussam forced the sights to remain on the others, awaiting the word from Mahmoud.

"Now!"

It began. The soldier carrying David reached the door, one foot on the plane, one on the steps. He was at the very point he thought himself safe when the young hostess made a sudden grab. Nooria moved so fast she was halfway down the steps with the child before he stepped forward in pursuit. But now a gap had opened between plane and steps. He fell headlong to the ground.

With one hand Nooria clung desperately to the steps whose driver was racing towards the terminal. With the other she clutched David. One soldier lay dead on the tarmac, hit in the chest. The other had time to loose a single shot which whistled past her before he reeled under the impact of Hussam's second bullet.

The Boeing was already moving, taxiing out towards the runway. Hussam observed it with an icy, calculated calm as Mahmoud reached into the large bag. "Not yet, not yet!" Hussam soothed as Mahmoud deftly assembled the gear. Without a pause, the big jet lumbered onto the runway, swinging round, gathering speed. "Wait! Just a little!" All four engines screamed. The aircraft accelerated down the straight, reaching take-off speed, rotate, and its nose lifted, rearing to take flight.

Mahmoud pressed the switch. The fireball lit the night, rolling down the runway in the path of the disintegrating Boeing. A second later the shock wave hit the tower, rattling the toughened glass panes. The twisted fuselage ploughed onward, engulfed in flames from the full payload of fuel. Metal sliced the earth and hurtled through the air scattering burning debris over a huge area, continuing to fall even after the echo of the blast died away.

Out on the runway, the wreck burned silently. Hussam rested a hand on Mahmoud's shoulder, squeezing it briefly, nodding approval and satisfaction. Then he raced down the stairs, across the tarmac to where Nooria stood, David in her arms, lifting him from her, holding the small body to his as the lad clung around his neck with a grip which threatened to strangle, refusing to let go even to allow Hussam to look at his face.

He turned to Nooria to tell her she'd done well but already she was locked in Mahmoud's arms. Hussam saw the tenderness between them, the love, the silent wonder of two whom God intended should be one. And now he thought of Jodi, closing his eyes against his son's hair lest the others see the tears.

CHAPTER 20

The day was humid, the night dry. She liked the night, the soft and gentle night. The day was harsh, bright, unkindly honest, demanding attention and action, summoning the world to come and go and work and strive, training its white light on a hot and alien scene.

In the night the breeze blew offshore, tumbling from the high escarpment, drawing down the desert scents of warmth and dryness which drowned in the cloying dampness of the day. They had a timelessness, a spirituality which spoke to the soul. They spoke of what had been and was to come. Jodi listened carefully. She had little else to do. She looked out on a land which wasn't hers and longed for England.

So many people came. Friends, doctors, Aref and, of course, Hussam. He was with her constantly at first but refused even to discuss letting her go home. He confused her, bullied her, even frightened her and the doctors told him to stay away. Now, usually he did but occasionally would come. His presence seemed to fill the room and she felt stifled, looking around for escape, keeping a distance between them until, abruptly, he would leave.

Aref was more gentle. He visited often, sitting with her, sometimes silent, sometimes talking like a father. She felt safe, almost relaxed. It was Aref who suggested the excursion. She confided her feelings of the night, the desert, and when next he came he said they would go on a camel ride, over the high ridge to the arid waste beyond.

All afternoon the beasts toiled up the steep and stony ground, heaving and complaining as she laughed and shouted to Aref that it was he who was mad, not she. Now, at the summit they looked back. It was dusk and beneath them the lights of Kahran pricked the darkening greys and greens of the coastal plain. Beyond, through a mist of orange and purple, the sun, subdued, touched the world's rim. She breathed the familiar desert scents, the welcome which had lured her upward through the heat of the day. A sudden practical thought occurred. "How will we get back?"

Aref smiled. "Trust me," he said, turning the camel and leading on.

It was dark when she glimpsed the light. Aref drew back level with her. "We're going there," he said and she nodded, urging the camel forward. She saw it was a campfire such as the bedouin made. Large enough to cook and give warmth but small enough to conserve the sparse fuel, enclosed so as not to attract distant raiding parties to an unsuspecting encampment. She could see a low tent, red in the firelight. A shadow crossed between the flames and herself. Someone there, waiting. She turned to Aref but he had gone.

Behind her was only blackness. She called his name but he did not answer. Momentarily she hesitated, then went on. There was nowhere else to go.

He reached out for the halter, looking up at her.

"*Salaam aleykom ya Hussam.*" She greeted him cautiously but formally, politely, as the rider should the stander.

"*Weh aleykom salaam.*" He seemed equally formal though he reached to help her down. She slid into his arms, pushing away immediately, walking to the fire, feeling in its warmth how chill the air was. Fat from an animal carcass on a spit crackled and hissed as it fell to the flames. The smell was delicious but she had no appetite.

"Remember when we played chess?" He was behind her, very close. "You won a gazelle but you never ate it. I got you another."

She looked at the sky, recalling the night on the way to Ein Mara, her despair at the vastness of the black endless desert. Now her despair was for the emptiness within her, and the loneliness of herself searching for an oasis. Hussam could only watch her. He had been warned not to force himself on her as he wanted so much to do. He felt if he could hold her, kiss her, gently persuade her as he had before, she would submit as she should, return his love, hold him as he held her. But she let no one touch her. The only man she trusted was Aref. Perhaps tonight had destroyed even that trust. He had to reach her somehow.

The doctors said a short holiday might be sufficient. And in England they were better able to deal with sickness of the mind. Hussam wouldn't hear of it. He was hurt, angry at her rejection of him. It was a shadow on the jubilation in Qmrah.

When they learned of the Sultan's death the people demanded Hussam as leader. He was reluctant but Aref persuaded him. "They want no one else. They'll riot if you refuse! There'll be chaos and more killing. All we have fought for will be gone," he warned.

So Hussam accepted, vowing it was temporary until elections were held. He had no clear view of his future, only that Jodi was vital to it. She would recover and they would return to a simple life with his son and what remained of his family.

The intrigues of politics and finance infuriated him. There seemed no point, and no end, to the complications raised by the people he must meet. He tolerated no bribery, no flattery and, while observing the customary courtesies of unhurried introductions, was uncharacteristically prompt and unyielding in his decisions. His bedouin background left him personally unimpressed with committees and collective argument. In the desert a *sheikh* had absolute power and wielded it ruthlessly. The best *sheikhs* were fair-minded men with the survival and prosperity of their people at heart. This he would be until a new constitution were forged and he could hand over to the democracy the people deserved.

It left him little time for the family he was trying to rebuild. His son demanded all his attention. Jodi, it seemed, wanted none. He glimpsed her sometimes walking alone through the gardens or riding, laughing with Aref. If Aref had been younger he would suspect their friendship and felt the torment of jealousy he had not known since Khadija.

One way or another it must be settled. If tonight he failed he must accept it as the will of Allah and let her go. She would be free to stay or leave as she wished. He walked to the fire, lifting the meat on the spit and placing it on a large leather platter.

"Sit," he said. "Eat."

Jodi did as she was told. Hussam's proximity here in the great desert was not as threatening as it was in Kahran. Here they were not thrown together in a space too small for both to breathe. For a long time they ate in silence. Then he began to speak.

"In the desert there are demons. We call them *djinns*, in the west you call them genies." He looked at her, awaiting a nod or some sign of comprehension that did not come. "They don't live in bottles or magic rings. They hide in the sands and lure men to their deaths. Mirages are the work of the *djinns* and a thousand other tricks which seduce us into thinking things are as they are not." He turned to her. "The bedouin believe the *djinns* destroy all men afraid to face them."

Jodi looked down. He touched her chin, lifting it so she looked at him. "Tonight we must face them. What is between us, *habibi*? Is it not as I believed?"

For the first time he saw pain in her eyes. They sparkled in the fire-light and a tear fell onto his hand. He brought it to his lips, tasting the salt. Soon the tears rolled down her cheeks though she made no sound. He fought to restrain himself. This battle she must fight alone.

She stood and now sobs wracked her body. He stood too, watching, waiting. She was wretched and alone but still she would not come to him, casting around for something to cling to, something, but not him. He thought for a moment it would end as his previous clumsy attempts when she recoiled like a cornered animal, wailing: "Leave me alone!" but now she took one step towards him, holding out her arms which shook with the violence of her grief. Still he did not move, reaching with one hand to touch hers which was deathly cold. She clutched it, using it as a drowning woman might, to pull her to safety.

Then she was against him and he held her properly for the first time in far too long. She was thinner than he remembered, the lithe, hard body, toughened by weeks of training, seemed wasted, frail.

"Hussam, too much has happened. I don't know who I am any more, only that I want to go home."

He nodded. "I know." She was so cold. He took off the *abba*, wrapping it around her shoulders, leading her to the shelter of the tent and sitting her between his knees, her back against the warmth of his inner thigh while his arms folded around her shoulders. "You said once you loved me."

"Yes."

"Do you still?" She nodded. He closed his eyes. It was not for him to question the will of God. "Then go. Get well and come back to me."

She looked at him as if seeing him for the first time. Quickly, almost shyly, she kissed him. It was but a drop in the dry well of hope beside which he waited. But in it he saw the new beginning of a stream from which he had drawn strength since the time he first saw her. He brushed his face against her hair, whispering endearments, reassurance, tracing with his hand the soft contours of her cheek, her neck, her shoulder.

"No, Hussam. No!" She reached for his hand to pull it from her breast but he resisted.

"It's time," he said. "Perhaps the last time. Only God knows, *habibi*." He bent to kiss her throat. She pulled his face back to hers, needing him to stay where she could see him, needing to know it was him, needing his eyes never to leave hers, never to close nor flicker or else she wouldn't know if the sensations he awoke were right or wrong. Patiently his fingers coaxed from her the moistness which told him at last she would have him but still she held his face, still she searched his eyes. He fed on her hunger, suppressing the remnants of her reluctance, the victor in him refusing to relinquish a fraction of the ground he gained until, with the violent, pulsating surge of her climax she acknowledged his triumph, his reclaim of her for himself and their future and his need and his body and the hurt and frustration and emotion which burst from him now as he closed his eyes, unable any longer to meet her gaze.

✻✻✻

The ships at anchorage shrunk away. The blue sea turned steely grey with distance, the white flare of the sun's reflection racing along beneath. In the safety of the jet she removed the scarab ring from her finger, placing it in the pocket of her jeans. She would send it back to him from England. Then he would know for certain what she hadn't the courage to tell him.

"It brought you back before. It will do so again," he said. But he was wrong.

She stared out of the window once more, the coastline had faded into the haze, or was it that the damned air conditioning kept making her eyes water. Either way it had gone.

With Hussam she could never have been just herself. She would always be in his shadow: his woman, his soldier, his wife, her own identity eclipsed. The spirit in her longed for freedom and the right to follow her destiny which life with him would preclude. And she was homesick and she did need time to herself, time to think, well beyond the sphere of his influence. What he needed was another Leila, an Arab who would happily conform to the role as she never could. No doubt he would find one. Already the wealthy of Kahran were offering their daughters. There wasn't a widower more eligible.

Call it fear, call it faithlessness. Whatever drove her from him, Islam would judge her guilty. East never seemed further from west.

She wasn't totally dishonest. Her mind was bruised, though not as badly as the doctors believed when she refused to let them touch her. She just couldn't risk them finding out the truth. Every morning she was sick and soon it would show. Had she stayed longer he must guess and then he would have never let her go.

THE END

If you enjoyed

THE SWORD – BLOOD DEMANDS BLOOD

it would be great if you would write a brief review. Online reviews are really helpful in bringing books to the attention of other readers who might also enjoy them.

To leave a review please go to

THE SWORD – BLOOD DEMANDS BLOOD

*On the **Amazon** website*

THANK YOU

GLOSSARY

ARABIC

Abba	Loose outer coat
Abu	Father
Ahlan weh sehlan	Welcome/greetings
Ana	I/me (male)
Annisatti	Young woman/Miss
Anti	You (female)
Aysh	What? Pardon?
Baksheesh	Bribe
Caravanserai	Town square
Chador	Woman's cloak wrapped around head and body
El Fatah	The Conquerer
Fedayeen	Arab guerillas fighting Israel
Habibi	My darling/love
Heloa	Beautiful
Hina	Here
Inglisi	English
Insh Allah	God willing
Jihad	Holy war
Kaffiyeh	Chequered head scarf
Kafi	Enough
Kaffirs	Non-believers
Kusumac	Obscenity/swearword
La	No
Laysh	Why?
Masa	Evening
Ma Salaam	Go in peace
Meshi	Go
Mezze	Selection of small dishes of food
Muezzin	Caller from a minaret summoning Muslims to prayer
Mukhtar	Head of the village
Nazrani	Christian
Salaam/aleykom	Peace/be upon you
Scarab	Beetle/symbol for luck
Shahadah	of God
Shari'a	Islamic law
Shi'a	Minority Muslim sect

ARABIC (Cont'd)

Souk	Market
Sunni	The majority sect of Islam
Tasbah alla khir	Sweet dreams
Thobe	Loose tunic
Umm/umma	Mother/mum
Wadi	Dry valley
Walad	Boy
Weh	And
Ya	O (form of address)
Yallah	Hurry/faster
Y'allah	Oh God
Yom el jumah	Friday/Holy day

HEBREW

Aman	Israeli Military intelligence
Ashkenazi	Jew from the West
Ayfo	Where?
Boi	Come/here
Erev Shabbat	Friday evening
Hora	Israeli national folk dance
Kibbutz/nik	Collective farm/farm worker
Knesset	Israeli Parliament
Le chaim	To life (a toast)
Memunah	Chief of Intelligence Services
Moshav	Collection of small farms
Mossad	Israeli Intelligence Agency
Nahal	Pioneer youth combining military training & farming
Persedah	Ok/all right
Sabra	Native born Israeli
Sephardi	Spanish or Asian Jew
Shabbat Shalom	Peaceful Sabbath
Shalom	Peace
Sheket	Shut up/be quiet
Shin beth	Israeli Internal Security Agency
Sikshe	Non-Jewish woman
Slee'ha	Please
Todah/rabah	Thank you/very much

Printed in Great Britain
by Amazon